To my Dormer, thank you for everything you didn't know felt real.

Bronte is from a small seaside town in the southeast of Kent, where she grew up. She has been an avid reader and keen writer from a very young age. Through her time at school, she fell in love with English literature and creative writing, finding sanctuary in books, science fiction and fantasy.

Her love for fiction then led her to complete a BA in Creative Writing and MA in Screenwriting from Buckinghamshire New University. Drafting prose and scripts alike, Bronte wanted to write anything and everything in pursuit of writing for a career.

The Last Royalist is her first novel.

Bronte Henwood

THE LAST ROYALIST

AUSTIN MACAULEY PUBLISHERS™

LONDON • CAMBRIDGE • NEW YORK • SHARJAH

A CIP catalogue record for this title is available from the British Library.

ISBN 9781528993227 (Paperback)
ISBN 9781528993234 (ePub e-book)

www.austinmacauley.com

First Published (2021)
Austin Macauley Publishers Ltd
25 Canada Square
Canary Wharf
London
E14 5LQ

Five Realms of Lexia

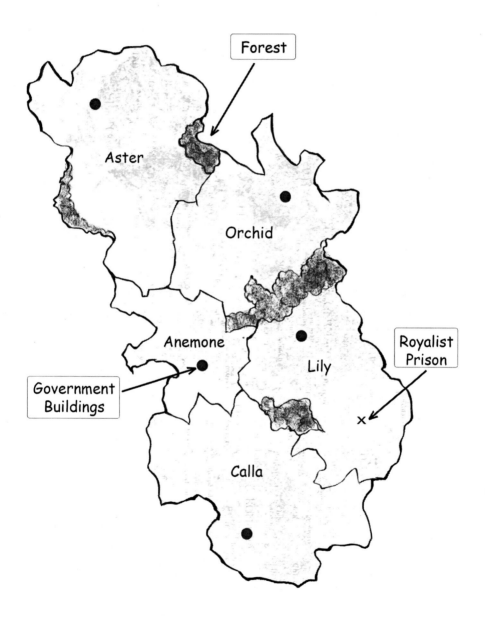

Forest

Aster

Orchid

Anemone

Lily

Royalist
Prison

Government
Buildings

Calla

One

Kick. Punch. Swing.

All movements that used to be the goal, the ideal. The trophy. But now, they're each nothing more than a memory.

Strands of long but thin light hair whip back and forth in a constant motion. Alia, a newly graduated Protector of her realm, hits the rounded hanging bag in front of her as if it was second nature. Which at this point, it kind of was.

Calla, her home. The realm of strength, physicality, agility and stamina. All the things that are beaten into you as soon as you can make the decision to leave or train. Train to be the best. While all the realms have known for the longest time is peace, there's nothing wrong with being prepared. And that's what Protectors, like Alia, have always been trained for.

She continues hitting the fraying fabric until the skin wrapped across her knuckles becomes dry and sore. Her breathing quickens, beads of sweat nestling, but not dropping, from her forehead. A feeling all but too familiar now.

So fixed on the easy patterns, Alia doesn't look up at first when the only door to the small room opens. Before even looking up, Alia can't shake the sudden tingle rising from deep beneath her skin. There are very few people she'd ever want in this room. While open to anyone, it became one of the few 'dead spots' within the Academy walls. Somewhere overshadowed by the nearer, more commonly known areas. But she felt this place had a meaning. A history. Her history.

"Alia?" She recognises the voice at the door to be her brother's. "The fireworks have started. Everyone's waiting."

"Everyone?" She responds before looking up. From the middle of the room, he might as well be a shadow. His small voice and plain features, matched with his skinny and not yet muscular physique. So ordinary, so simple. Yet a part of Alia had always been jealous of her little brother Eli.

"Mum's waiting." Throwing another, but lighter, punch at the constant swinging bag, Alia lets her breathing slow until she is able to keep her eyes on Eli without also panting like a dog under a hot summer's sun.

"Tell her not to wait for me. You guys go ahead. I'll catch up." She pauses, fiddling with the tape tightly wound around each hand. While she knows she doesn't really need it, she still wants it. Like many things, she doesn't feel ready to let go of yet.

Eli remains in the doorway, so still he may as well have become a part of the room. It shouldn't irritate her, yet it does. This isn't his home, it's hers.

"What?" She doesn't quite shout but makes it known that she doesn't want him there.

"You know she's not coming. At least not here."

"I know," Alia responds, too quickly upon realisation. "This isn't about her. I just, need time, here. You wouldn't get it."

"Maybe not yet." He pauses this time, shifting his weight between his feet. "But this isn't just your place anymore. You need to let it go."

Squinting, instinctively trying to hide what she can't keep to herself, Alia looks away. She can only tell he finally leaves when the slight light from the open-door swings back to darkness. As much as she'd love for him to understand, and he'd try, she knows he wouldn't get it. Not yet. He hasn't walked the halls or been thrown to the floor yet. He doesn't know what it's like to have no one there to pick you back up. That's something you have to do for yourself. He doesn't know what it's like to say goodbye to a space that's been more like a home for as long as Alia can remember. Not yet, anyway, his time is still to come.

Throwing the last few, harder, punches, Alia eventually sips some water and begins taking off the support still secured across her hands. Unwrapping it layer by layer, Alia knows she's making more of a deal out of it than it needs to be. Everyone else has already been and gone.

Collecting their awards like they were nothing more than simple gold stars and have gone to join the night's festivities. They've earned it. They've already moved on. They feel ready, but Alia still doesn't.

Eventually dragging herself to the door, small bag slung over her shoulder, supports now sprayed across the sweat beaten floor, Alia takes a breath. Tears forming, chest tightening. She knows it's time to say goodbye, even if she's not ready to yet. Switching off the lights, casting the whole room into one continuous shadow, every part of her leaves, aside from the part of her that will forever beat between the walls.

Two

First, there was the Academy. The next stage in everybody's lives, but the initial stage in your journey of whatever realm you choose to be a part of. Each one is different; everyone has the opportunity to choose their own path. Like many before her, including her parents, Alia decided long ago that she wanted to stay and try and find a place within the only realm she's ever really known. While she may eventually be relocated across any of the five realms that make up her world, for now she'll train and just try to live, like anyone else in Calla.

From basic techniques to the psychology behind each role, the Academy gave Alia every aid in order to prepare her for what lies outside its walls. Well, at least in terms of her ability to do her job. As for how to survive truly on her own, Alia feels as unprepared as she did her first day at orientation.

But no matter how young and unprepared she feels for the world, Alia knows she's earnt the right to hold her head up high as she accepts her place in one of the most prestigious institutes that anyone can hope to be a part of following an Academy graduation.

All new graduates are seated in a large hall. Each row of chairs exactly positioned one in front of the other. Everything in its place. Just like every one of them will be.

Between the General's words of wisdom or anything she says that's clearly meant to be inspiring, Alia attempts to steal looks in each direction, searching for any familiar faces. While she knows everyone in this room would have come from the Academy just like her, it means nothing. In such a big place with every class seemingly bigger than the next, it would be impossible for someone to recognise everyone, especially now they all share the same standard black uniform that every new recruit will wear until being sorted into their roles.

"On behalf of everyone in this room, I welcome you, and congratulate you, on making it here. As long as you work hard and serve your purpose, there will always be a place here for you at the Bureau."

Commander Jackin. *The General.* Some would say the sole beating heart of Calla. A big title for such a seemingly weak older woman. While still clearly strong in her arms and a certain determination in the face, from the outside, she could pass for anyone's loving grandmother. At least until she opens her mouth.

"Congratulations aside, you should remember that you all deserve to be here. While the Bureau is big, yes, it still has a place for you. We chose you to be here, and now, it's just a question of placing you."

The tests. The trials. The results.

Everyone in the room seems to stiffen at just the thought of any more trials of competence. They've all already passed all the tests to be here. Their time at the Academy made sure of that. But now there is even more of a grapple, for nothing more than to get a higher position. Out of every realm, no matter how different, Calla has always been known to be the most cut throat. Over time, things have changed across the realms; across their values and practises. But Calla's main Protection Bureau still works the same way it did when it was first created. Alia has never been able to truly decide whether their stickler for tradition is good or bad thing. Or maybe, it's a little of both.

"Whether you're placed in the Force, Defence or another service, each one of you is and will be equally as valued. I need you to remember that."

While Alia wants to believe her, she knows better than anyone that everyone's goal is to be a part of the Force. The most elite of all the Protectors. The chosen ones to be the first port of call if the time were ever to come that they could be needed, again.

While the realms have each known peace longer than any war, it doesn't mean that there may never come a time where they will be forced to make another impossible choice for the safety of every life under their protection.

Aside from fighting in a real war, which none of them would ever wish for, being a part of the Force instantly earns anyone the highest level of respect. In many ways for any Protector across any point their history, respect and honour is something they will fight for above all else. While this is something that Alia doesn't really care for, she does value all the other little perks there is to being a part of such a highly established group. She knows she wants it for all the wrong reasons, which only makes her crave it more.

Everyone in the room seems to radiate Alia's sudden itch. The want, the need, to just get up and be able to prove their worth. In a world where you get to choose what you want to do, you still have to be able to prove that not only can you do it, but that you want it. Even if you want it for all the reasons that you shouldn't.

"I could ramble on forever about what you could all achieve here and what the people before you have done. But for now, I'm going to let you go and allow you all to prepare for the upcoming trials." The General takes a breath, while everyone else in the room continues to hold onto all the oxygen they've gathered in their lungs. "You are all amazing. And now, you have the opportunity to prove it. Dismissed."

***

Each and every training room across the entire Bureau is filled with eager new recruits as soon as the doors to the main hall open. Everyone who previously sat in front of the General is now within the walls of one room or another, preparing for what many of them believe will be the biggest tests of their lives.

Alia stands in the corner of one of the larger training rooms, a water bottle tightly grasped in her sweaty hands. She wants to train. The urge is there, like a constant tingle that won't shift unless she gets her body to move. To feel the sweat teeming as her nervous breaths become controlled and she feels every bone begin to burn. That's how she knows they're working. But something is different here.

Something is wrong.

As hard as she tries to get back to what she knows, punching a hanging black bag until her knuckles split and she's overcome with a new surge of power as her leg lifts high above her head onto its next target. But at every movement, she feels herself almost falling. As if her body's simply forgotten how to move like this. As if it wasn't just her surroundings and the people that were new. It was everything.

Keeping hold of her water and grabbing her small bag from one of the provided lockers, Alia quickly exits the room, making her way out into the quiet corridor that leads back to the main hallway. She almost falls against one of the walls, her back sliding across the smooth surface. For minutes, she feels herself just standing there, her heart still racing while her mind is just confused. She knows what she's supposed to do, so why can't she just do it?

"Hey, you okay there?" an oddly familiar voice speaks. Slowly turning her head, blinking a number of times in order to clear her hazy vision, Alia finally looks to the side of the remaining empty hallway.

"Emmett?" Alia's voice is quiet, as if on top of everything else she's forgotten how to speak. Although she's barely had the need to open her mouth since entering the Bureau.

"I thought I recognised you. Still at it I see?"

Alia smiles, almost too widely, at the sudden company of Emmett Stains, one of the only true friends she made at the Academy.

Although she's never paid much attention to anyone's physical appearance, Alia can't help but notice just how much Emmett looks like he belongs here. With his sun kissed skin, true to most who spend their summer days training in the bright outdoors, his precisely trimmed hair and muscles that aren't obviously toned until he moves his arms a certain way. It doesn't matter that they did the same tests, passed the same exams and completed the same physical training to gain entrance to this institute. In Alia eyes, Emmett is the ideal Protector and next to him, she as well be a ghost still fighting for people to see her as more than just a blood and boned individual with strong hits.

While Alia will never not be happy for someone who spent hours training with her when everyone else went home and always had her back whenever she needed him, she knows she can't help being a little jealous of him. He's prime Force material, but does he want it as much as she does?

"I'm glad we ran into each other!" She stiffens at her own lucid tone, both happy to see him but not feeling ready to talk to anyone while she needs to remained focused on the task in hand. "You not training?" Emmett shrugs at her question, pulling tighter on a bag Alia didn't notice was on his back.

"I think I've done enough. I'd rather take it easy today, save my energy for when it really matters." Alia nods, as if silently agreeing with him.

"You were always great at the whole calming your nerves before stuff."

"While you were always the best at punching things." Emmett can't help but laugh a little at his words.

"Only when I needed to let off steam."

"Which was always if you remember." Alia joins him laughing at this, as if they were still back at the Academy joking between classes.

"Well, I had a lot to work through." She suddenly adverts her eyes, panicking that she's said too much while still knowing that between them; it will be conceived as nothing more than a passing comment. "So, what position you aiming for? Will I have competition?" Emmett laughs.

"Oh, no, I would not want to go up against you. You're destined for that Force. I can feel it." Alia smiles, knowing the words themselves mean nothing, but his belief behind them means everything. "No, for me, I'd rather just see what happens. I'll end up in the place they think is best for me." Emmett continues.

"I wish I could be as chilled out as you about all this."

"Yeah, well, I wasn't always. The Academy Commanders are going around and speaking to everyone in the training rooms, trying to get us to remember that at our stage, these tests and our positions don't mean everything. I know it was just routine, but I don't know, it helped. I'll try my best, but it's just a job at the end of the day. And any Bureau job, no matter how small, is more than enough for me."

"What commanders?"

Emmett frowns at first, clearly expecting another reaction from what he's said. But then he smiles, as if piecing together what she really wants to know. What she really cares about in this moment.

"She was here, along with Thornbe and another guy, but I didn't recognise him. After they've made the rounds they'll probably be with the General." Alia smiles, a new surge of something she can only identify as comfort, flows around her as if it was another type of blood in her veins.

"Thank you." Alia smiles, even more than before, as she can feel her attention quickly sliding away from Emmett. "You may not care about your position, but I hope you're happy with whatever they give you. It would be even better if you were on the Force with me."

"I'll try my best, Alia."

"I know, you always do."

"As do you, which is what makes us such a good team." Alia laughs, conscious of keeping the volume of her voice low. She then frowns a little as she looks quickly around their new surroundings.

"Emmett, I know this is what I wanted, what we all did. But, I'm not sure about this place. It's, weird."

Emmett smiles but not in the mocking kind of way that she'd expect anyone to. When one thing is all you've thought and talked about for years, but when you get there, it's nowhere near as good as you thought, it's almost embarrassing to even admit that you could have been so wrong.

"I get it. And I feel the same, almost."

"Yeah?"

He nods. "It's just going to take some getting used to I think. But I get that it's odd and it will be, after just training all our lives and never getting any real action. And now we have to do it, like, for real? That's scary stuff."

"Agreed," Alia replies, her body present, but her mind still elsewhere, as if she can only half hearing everything he's saying. Emmett smiles once more, straightening his body, clearly getting ready to depart.

"I better head off. You take care, Alia. I hope I see you again soon. In or out of whatever positions we get." Alia smiles, knowing for once, someone means exactly what they say.

"You can count on it. At least from my end." They exchange one last smile before Emmett begins to walk away.

Taking a long breath, trying to ease herself into some sort of stable state, Alia takes a couple of gulps of water and straightens her own body, wanting to appear like anyone else she may cross paths with.

Putting one foot in front of the other, she takes slow steps down the corridor before taking a left and finding herself lost in another. She continues to wander, feeling more at ease the more she walks, until she reaches the part of the building that she only has vague memories of. The building of the commanders' Offices and Meeting Rooms. While no section of the Bureau is strictly forbidden, you will be asked more questions in more sections than others, but luckily for Alia, currently all seems quiet. Although not the type of quiet that you tend to worry about, the type of quiet that is relaxing, like you know it's only temporary so you enjoy it while it lasts.

Making her way towards the end of another empty corridor, leading straight to the General's office, Alia stops at even the whisper of approaching voices. She both does and doesn't want to be seen. She wants to be questioned and she doesn't. She wants to fade into the background yet at the same time stand out as if she had a giant luminous sign above her head saying see me.

As the bodies of the voices come into light, Alia stiffens at the presence of so many familiar faces. They do exactly as she thought they would; go straight into the General's office without even a thought to check their surroundings.

Now off duty, with their uniforms off, their hair down, Alia almost wouldn't recognise them if she hadn't spent every day in their presence for so many years.

The two she recognises most linger for a minute outside the office, clearly caught up in some kind of conversation. The first is Commander Thornbe, one of the toughest Academy tutors, responsible for so many dropouts and late-night tears. It occurs to Alia that until now she never thought she'd see him outside of uniform. But then, she never thought she'd see him again, at least this soon, once the Academy was done with and her place here was secure.

She concentrated more on the other. From her wild hair, that she's never actually seen down before, right the way down to painted toenails that can for once be seen from the sandals that she wears. One of the highest-ranking Academy Commanders, Bureau Alumni and previous member of the Force. Commander Dormer, Alia's personal Academy tutor and the best woman she's ever known.

Three

For Autumn, the skies are unusually light and the air equally as clammy. Alia feels herself burning up as she sits uncomfortably in her new uniform. It's woollen fabrics, clearly designed more towards their bitter winters, irritating her hot skin. She's normally resistant to the heat, finding herself thriving more in the high climates. But not today.

Sitting at a high wooden table, Alia rests her hands on a cup of barely touched coffee, letting it radiate against her hands as if the rising heat was a form of punishment. Her legs kick the wood of the seat in a constant yet quiet rhythm. Her eyes are still, keeping to the same spot, but her mind is racing.

Flashes of the tests bore into her as if she was living in a nightmare. Sparks of commands and aching breaths seem to echo in her ears the more she tries to forget. Nothing could have prepared her for what she had to do, what they made her do. Yet she did it, but not well enough.

"Sully, make sure they get my order right!" An almost too high-pitched female voice shouts, bringing Alia back into some kind of consciousness. She suddenly realises that the room around her is teeming with more people than when she first sat down, all clearly in a hurry for something they're meant to get to.

The room itself isn't the biggest yet it seems to be crammed from corner to corner with people from every position. As the tradition goes, when the tests are over and all new recruits are sorted in whatever position they begin their life long careers with, their uniforms are slightly altered to match their new way of life.

While they all remain in black, two new colours are also present, creating a slight divide. One is yellow, represented in a stitched Calla flower on the left arm, the flower of her realm, something that everyone, when qualified, will always share. However, the second is more particular. Each position has an assigned colour and is represented by a pattern of triangles on the top right corner of the buttoned jacket Alia wears. Although as a new recruit and at the beginning

18

of her first year, Alia only has one triangle to show. Looking around she spies many others with multiple triangles, meaning that the room is currently full of people who've been here a week, and others several years.

It takes another look around for her to see how many different colours people are also wearing. Blue, green, orange and pink. Each one means a different position, a different kind of ranking. A different kind of life.

Looking down at her single blue triangle, Alia sighs knowing how much she wanted to wear green but also knowing how her time to do something about it has passed and all she can do now is make the best of what she's been given.

"Hey," a new voice speaks right in her ear.

A guy who appears to be a complete stranger, smiles as he takes a seat on the other end of her small table. Alia would be both more annoyed and concerned at his decision to just sit and join her if it wasn't for his uniform, identical in every way to hers. Apart from the fact that he has two triangles.

Much like Emmett, from the first look Alia can tell that this guy just belongs here. With naturally darker skin than Emmett, matched with his midnight hair, he has the overall look that she's seen girls fall for far too often. Through the years of the most intense training, it always surprised her just how much everyone else seemed to make sure there was still always time for romance.

"Hi," Alia responds, unsure of exactly what to say to fill the sudden awkward silence they're wrapped within. "I—"

"I'm Marne." He smiles again, holding out a hand for her to take, which she does.

"Um, I'm Alia, hi."

"Yes, you are." Alia feels herself smiling for the pure sake of it as the motion of her swinging legs quickens. "Sorry, you just looked a little lost here and, I think we had a session at the Academy together once."

"We did?" She frowns while Marne nods.

"Yeah um, just one of the open classes. I remember you being like the only second year to even attempt to participate in one of the third-year advanced aiming sessions. You were amazing." Alia can't help but smile at his compliment, now desperately trying to place his face.

"That sounds like me, I guess." She laughs. "Not the being amazing part, I mean just the actually doing the class part." Marne laughs as she feels her chest tightening. "I'm so sorry for not recognising you, um—"

"Marne."

"Marne! That's right, I'm sorry."

"It's okay. I remember you being so focused that day. I mean, if the roof suddenly caved in you probably wouldn't have noticed." They're both overcome by a new kind of laughter.

"Should I be concerned that you took that much interest in me?" At this Marne is suddenly taken back, from embarrassment or something else Alia can't quite decide.

"I'm sorry, that did all sound a little creepy." Marne leans back a little, throwing his hands up. "I just meant that, it was unusual to see and it made people notice you in a good way."

"Okay, I can get behind that, I think." She smiles as she takes another sip of her coffee before pushing away the still nearly full cup.

"You not a fan of the coffee?" Alia squints and shakes her head, marking her distaste.

"Not really. It tastes weird." He laughs again, this time emphasising the matching dimples that appear on either cheek. As if, he didn't need anything else to add to his 'pretty boy' exterior. Although Alia isn't thrown by it like she knows many others would be. Guys have never had that effect on her, not one. Or girls, for that matter. At least, not in the traditional sense.

"It's nice to see someone else not falling over the stuff just because it's new. A buddy of mine is on at least three cups a day now, it's mental."

"Jeez." Alia laughs, now focusing on how to bring up what exactly she really wants to ask him. "So, I'm guessing that you were at the Academy quite recently?"

"That I was." Marne nods. "Only a year above you. I'm surprised we didn't cross paths other than that one time." Alia nods.

"Me too. I'm sorry I didn't recognise you though, there were always so many people around".

"Well, it was a big place."

"The biggest." They laugh together before another silence falls over them, although neither of them feels as awkward about it. "Ready for your first official day then?"

Alia bites her lip, quickly feeling all her first day jitters come rushing back in one big swoop. While she wants to walk around with her head held high and at least pretend she feels like she belongs, she still can't shake the feeling that she's not up to the tasks they have for her. At least not yet.

"I guess. I just feel a little unprepared."

"I know it's all new and always scarier than anyone openly admits but don't worry, you'll be great." Alia smiles, feeling the tiniest sense of hope that he's being honest rather than flattering. "Besides, you're going to love your first assignment."

"Oh yeah?" Marne smiles, his body tensing through excitement rather than nerves. "Impress me."

"We have been selected to take up a position in the dusty, rarely touched, Lexia chambers outside Meeting Room A." As if what he said had meant nothing, Marne continues to smile as he gets up from the table and starts walking towards the exit.

Still having trouble processing exactly what she's heard, Alia gets to her feet and makes sure she's quick on his heels.

"Are you serious?" She asks as she pushes her way through crowds of people to walk besides him.

"Yeah." He laughs again as they turn a corner down one of the many long and winding corridors that Alia is happy she doesn't have to walk alone. "I can't quite believe it either."

"But it's my first day! And I swear that room is never used anymore."

"It's not, that's why it's exciting. But also kinda worrying." They turn another corner leading them down yet another corridor where Marne quickly steers them to one side, out of the way of everyone else who continues to rush around, all going about their individual business.

"Have you heard any of the rumours going around?" Alia shakes her head.

"I've been here officially all of about two hours, I doubt news travels that fast."

"I don't just mean here, I mean across Calla." Alia shakes her head.

"I try and avoid gossip. It usually does more harm than good."

"I agree, but people are saying that the meeting today, it's about the Royalists."

The Royalists.

Alia shivers at just the mention of the name, like she's been programmed to be scared of the very thought of the Royalists. The last living members of the Royal family in the land. Although few remain alive, they still have to die before the people of Lexia can finally feel like they can be truly free and really begin a new way of life.

Although now more of an old tale rather than something you learn in a history class, there isn't a single person across any of the realms who doesn't know the story of what happened to the Royalists.

"Could it be?" she asks, her heart quickening from both sudden excitement and complete terror.

"I don't know. But is it bad I kind of want it to be? Just the thought of finally being involved in something real." Alia laughs.

"It would be amazing to be a part of something that would be remembered for years to come." She pauses, as if suddenly realising the truth behind what could really happen. "But if it's real, then what does that mean? A war?"

"I wouldn't jump to conclusions, but I wouldn't rule it out either." He nods, neither of them knowing quite what to think.

"I just can't believe this is my first assignment." Marne laughs at the sudden glow in Alia's eyes. "Are you sure though? It's literally my first day, surely people like you who've already been here at least a year, should be chosen for it?" Marne shrugs.

"Orders from above I guess. Our assignments are usually mixed with people who've been here different lengths of times. I guess someone high up just likes you." Alia huffs, biting her lip.

"They would like me now."

"What?" Alia feels her throat tighten, not aware until his question that she'd just spoken out loud.

"Nothing, um, I just." She sighs. "This isn't exactly the position I was aiming for."

"Ah." He smiles, leaning back against the wall like he was at some kind of party rather than just about to go on duty.

"You're one of those you think you deserved better."

"Don't make me sound like a spoilt brat." To Alia's annoyance, Marne sniggers. "I'm not being ungrateful. It's just, not what I was aiming for, alright?"

"Okay, okay." There's a sudden silence as Alia takes a small step away from him. "So why don't you appeal?"

"What?"

Appeal?

"What do you mean appeal?"

"During your first six months of being placed, if you think you'd be better suited somewhere else then you can appeal it."

"How?" Marne shrugs, swallowing as if he's just taken a swig of water.

"I don't know anyone who's actually done it, but I've heard about it. If you're sure you want to change, you probably just have to make your case to the General."

"I don't want to make any trouble. I'd rather just get on with it. They clearly put me in this position for a reason." Marne shrugs again, like it's his go to respond without actually having to speak.

"Up to you. But if you're aiming for the Force, I think you'll get there. If I were you, I'd take the chance."

Since coming to the realisation that she didn't make it into the Force, Alia felt nothing but shame about the position of Surveillance that she's been placed into instead.

It's just a fancy word for guard dog,

Although hard to remember, Alia knows she has to get past it all feeling like a disappointment and see it as an opportunity. Above all, she's made it to the Bureau which is something to be proud of. And now, her first day on the job, she gets to stand outside while one of the most important meetings of the last decade takes place. As much as she knows she can still do better, that at least is something she can be proud of, no matter how many people she still feels like she's letting down.

Four

Alia and Marne are joined by several other members of their Surveillance team outside Meeting Room A. Marne is positioned right next to the large brass doors, decorated with golden carved flowers, representing each flower of all the five known realms. If it weren't for what they think is about to happen, Alia would be admiring the whole room a lot more. Even from the outside, she can feel its beauty, its power. As if a little bit of pure magic still lingers in the settled dust.

"You will remain here until you are instructed otherwise," Commander Thornbe speaks as he paces up and down in front of them.

As an Academy Commander, Alia isn't sure as to why he is the one giving them instructions rather than someone who actually works at the Bureau. But then she knows better than to question him, especially on her first day.

His round but strong body seems even larger in the shadows cast by the fading light of the day through the small high windows, placed at the top of the golden walls. While Alia knows she has to keep her eyes open and head still, every other part of her wants to be able to follow the commander as he continues to pace, his mouth still open.

"No matter what happens, no one will enter that room unless given express permission to do so. Understood?"

"Yes, sir!" Everyone shouts in unison.

Commander Thornbe then nods but says nothing more as he points to where he wants everyone to stand. To Alia's annoyance, she's made to stand in one of the corners with her back to the room and no clear eye shot on any of the exits. It appears she is condemned to spend this meeting watching one of the small windows which isn't big enough for anyone or anything to go through.

When everybody is poised in their positions, Commander Thornbe opens the doors, exposing them to a new kind of light.

As if the doors were some kind of signal, an array of people quickly begin to enter and file into the room. While a lot of them pass too quickly for Alia to take a proper look at, especially without making it obvious, she does recognise each and every Council member that enters, taking their place in the room. Although they go quiet when close enough to be heard, Alia is sure she recognises the voices of the General and Lady Talia, the elected body of Anemone, deep in conversation before they enter the room one after the other. As much as it's killing her not to turn around and look at them directly, Alia knows that now she's at the Bureau, everything has to be done exactly by the book.

If all of them are here, this must be serious.

Alia holds her breath as more people funnel in. She always imagined being able to meet a lot of these people one day, in some situation or another, but she never imagined it being like this, let alone on her first day. Once all the officials have entered, a series of Commanding officers then follow, none daring to speak a word to each other until they've safely made it within the walls of the meeting room. When there seems to be no one left to enter, Commander Thornbe approaches the doors, taking one last look before disappearing inside and closing the doors behind them. From the inside, Alia is sure she hears the door lock.

***

Several long minutes, or more likely hours, pass before Alia hears anything she deems the least bit exciting. If that is the right word for it. While the room clearly has thick enough walls for most of the conversation to be safely concealed, it's when the volume of voices begins to rise that Alia can almost feel her ears prick up.

Having not heard a lot of the people inside the room speak before, she feels at a sudden disadvantage when trying to hear what is being said. But as the noise once again begins to escalate, Alia is able to guess with a lot more certainty which voices belong to which people.

"I don't care if some of your best people were killed on site, the fact of the matter is that it was your people we left in charge of everything that happened in Lily and this was their mistake. Now we all have to pay the price!" Lord Ion, the elected leader of Aster, shouts.

His voice is the loudest so far. Everyone else on duty can feel a new type of tension ripple through the room and out to them. But as much as they may want to, no one can look at each other to confirm what they think.

While still having to be on alert, all they have is what they can hear. And what they can learn.

"I hardly think that anyone could have seen this coming. Most of us have only ever lived through peace among the realms, including Lily." This voice is a lot softer than Lord Ion's, although Alia cannot be sure exactly who it belongs to.

"I will not have any of you disrespecting the skill of my people!" General Jackin shouts as clear as day. "It doesn't matter how this happened, what's important now is what we do next. How we come back from it and deal with the crisis at hand, that's what people will respond to. We can figure out who to blame later, but right now, we need to figure out what the best course of action is."

Everyone surrounding the meeting room remains silent and continues to listen, sharing uncontrollable smiles on their faces filled with pride for their General. Each one of them knows they shouldn't be listening, they should be blocking it all out to keep their attention to the task in hand, but curiosity is a part of human nature that none of them in this instance is able to put to bed.

Through all the intrigue and wonder, Alia knows she feels alive for all the wrong reasons. For this she knows she should stop listening, yet she doesn't.

The buzz, the little tingle of excitement, all the things Alia hasn't felt since her time at the Academy. Feelings she never thought she'd find again. Especially here.

"We have to contain this before it's too late. I suggest, after formulating some sort of plan, we make a formal announcement tomorrow." General Jackin's voice, although with a clearly lower tone, can still be heard. "If she is as greater a threat as we fear her to be, then the people deserve to know. It may be the only way to keep everyone safe."

Alia releases a breath she hadn't realised she was holding. *If she is as greater a threat as we fear her to be,* the words of the General seem to echo around the exterior of the room. She knows the others can't hear it, but by the way she can just feel everyone stiffen, she almost thinks they can.

"But we also do not wish to alarm anyone until there is cause to." Lady Talia, at least Alia is sure that is who's speaking, interjects. Her voice is soft and light compared to everyone else who has spoken, it's almost inaudible. "The most important thing right now is finding out what they're looking for."

While everyone then proceeds to go quiet, leaving Alia more in the dark than before, it does make her question not what she heard, but how it was said. Between all the raised voices and cryptic sentences, everyone inside shares something more than a title. Right now, Alia can only guess that there is something hanging over all of them. But whether it's confusion or fear, Alia can't quite decide.

Five

For a meal dedicated to the purpose of several celebrations, Alia spends the first quarter of the evening trying to decide whether to laugh or be concerned by the single deafening noise of metal cutlery scraping everybody's individual china plates. Especially as this event of a family meal is an almost unheard-of occurrence within Alia's *close* family circles. Since declaring herself an independent adult, Alia has almost cherished every moment she's been given away from the ties of what she used to call home. She can finally begin to learn who she really wants to be, who she can be, what she can become without the feeling of anyone holding her back.

After the brief *hellos* and *how are you* questions at the very beginning of the evening, the conversation seems to have withered down to silence. As far as Alia can tell, it's become neither a comfortable or uncomfortable one. Simply just silence.

"Would anyone like a refill?" Arna asks, holding up her glass. Although they're only midway through the main course, Fiona has managed to empty her glass twice with no hesitation of further refills. Alia can only wonder if the real reason her mother has gathered them all here was to announce that her girlfriend has acquired a drinking problem. Although unlikely, it could be a logical explanation as to her somewhat abnormal nervous behaviour.

Through the next silence, Alia takes a long look at Fiona, still trying to deduce exactly why she's being odder than usual. It's only when she really looks at her that Alia realises how different Fiona is compared to the rest of them. With silver tints streaking through her otherwise vibrant short blonde hair, and piercing, somewhat stern, dark eyes, Fiona is everything that the rest of them isn't. And yet, Fiona seems to fit better than Alia ever has.

"Yes, please," Abella replies, her usual polite and cheery tone as perfect as it has ever been.

Alia never minded being one of those middle children; classically so jealous of her eldest sibling, being the one to never put a foot wrong, and the youngest being the one raking in all the constant attention. Although in many ways, she almost liked being the invisible middle one; especially if it meant she could be herself while everyone else turned a blind eye. She was always more than satisfied. But sitting between the two, just like she always has, Alia remembers all those times, particularly in the recent years, she's admitted to herself that maybe, she needs and wants that little bit of extra help and attention from the people she's supposed to be able to turn to so easily. But a lot of things never seem to happen as they should. And sometimes, help can come from the most unexpected places.

"Are you sure you can manage anymore?" Alia says, feeling the need to comment on yet another top up of Abella's glass. "Aren't you back to work soon?"

"No, I still have a few days, so another glass won't hurt." Abella continues, clearly feeling the need to justify herself as she smiles her usual sweet happy smile.

"I thought you had a big project you were working on and needed to get back to?" Eli speaks up. "Since your promotion, I thought it was a big deal." His voice, although quiet, feels like a sharp prick in the eerie silence that Abella wasn't able to completely crack alone. These are his first proper words throughout the whole dinner and all Alia can think to rationalise this weirdly quiet behaviour is the fact that he's now the one left living at home alone with Fiona and Arna. Maybe living within this odd dynamic is finally taking its toll.

"Yeah, I was, but—" she tries to continue between mouthfuls. "Something more important came up and it's been shelved for the time being. We've been told everything should be back to normal within a few weeks. I don't know any more than that just yet."

"What's come up that's more important than researching the most effective idealistic ways to make people feel secure in their homes in an unlikely crisis and how to make these ideas become more realistic than fanciful?" Alia pipes up before swallowing another large forkful of food. They each stare at her almost in shock for a brief moment. Eli soon decides it's more funny than shocking. "What? I do listen and I'm not that dumb."

"No one ever said you were, dear," Fiona replies. *Dear, really?* Alia does her best to not make eye contact and wishes she'd never spoken at all.

"Um, Al, I'm not sure. Apparently, only those with the highest security clearance have been told why everything's stopped. For now, at least. We'll be told more when it's time, but we'll just have to wait it out and work on whatever they need us to."

"Oh, you're not one with the highest security clearance?" That got to her a little.

"No. Just because I had one promotion doesn't mean I have the highest clearance." She laughs. "You know Fiona has a higher security clearance than I do, it just takes time. And I know enough, for now at least."

"You'll work your way up there, dear, and you're right, it does just take time. Besides, you've already managed to get promoted and now you get to work with the best of the best from every department within Aster's Bureau. You've already done so well." Fiona smiles. "Remember I worked there for a long time—"

"Yeah, a very long time," Eli murmurs, whether purposely or not loud enough for everyone to hear. Alia smirks to herself as Arna gives him a stern look. When her eyes turn the other way, he and Alia both look happily towards each other. Eli's not all bad, most of the time.

Another silence laps around the table as they each clear their plates and wait for Arna to return with dessert. While dinner itself wasn't very filling, Alia's stomach worms into constant knots as she prays the attention of the evening doesn't fall onto her.

The experience of having to tell her mum the disappointing news that she didn't gain her place on the Force, while wasn't as bad as she expected, still isn't something she wants to relive anytime soon. She knows full well that her embarrassment has been passed around to both Abella and Fiona and even though neither of them gave her nothing but encouragement straight away, that doesn't mean no further comments will be made later on.

But Alia knows she can at least be thankful for the fact that Eli had been the most encouraging after she didn't achieve her goal. And by far the most accepting. The type that, she knows full well, no other member of her family would be.

"So, Eli, how's the Academy treating you? Fiona and I barely see you around the house anymore!" Arna asks, returning to her seat now everybody has their desserts neatly placed in front of them.

"Err, it's good, really good thanks." He pauses, putting down his fork and placing his hand in his lap. "Yeah, my tutor is really impressed so far. She says

I still have a long way to go but believes I could be one of the best. She has a few of us attending extra training sessions every other week to keep on top of things. That and I like to use the training rooms a lot. The facilities are amazing."

"I'm so pleased you like it. Alia really flourished there, of course you will as well." Eli smiles almost awkwardly as Alia tries to conceal her face at the similar speech she also received at the time she had first joined the Academy. "And it's good you like your tutor. I always think at whatever Academy you end up at, your tutor can really make or break your chances of getting the job you've always wanted. Don't you agree, Alia?"

"Yep." She coughs between sips of cold water. "Absolutely."

"Yeah, she's great. One of the best actually. She really gets me and where I want to get to. I think she can really help me improve, a lot! And everyone else. She's great."

"Yeah, which tutor do you have again?" Alia asks, more intrigued at the conversation with every passing word. "I might know them."

"I don't think so. I've got Commander Sutton, she's new this year. She's amazing though. Some people are just made for teaching, I guess."

"Yeah," Alia replies, disappointed yet simultaneously relieved. "I guess so."

"That's nice," Arna remarks, her eyes slowly drifting towards Alia. "Who did you have again, Alia?"

"Commander Dormer," Alia responds a little too quickly. "If Eli had her, then maybe I could have helped. You know, pass on some knowledge and stuff."

"What kind of knowledge?" Abella comes in, her raised eyebrow making Alia more uncomfortable than it should.

"Just, training tips and stuff. I know how she works."

"Yeah, I bet." They give each an off-putting look, their eyes connected for a second too long. Alia resumes trying to finish her desert.

"How is Commander Dormer? Is she still at the Academy?" Arna speaks, leaving Abella to sit smugly in her seat.

"Yeah, she's around," Eli responds.

"I haven't seen her since your last day at the Academy, Alia."

"Well why would you? It's not like I still see her."

"I just thought you might have that's all. After all, she did help you a lot at that place; I still need to properly thank her for it."

"You've thanked her enough Mum really, she knows how thankful you are." She pauses, caught between frustration and a little embarrassment. "And please do your best to remember that I'm not at the Academy anymore. I've moved on, so has she. New year, new bunch of recruits for her to train, that's just how it works."

Another fresh silence surrounds them all. Alia shifts in her seat again, silently pleading for this dinner to finally be over. Eli slouches in his own, clearly thankful for the shifted spotlight while Abella sits poised, almost too happy to see Alia looking so shaky. They all sit and pick at their crumbling desserts.

"I didn't mean to upset you, Alia," Arna says, her voice soft and almost natural as if nothing had been said. "I know moving on hasn't been easy for you, but I thought that you and Commander Dormer were still in contact and that you could get her to help Eli if he ever needed it, that is all."

"Mum!" Eli begins to outburst.

"Well, we're not, okay? We've both moved on, that's the way it is. Things haven't changed that much since you were there."

"Didn't she say she would come and check in on you at the Bureau during one of her visits?"

"Well, she hasn't!" Alia shouts, feeling as if she'd just expelled all her built-up frustration from this evening alone into one single shout. "She cancelled her recent visit, I haven't heard from her since before graduation," she continues, her voice slowly calmer and back to its usual volume. "Like I said, we've both moved on. Now if you wouldn't mind, I have a slight headache so please may I be excused?"

Fiona and Arna exchange a nervous glance and Alia can sense that this dinner is far from over.

Clearly picking up on the sudden change of mood, Eli straightens up and looks as if he has quickly become far more alert. Abella's face doesn't change, as if she knows what is coming. With her being the one closest and most friendly to both their mother and Fiona, it wouldn't surprise Alia in the slightest if she knew what they were keeping secret.

"Actually, Alia, if you wouldn't mind staying for just a while longer," Arna says, her voice distant and clearly worried. "The real reason that we called you all to dinner tonight—"

"Not that we both aren't so proud to celebrate all of your wonderful achievements," Fiona cuts in.

"It's well," Arna smiles, grabbing Fiona's hand on the table, "we're engaged!"

This silence is full of complete shock, more on Alia's part than any. After everything that happened between her mum and dad and how complicated their whole marriage became, she never thought her mum would ever try it again, with another man or woman in this case.

No matter the person, Alia wants to be overjoyed for her mum more than anything that she's found someone new to love. Someone who she can share everything with now that all her kids are nearly grown up and are out in the real world. Through her dislike for Fiona, she wants to push past it all and be happy for the only person that really matters.

But she's just not…

Abella grins from ear to ear, smiling so widely at them both she may as well be sitting at their wedding right now. Quickly rising from her seat, Abella swiftly rushes over and embraces them both in a hug.

"Finally! I'm so happy for you both!"

"Thank you so much, darling," Fiona says, embracing Abella as if she were her own. "I—"

Before anyone can say anything more, Eli stands up abruptly and storms out of the room without a single word or look to anyone. Slamming the door behind him, both Alia and her mother get to their feet as everyone becomes trapped in another silence. One that none of them want to be the first to break.

Six

The morning's air has a slight tinge of unusual chill for the season. While Alia walks her usual short route to the Bureau, she finds it hard not to shiver at every fresh gust of bitter wind. Something in the air is different, something is changing, she can feel this for sure. Each leaf still hanging onto the surrounding trees has almost completed their effortless morph from a collection of dull greens to florescent yellows, oranges and reds alike; signalling the yearly wave of the summer season and the welcoming of the autumn tides. Yet Alia feels as if she's tiptoeing along the border of late autumn and the early chill of winter. Even though her world has been without magic since before her time, this morning Alia almost feels as if a little magic has been caught in the air and has come to circle her realm. She knows it can't be, but she almost wants it to be.

Magic has always been a curiosity to the younger generations of the realms. Especially during their first weeks in a real position like Alia's. They each grow to wonder what having magic must have been like. Did it make your job easier? Harder? Neither? What must it have been like to use magic when you find yourself in a position where it is greatly needed? For tracking someone or simply growing a tree. Through all the history that every child is now taught, no matter what realm you grow up in, the question of what really led up to the outlawing of all magic is something that doesn't seem to have a definitive answer.

Alia has heard the many growing tales of the Royalists, the elected family across all realms, who became too desperate for magic and the extraordinary power it gave them. So hungry it led to their greatest downfall of which none of them have been able to escape from. But one underlying question is always on everyone's lips, was it just the Royalists that caused people to outlaw magic completely? Or was there an untold part to the tale of the war that everyone has only ever heard about. Is it possible there could be more?

A constant vibration suddenly begins to radiate from Alia's pocket as she's pulled back into the present, surrounded by nothing but theories and whispers.

Ever since the meeting, everyone has been trying to keep a low profile and not let on that they heard anything they shouldn't have while on duty. But from the volume of shouting and raised voices that occurred, General Jackin can't really be surprised that some of their rather delicate discussion points are no longer as secret as she wanted them to remain. And since no one has been directly told anything further during this past week, people have had no option but to speculate amongst themselves as to what they really think is going on.

The buzzing stops for the briefest of seconds before beginning again, even more persistent than before. Alia has never been keen on the whole phone idea. Since magic became obsolete, people have been searching for a new method to communicate across large distances and it wasn't until only a few short years ago that the technological works of Anemone created portable speaking devices. Some even include the feature of word messaging which is a whole new kind of weird. But no one ever calls Alia. Everyone knows she much prefers to talk to people face to face or not at all, so this must be important. Stopping just outside the Bureau's front gates, Alia pulls the phone from her jacket pocket and tries to contain the shock of the caller ID.

"Hey," she begins, her reflex to start a usual conversation clearly working.

"Alia, finally!" Eli's tense voice replies from the other end of the line.

"What do you mean finally? No one's seen or even heard from you since that disaster of a dinner last week. What the hell happened, Eli? You can't just walk out like that and then just disappear! Mum's been—"

"You can cut the crap, Alia. I know you feel the same as I do about the engagement. If I hadn't walked out, then you would have and we both know that would have looked even worse." Alia finds herself hesitating to answer. This whole conversation has taken her completely by surprise, yet she still feels the need to end it as soon as possible, even if she's finally getting some of the answers she's been looking for. She doesn't want to get herself or Eli into any more unnecessary trouble.

"You don't know that," Alia says, her voice momentarily soft.

"Yes, I do." He pauses between deep breaths. "Trust me it could have been a lot worse. You should be thanking me."

"If the only reason you called is to ask for my thanks, then you might as well hang up. I have a job to get to and you have classes."

"Which don't start until this afternoon actually. But I didn't call about that, this is important."

Alia doesn't speak. Eli's definition of important compared to Alia's is usually two majorly different things. Eli would say that being able to walk in a straight line after drinking too much was important if it meant he could get what he wanted. A quality that Alia always fears will become a lot worse after being in the competitive grips of the Academy for too long. Even so, she wants to hear him out.

"Fine, but be quick. Like I said, I have a job to get too."

"Is it true that something happened in Lily and at least one of the Royalists might have escaped?"

Alia finds herself almost speechless. After nothing concerning the Royalists really came up at dinner, Alia thought it was the end of it until she was told more, if there even was anything to tell. Now Eli is asking questions, news must be spreading fast, which can only mean that there has been a further development. But what exactly she can't be sure of, at least not yet.

"I can't talk to you about it, Eli, you know this." She pauses, trying not to let her tongue slip further. "What have you heard?"

"That the reason Lily has just been completely closed off is due to an attack by the Royalists. But, aren't they all meant to be old by now?"

"First of all, if there was an attack, I couldn't tell you about it. And secondly, Lily could have been closed off for all kinds of reasons. It's an old, uninhabited realm. What makes you think it has anything to do with the Royalists?"

Alia sighs, not sure whether she's frustrated of just how much Eli seems to know or how much she still isn't sure of the facts herself.

"Well, firstly, the Royalist prison was right at the centre of where it's been closed it off. And secondly, everyone at the Academy has been on edge all week and it's getting worse by the day. Especially Commander Dormer, I've never seen her so freaked."

"You've seen her? Recently?" Alia's breath quickens.

"Briefly, in passing. But every time she nods or says hello, it's like her mind's clearly on other things. She seems more, further away from herself every time I see her. Something's up, Alia, and I don't like being kept in the dark."

Suddenly feeling that all Eli really wants is the truth, without any hidden agenda, Alia feels as if it is her right to ease his worries and hopefully if he knows more, he might be able to pass on his calmer manner to the people of the Academy while also not saying too much. Just the thought of Commander

Dormer, or anyone important at the Academy, worrying for the sake of it makes her ache a little.

"Okay." She breathes deeply. "But this didn't come from me and you can't say this directly to anyone. You can hint all you want, but do not say I told you directly under any circumstances. Clear?"

"Sure."

"Eli!" She shouts.

"Fine, yes! I promise. Now tell me."

"Alright." She pauses, wondering where to start that won't make it seem as if she'd taken the opportunity to eavesdrop while on a job. "I heard, almost directly, statements from several of the Council members that make it seem like." She pauses, already feeling like she's betraying secrets that weren't even hers to protect. "There has been a breakout at Lily."

"I knew it!" he says almost excitedly.

"General Jackin, Lord Ion, everyone, they're afraid. There might be more to it but, I think we can take a very good guess."

"The Royalists?"

"Seems like the most logical answer." They both pause, failing to think of any other explanation, however unlikely it may be.

"But, Alia, if this is true, and the Royalists really have escaped, then why now? Why wait all this time? Those actually still alive must all be old by now; surely it would have made more sense to break out years ago."

"I really wish I had the answers, Eli, but I don't. I really don't know any more than you do right now. Maybe there is a reason they've waited, if they really have escaped, or maybe it was an accident."

"You can't accidently break out of a prison cell."

"You know what I meant."

"Yeah," he stops, as if he's finally run out of questions. "Thanks for trusting me, Alia, and for, you know, actually picking up."

"Well, you were very insistent and I woke up in a pretty good mood today."

"That makes a change."

"Shut up!"

Hearing him laugh, even through the mechanics of the hard-shelled device, makes Alia break out into a small smile. They used to get on so well, they were even close for a while. She misses those times. She's sure he does too. But things have changed now, they've changed. Things are just, different.

"Just promise me you'll talk to Mum, please," Alia practically pleads.

"I already have. She's still pretty pissed at me, but she'll get over it. She always does."

"I wouldn't hold your luck about her forgiving you so quickly. Not for this."

"I don't expect her to be quick about it, but I expect her to cave and do it at some point. Whether it's in a few days or a few weeks. Now I'm at the Academy, I'm barely at home anyway so what does it matter when she gives in." He stops. "Just like you."

"That was different," Alia defends herself quickly. "But even though you know she'll forgive you in time, just make sure you don't throw it all away. I know how close you are with her."

"How close I was. Past tense. Times change, Alia. People change."

"Not that much and you know it." Focusing her eyes back on the Bureau, Alia finds the entrance to be unusually quiet, even for this time in the morning. "Eli, I've gotta go. We'll talk later."

"And you'll keep me informed?" Part of Alia wants to hesitate, as if she knows she's having to choose between keeping a good relationship of sorts with her brother and protecting the duties of her job to the realm. Why has balancing the two suddenly become such a juggling act?

"I promise." Alia smiles.

"Thank you."

"And, Eli." Alia pauses, taking a breath, giving her mind the time to catch up and focus on what she really wants to say. What she wants to but can never quite get out. "Keep an eye on Commander Dormer. If she's got the jitters, things are probably worse than they seem. So just look out for her, please."

For a minute, he's silent. Alia knows she's gone too far. Crossed the line. But she doesn't want to have to hide the fact that she cares, not anymore. Why should it matter? Why should it ever be seen as a bad thing? Why can't she just want to be there for her like she would for anyone else?

"Okay," he agrees, causing Alia to smile to herself. "You can count on me."

"I know. Thank you, I mean it."

With no more words needed, Alia ends the call, holding the phone to her chest, which is now suddenly tight. With everything going on, all the new ideas and theories now swirling within her. Alia knows her most prominent thought shouldn't be whether Commander Dormer is okay. Whether it's just the Royalists she's worried about or if there is something else going on behind the scenes. Alia knows she shouldn't even be thinking about Commander Dormer right now, yet she is.

With Alia's mind still caught up in her conversation with Eli, it takes her longer than it should to notice the shared panic as she enters the Bureau through the main revolving glass doors. Taking a second to get her bearings, she quickly makes her way to the assignment board to find it completely blank.

It's never been completely blank, ever.

No matter how trivial she believes some of her tasks to have been during her time at the Bureau so far, there's always something to be taken care of each day. As she looks more closely around the main room, Alia is astounded to find that the rest of the notice boards, for people in all other positions, are also completely blank. As if everything they know is about to be completely reset.

"Alia!" a familiar voice shouts behind her. Through the growing crowds of people, she's just able to see Marne fighting his way towards her. "Alia! Thank god you're here."

"What the hell is going on? We have no assignments, everyone is so frantic, what—"

"They've called a meeting." Alia gives him a confused look.

"Alright, but they schedule meetings all the time."

"No, not like that. This is a complete Bureau meeting, everyone from every single position in the same room altogether."

"But that never happens." She pauses, trying to understand the abnormality warping around her.

Nothing sporadic ever happens around here, it's as if everything and everyone within this building from the moment they step inside each day is hooked up to the same machine until they step out and away to signify the end of another mirrored day.

"Who called the meeting?" Alia asks, her heart already starting to quicken.

"The General."

"Are you sure?" She pauses, clearly trying to process all the new thoughts erupting within her. "Apart from introductions and celebratory assemblies, she never addresses large crowds anymore."

"Well, today she does. I haven't heard much more than that."

For a minute, they stand together in silence, simply watching the actions of the morning unfold around them as if they were statues cased with the task to only observe, never interfere. In Alia's position, she's felt like a living statue already more times than she'd care to admit, but this time feels different. This time feels, wrong.

'Will everybody please sign in and then go straight to the main hall. I repeat, everybody must gather in the main hall immediately. Thank you.'

The voice over on the usually unused loudspeaker booms throughout the reception. For a split second, everybody stops and just listens before going back to rushing around and not seeming to have time to hear the message repeated.

"I guess we better go," Alia says.

"Dump your stuff and let's do this. Is it bad that I'm a little excited?"

Alia smiles as she crosses the room quickly, heading towards her usual locker that's located just around the corner from the reception. Marne remains at her side, pulling a little on his jacket as if it feels a lot tighter than usual.

Alia manages to get in and out of the locker room without much fuss, dumping her coat and bag in her allocated space. She and Marne then exit the room and start walking in the direction of the main assembly hall.

The large crowds of people, all attempting to remain in some kind of order by lining up with others from their positions, make trying to gain access to the hall a rather difficult task. Standing there, waiting patiently to be able to enter, Alia turns back to Marne.

"So, do you think they're finally going to tell us the truth?" Marne shrugs, his eyes constantly moving between Alia and the open door.

"I guess there's only one way to find out."

Seven

Alia has never seen so many uniformed people in one place at one time.

The main hall is full to bursting, people taking up every inch of the available space. Although not directly informed to, everybody seems to have the same idea about staying within their positions and there is a clear divide of four groups within the room, each one gravitating towards a certain corner, leaving enough space for people to walk between each group.

The stage in front is set out much like it was when Alia had her only other assembly here. There is a chair at the centre, clearly for the General, but this time, there are also four other chairs, two either side of the Generals. Although Alia is sure these will be for the other Council members, who she has no doubt will also be joining them, it doesn't explain why there are four. Yes, there are four other realms, but since Lily is no long inhabitable and doesn't require an elective Council representative, why would there be an extra chair?

Although thankful to be standing with the people she's slowly getting to know, including Marne, Alia can't help but look around and feel disheartened that she still doesn't feel as comfortable here as she did at the Academy. While that also took its time, she knows that she'd be feeling a lot less skittish right now if this had all happened a few months ago. But she can't think like that, especially not with everything all up in the air. If things are really as bad as she fears, maybe this could all help her to get over everything she should have already left behind and focus on all that is yet to come.

A dull whisper fills the slightly stuffy air as people try and keep their voices low, all clearly still theorising amongst themselves about what they will shortly be told. It's only when the main door is pushed all the way open that the whispers subside and a new silence takes hold.

To everyone's surprise, it's Lord Ion, the elective for Aster, who is first to enter. As much as she knows she shouldn't stare, Alia isn't alone in her gaze as everyone seems to have caught on that this may be their only opportunity to take a good look at current leaders of their world up close.

While clearly not as old as the General, Lord Ion still carries several lines under his tired but wide eyes, suggesting that he was as young as Alia's parents during the Royalist War and that this will be, like it is for the most of them, his first time having to deal with any kind of real conflict.

Lord Ion strides down the allocated walkway towards the stage. His focus not shifting from his objective, not giving even a second to return one of the many stares everyone is currently giving him. Even when he takes his seat on the far left, his eyes do not waver from the doors that remain open.

Commander Thornbe is next to enter, taking quick and long steps towards the stage. Instead of sitting, he stands just behind Lord Ion, again keeping his full attention on the doors and nothing else.

The next elective can be heard long before they are seen. The clump of thick high heel shoes thuds against the stone flooring of the hallway before their echo reaches the main hall. Lady Talia has arrived.

She is one that Alia does recognise. It's no secret that she and the General have been seen to be rather cosy from time to time, which has meant that Lady Talia more often than not has a personal invitation to majority of Calla's events.

Alia always thought that the Lady Talia was the type of woman who used to turn a lot of heads. The combination of elegantly braided blonde hair, with only subtle hints of aging silver, along with her poised, skinny but strong exterior are a combination that usually peeks people's interests. Never mind the fact that she's probably one of the more intelligent people of their time. Being the first to pave the way for their technology revolution after the loss of magic to aid their inventions, Lady Talia is someone that everyone has heard of at least once in their lives. If it weren't for something odd in her eyes, like a type of hunger that you'd see in the eyes of any predator, Alia would feel humbled to finally be in her presence as someone in a remotely respectable position.

It's then no surprise that the General is close behind her, dressed and composed as well as she always is. The two make their way to the stage together and Lady Talia sits closest to the General who herself stands behind her seat with clearly no intention to actually sit in it.

The final elected body to join them is Lady Dany. Having only taken over leadership of Orchid a year earlier, she is by far the youngest compared to her fellow Council members. With fiery hair matching the colours of her Realm,

Alia feels like she fits her role better than anyone ever did. Unlike her fellow Council members, Lady Dany elegantly nods as she passes each group of people before stepping onto the stage and taking the seat opposite Lady Talia's, leaving just one.

In the long breaths before anyone else approaches the door, Alia can't help but take one last stretched look around the room. Everyone around her is now divided between studying the faces of each other and those sitting on the stage before them. Taking one last look to her right, Alia smiles as she locks eyes with maybe her only true friend in the room.

Emmett stands tall, his hands wound behind his back as if they were tied with real rope. Although his eyes are still kind, there's also something else hidden within them. It takes Alia longer than it should to notice the single green triangle present on his uniform. While Alia doesn't want to make it known that this new position bothers her, in many ways, it kind of does, and Alia is sure that Emmett knows it too. Releasing the smile from her lips, Alia gives him a slight nod before moving her attention back to the stage and briefly closing her eyes, knowing now is definitely not the time to get caught up in too many past emotions.

It's several minutes before further footsteps are heard approaching the main hall. Alia tries to be professional and not let her eyes wander further when she hears someone close the doors, feeling both satisfied and suddenly nervous that soon enough, everything will finally begin.

Only letting her head move when they come to pass her, Alia is surprised to see Commander Peircly, someone she's only ever seen from a distance when he visited the Academy. From her knowledge, although a Force member, he's spent the majority of his years in Lily, assisting with both the prison and anything else people need him for. This at least makes more sense as to why he takes the last remaining seat, but why he's the one to do it over another she isn't sure.

The stage is now full, yet someone else is still walking.

Keeping her focus on the walkway, Alia feels every bone inside her stiffen as Commander Dormer walks past, her own head held high and not dropping to look at anyone on her way to the stage. Taking a breath, Alia's eyes don't move from the commander as she takes her position behind the chair of Commander Peircly.

Although knowing she has no right to, Alia always like to think that she knows Commander Dormer better than most meaning that right now, she knows something is wrong just from the way her arms are placed behind her back and her neck seems oddly stuck in place. But as to what exactly is wrong, she hopes they will now be able to find out.

With everyone seated and in their place, the General moves away from her chair to the edge of the stage.

"Thank you for coming." The General begins, already unable to stand completely still. "As you all know, for the past forty-six years, all the realms have known is peace. But it's been the type of peace that could only come out of a war." Although no one speaks, several people steal glances at one another and many people's hearts begin to quicken. "The Royalists, the family originating from the first person to find and use magic, thought they could handle it. We all thought we could trust them. But after failing to safely execute their duties, it became clear that they had to go." Giving a slight nod, the General steps then aside as Commander Peircly steps up to talk.

"Thank you General." He nods towards her, obviously more out of politeness than real gratitude. "When the Royalists were overthrown, it was decided that killing them could have too many disastrous consequences, given all the magic we were unable to take from them, even at the end. So it was decreed that they were to live out their remaining days together in a structure designed in order to keep everyone safe. We then went on to outlaw all remaining magic, meaning that anyone caught trying to use it, or retrieve it, would face the punishment of execution." A new wave of yet more unspoken questions ripples through the room before he continues. "It was ensured since the beginning that the Royalist prison had round the clock protection. I myself have been a part of this on several occasions. But then last week, there was an incident."

An incident? Is that really what they're calling it?

"We are still trying to find out exactly what happened. But we can tell you that there was an explosion at the prison, resulting in the death of everyone in the realm, except for one."

The words, *except for one,* are more than enough to break the silence and let a new surge of voices erupt throughout the room.

"Quiet everyone, please!" The General shouts, resulting in a quick and sudden silence.

"It seems as though one Royalist managed to survive and has escaped our custody." He pauses as if waiting for a further reaction, yet everyone remains still and hushed. "While we don't know how much magic they still possess, we do believe it's enough to make them dangerous." Nodding again, Commander Peircly retreats back to his seat, letting the General once again move to the position of speaking.

"This is very delicate information that we do not bring upon you lightly. Over the coming weeks, or maybe months, you will all have a part to play."

As the General takes a minute to compose herself, probably trying to find exactly the right words for what she next needs to say, Alia finds herself sneaking a glance in Commander Dormer's direction. Although she hasn't moved, she's now discretely biting her lip and blinking in a constant rhythm that she has been known to do, by people other than Alia, when feeling uneasy.

"While we cannot be sure exactly what they will be aiming to achieve, we do believe that they will be trying to seek out where any further magic is kept in order to ingest it, thus expanding their power for their next move."

And here it comes…

"Although the information has never voluntarily been shared, it has never been a secret that when the war was over and the Royalists were locked away, we chose to keep the last remaining bits of magic in case we ever reached a time when we felt we had no other option but to use it."

There it is, finally said out in the open. For long as Alia can remember, every now and again, people would talk about magic and how there is still a little bit of it left. They would joke about the ones to go and find it and when they do, be the beginning of a brand-new age. As much as Alia has thought about what it would be like to live in a world with magic, she never imagined herself, or anyone, ever going to actually find it. But now the Royalist is going to try to and as much as she'll never admit it, she kind of wants them to succeed. Just to see what the world be like, what her life would be like, if it still existed. Even if it meant the destruction of everything she knows and loves.

"While it works to our advantage that the magic is being kept in Aster while we believe the Royalist to still be in Lily, I have already put procedures in place to triple security across all the realms, but with particular focus on Aster and where the magic is being kept." She pauses, sharing a reassuring but small smile with Lady Talia before continuing. "It is situations like this where our divided positions come as a great asset. We already know the strengths each of you hold and where you all best be placed to help with this current crisis. However, it is very unfortunate timing that the group of Force members we would use as our primary defence, are on their routine exploration beyond the realms, meaning, we need replacements, and fast."

Alia's chest tightens as she tries not to get too excited about the prospect of possibly having a second chance to prove herself while also being a part of something real.

"It has been decided that all remaining Force members will be divided across the realms with the sole intention of disarming and recapturing the Royalist."

"But we have also decided on a second group." Commander Peircly adds, once again rising from his seat. "We are giving all of you the opportunity to volunteer. But this is not a decision to be made lightly. Yes, it would be a great honour, but what we are asking of you is no easy task."

"We are searching for five volunteers, to be accompanied by three Commanding Officers, who will attempt to track the Royalist as she moves towards Aster. If possible, you will engage and try to restrain her. But only if it is deemed safe enough to do so." The General says, now sharing centre stage. "Due to this being a volunteer mission, we are also opening the opportunity to anyone currently at the Academy. You are all of the age to volunteer, just as the people were when the Royalist war began. To that end, if any lives are lost, we take no responsibility."

"If you wish to volunteer, please write your name by the end of the day on the main board in reception. A decision will then be made and announced tomorrow morning, with the chosen party leaving the following day."

"While it would be a great honour to be chosen, I stress now that no one should feel disheartened if they're not. We aim to put together the team of people which we feel are both ready, but also have space to learn. Over the coming days when we have more information, more of you will be assigned further tasks so above all, I ask for your patience."

A short sweep of whispers snake through the crowds but dies out pretty quickly when it's clear that they haven't quite finished speaking.

"Due to the number of lives at risk with the Royalist still out there, you are the only ones being directly told of the situation. The people of the other realms will be informed when we deem it necessary so I urge you to keep everything you have been told here today to yourselves, unless in the event that lives will be at risk."

Commander Thornbe then returns to his seat with Commander Dormer finally releasing her sweaty hands from behind her back.

"That is all, I believe." The General's voice is suddenly soft, as if she's released all the tension that sharpened every word she spoke. "As we said, please sign up by the end of the day if you wish to and see your Position Heads for further instructions for today. Thank you, you are dismissed."

The swift movements of the crowds suddenly forgetting the order in which they arrived as they funnel out the door like water trying to escape, reminds Alia very much those moments at the Academy where everybody would always be in a hurry to escape that one class. Although no one is directly letting on that they're worried, a state of infused panic lingers in some form or another upon everybody's face.

It's obvious that the majority of people, if not all of them, are now going to fight their way to the reception board in order to write their name first. Alia feels as if it's one of those times where the answer is obvious, yet she's still unsure. She wants to do this; she wants to be a part of it. But what if she's not chosen? Or worse, what if she is and fails once again? The unease of everything swirls within her, so much so that for a second she feels a little faint. Without much thought, she holds out a hand towards Marne, who remains at her side while talks to others from their group, to steady her.

"Woah, you good there, Alia?" He laughs, but the concern is clear in his eyes.

"Yeah, I'm okay." She smiles briefly back before turning around back towards the stage which is now empty.

They all went out the back. I wonder if she saw me?

Shaking her head, as if shaking away all the sudden questions she has about where the General led them all, Alia brings her attention back to Marne.

"Sorry, um, I'm fine. Very fine." She pauses, still unsure of what exactly to do next. "You guys go ahead, I'll meet you out there."

"You sure?" He frowns.

"Yeah, absolutely. I just, need a minute, okay?" He nods, briefly touching her arm as he passes, bringing everyone he was talking to with him.

It's when she watches Marne leave the room that Alia realises how few now remain. But of course, she would recognise one of the only people still there.

"So," she says, crossing the room to come face to face with Emmett. "I guess congratulations are in order." He laughs, not able to look her directly in the eyes. "Which is why I think you haven't reached out to me since right after the tests?"

"Look Alia, I never meant, um—"

"Honestly, it's okay." Alia attempts to laugh but in a way that it comes across as more of a cough. "The last thing I'd want is for you to feel bad or awkward, or, anything. I just, I'm pleased for you." He smiles.

"Thanks. I'd believe you more if you wouldn't say it through gritted teeth." This does make her laugh, real genuine laughter for the first time in a long time. Probably something she shouldn't be doing after just being told they're on the very brink of another war.

"Shut up." She laughs again, with Emmett this time joining in. "So, you gonna sign up." Emmett tenses at her question all before Alia realises what she's actually said.

"Well, I actually can't, um, the General said—"

"Oh right, yeah sure. Of course you can't, you're a Force member, you've already got your assignment."

"Yeah." He nods. "But you should definitely sign up. I'd vote for you, all the way."

"Why thank you." He rolls his eyes, more from her sarcastic tone than what she actually said. "I dunno though, is there any point? I'm still new here, I'm sure the General has far better options than me for this." Emmett shrugs, suddenly feeling the need to bounce a little on the balls of his feet.

"I wouldn't be so quick to put yourself down. So you put your name in and you don't get picked, so what? At least you were in with a chance. A far better one than if you do nothing. Just go for it, you know you want to." He teases, play punching her arm.

"You know I'd hit you under lighter circumstances."

"Oh, that I have no doubt." They laugh again, only noticing now that aside from a few others, they are the last people remaining in the room. "I better go catch up with my lot."

"Oh yeah go. I'm sorry to have kept you." Alia takes a breath before letting further words tumble out her mouth.

"That's not what I meant." Emmett sighs. "I don't want things to be weird between us, okay? I didn't choose this but it's what I was given and now I'm going to enjoy it because it's far better than going around thinking that I don't deserve it." He sighs again, finally getting the courage to look directly into the eyes of the girl he cares about far more than he'd ever let on. "I don't want you to miss this opportunity. So get out there and put your name down, whether you get it or not. Whatever happens, I'll see you on the other side, okay?" Going to bite her lip but then deciding against it, Alia nods, letting Emmett embrace her in a hug she didn't know she needed until she's in his arms.

Letting her go, Emmett smiles down at her once more.

"Be careful." At her words, Emmett playfully, yet dramatically, puts a hand on his heart and stumbles back a little.

"Oh my, are you actually showing me some affection?"

"Get out!" She laughs, pushing him towards the door. "But I mean it though, no dying out there. God knows where they'll send you." He nods, his smile quickly fading.

"I'll promise to stay alive if you will."

"Deal." They exchange one last smile before Emmett jogs out of the room.

Watching him go, Alia takes hold of one of her arms and squeezes it, unsure whether she's happy to be alone or secretly still wanting someone to be there.

Even from the now quiet and almost peaceful room she stands in, she can still hear the voices and commotion from reception where everyone is likely to still be gathered.

Taking one last look back at the empty stage, Alia focuses on where Commander Dormer stood, imagining what she'd do if she was still standing there now. What would she tell her to do? Write down her name? Leave it?

Breathing in, Alia turns her back on the stage and looks towards the door knowing that from now on, she really is on her own.

Eight

For a building as big as the Bureau, Alia always expected there to be more windows. From the few times she visited during her time at the Academy, Alia never seemed to notice how dreary it all was. How little light was allowed to enter such confined and sometimes cramp rooms, no matter their size.

As the central and most formal room in the Bureau, of course the main hall would be the place to have the most windows.

Now sitting comfortably on the ledge on what is probably the largest window in the Bureau, Alia no longer flinches as eyes constantly skirt over her as people pass, going about their business.

She had a lot of this back at the Academy. When her training room was unavailable and she had some time to kill between classes, she'd go and perch on the ledge of one of the windows there. It wasn't the largest thing in the world but she loved it all the same. Looking out to the other side of the building which housed all the commander's Offices, she found pleasure in being able to capture them in a moment of what she can only describe as innocence. Alia always believed that if you really want to know someone, you look at them when they're caught completely off guard and in their own head. Only then will you have the privilege of seeing the person behind the mask, no matter how much or little they usually allow you to see.

While some always looked down at Alia for her odd seating choice and considered her interest in others spying, she grew so accustomed to her window seat that in the end, she didn't need to care what anyone else thought.

Her window was one of the things about the Academy that Alia hasn't yet been able to shake. The comfort of sitting in one particular place and watching the world pass on while you remain still is a feeling she longs to have again. She hopes that here, this could be her new place, her new comfort. But then here all the stares and whispers actually mean something and are more than just teen gossip.

With her back to the wall and knees to her chest, Alia lets herself get lost in seeing the world through the glass that separates her with the chilling morning outside. This particular window looks out onto the central courtyard, mostly used for drills and daily exercises, there isn't a lot of natural ground still untouched.

Alia watches leaves fall to the ground, concentrating so hard it's like she's trying to find a pattern that she knows isn't there. The whole thing may seem pointless, and in many ways that's exactly what it is, but right now, Alia finds it almost comforting.

It's been hours since she's arrived to begin her day and there's still no word from anyone about who will be going on the Royalist mission. She can only assume that whoever is chosen will simply be told and sent on their way while the rest of them just have to sit back and wait for further instructions.

Alia saw every Force member leave this morning. As she approached the Bureau gates, she marvelled at the site of so many of them in one place at one time. Each travelling light and only carrying a small bag on their back along with their bows and arrows and probably phones for those who think they're needed.

While she couldn't spot Emmett directly, she knew he'd be there, somewhere. Standing in line, just another number amongst so many others. Alia hopes, more than anything, that he makes it through this and doesn't come back as just another number, but this time on a casualty list. It's only when she thinks about it that Alia regrets not giving him a proper goodbye. Not taking the time to tell him how much he means to her and how much she'd miss him if she were to never see him again. But then she knows much like anything else, it's only when you're faced with knowing that someone is gone for good that you regret everything you never said. As much as she knows she will still never have the courage to say a lot of things she truly means to the few people close to her, Alia is determined to not let someone else leave without getting out everything she has to say. No matter how difficult it may be.

"Miss Alden." A voice, a man's voice, speaks, reminding Alia that while she feels alone, she's also currently sat in the middle of a very busy corridor.

Looking up, Alia is surprised to see Commander Thornbe standing in front of her, looking down with the same confused frown that he did every time he saw her perching at her window back at the Academy.

"The General would like to see you." Alia frowns this time, her palms suddenly sweaty.

"Are, are you sure it's really me she wants to see?" slightly stumbling over her words, Alia sits up but doesn't move away from the window.

"Yes, she definitely sent for you. If you'd like to follow me," he says with such little emotion that Alia has no choice but to follow him, still convinced that he's made a mistake.

While her thoughts instantly move to the only reason for this being is that her part in the fight against the Royalist has been decided and the General feels she has to individually speak to everyone about what they'll be doing, it's like something doesn't quite feel right about it all. But surely, it can't be about anything else?

***

The General's office is not at all what Alia expected. While having the odd few homely touches, like a few framed photos and a hanging painting, the rest of the room feels rather clinical and far too clean. But then again, she could say the same thing about the Bureau. Everything and everyone present and correct, always in their place with little to no fuss ever made.

Being the only one in here, Alia takes a moment to really look around, not moving far from her position in front of the General's wooden desk. To her left, there is a whole wall dedicated to medals which without doubt all belong to the General. Each one hangs pride of place within a painted glass frame and all probably have rather interesting stories to tell.

To her right, Alia takes particular interest in the map pinned up on an otherwise empty wall. She takes a step towards it, engrossed in all its little details that others usually miss. The sharp sea rocks of Aster and the slightly bumpy hills that surround Orchid.

Each realm is painted with its flower at the centre, everyone coloured in while the rest of the map remains in black and white.

Reaching out and tracing the map with her fingers, Alia's eyes are then drawn to the blackout regions of places beyond the realms.

For a realm with such history, Alia always felt they were never taught enough about how their realms came to be and everything they've had to do to survive. Since magic was outlawed and seen as the ultimate poison, the elders and teachers across Lexia have deemed it unnecessary to tell them how magic first came to be and why it always affected Lily in ways it never touched the other realms.

There was so much Alia still didn't know or even try to understand. While she knows that things will never change, she can only hope that when all of this eventually passes, there will come a time where people will no longer be ashamed of their history and the truth about where they all began all those long years ago.

"So sorry to keep you waiting." The General says as she bursts through the door, causing Alia to jump a mile and return to her place in front of the desk.

Alia smiles, trying to do her best to make a good first impression while hiding how terrified she really is to be standing in the presence of the General in a place she can really be seen. While she's sure that the General at least knows of her, as nothing more than another new recruit, she still can't imagine why she'd feel the need to talk to Alia personally.

It's only when the General takes her seat that the door opens again. Alia tries to smile discreetly but can't help at the feeling of relief when Marne enters the room. He subtly tries to return her smile as she takes his place next to her in front of the General.

Seconds later, the door opens again to reveal someone new. From the two blue triangles on her uniform, Alia can see that this girl is also a second year Protector, who she has no doubt was at the Academy along with Marne. From their familial gaze and lip biting smirks, Alia tries not to laugh at just how familiar they clearly are with one another.

"I'm sorry to be late General. I—"

"Yes well, there's no time for that now." The General speaks quickly, as if forgetting the fact that she's only just arrived herself. "As I'm sure you're all aware, time is very much not on our side so I will get straight to the point." They all nod but don't dare say a word. "As I'm sure you've all probably guessed, you have all been selected to be a part of the group who will try and track down the Royalist."

Both Marne and the girl look at each other and gasp with clear excitement. Her heart beating fast and throat suddenly dry, Alia smiles but feels overcome by a sudden wave of nerves. Yes, she put her name down but she never thought she'd actually be selected. Can she really do this?

"I understand that this is very exciting but also maybe a shock." The General narrows her eyes to Alia who feels that as much as she wants to, she can't look away. "I would advise you all that while you volunteered and have been chosen, you still have time to change your minds."

"No way!" Marne says before he can stop himself. "I mean, um, not at all, General, ma'am. We're all grateful for this opportunity." He smiles, looking briefly at both Alia and the girl.

"Good." Oddly, the General finds herself smiling. "You have all shown great skill and potential for more than you've been able to show us so far. I'm confident that you'll all do us proud." They all smile at this, all in disbelief that the General is really talking about them.

"You will meet with the rest of your group in the main Courtyard later this afternoon and leave first thing tomorrow morning. As I said in the meeting, Academy members also had the opportunity to volunteer. I have since chosen two of them who will also be joining you along with Commander Thornbe, who I believe you all know from your time at the Academy." Although it's not really a surprise due to his immaculate reputation, Alia can't help but feel disappointed that she couldn't have chosen someone else. Someone, a little more, likeable.

"And of course, Commander Peircly."

Of course.

"But you will be led by none other than your previous Academy teacher, Commander Dormer."

Nine

As she expected, Alia is first to arrive. Not quite sure what to do, she lingers in the corner of the Courtyard for several minutes before moving to an empty wooden bench. While making sure to stay alert at the entrance of anyone else, she's also wary of not letting her eyes stay on one spot too long, wary of not wanting to appear odd to someone who doesn't know what she's waiting for.

To her surprise, it's Commander Dormer who appears first, approaching the Courtyard alone. Even from a distance, Alia notices a slight scuffing to her uniform, paired with crumbs she hasn't successfully managed to brush off. She always was one to eat on the go, never stopping to sit down if she could help it.

Now wearing the same woven fabric herself, Alia pays close attention to the uniform that Commander Dormer has chosen to wear. Being an Academy tutor as well as celebrated Commander in the Force, she has more than just a few options as to what she should wear. As expected, Alia sees that she's gone for her Force uniform, identical to Alia's in every way aside from the five Green triangles, signifying her length of time with the Force. Although a part of the Force for far longer than five years, it's only after this time where you're expected to be known by your reputation, rather than the number of triangles you wear.

Having not yet noticed Alia sitting alone, Commander Dormer spends mew minutes tying back her thick dark curls into a style that Alia has always been envious she's never been able to copy.

Alia then smiles when she notices her shoes. Not the standard black ones they're all issued with as a part of the uniform, but ones that reach her ankles and have a slight blue tint to the otherwise dark exterior.

She always was one to do things her way.

To anyone who doesn't know them, they'd think Alia's staring was weird. That her clear fascination of her former tutor is creepy and something that should be addressed. But Alia knows that no one can ever really get it. What it's like to never be able to truly count on anyone until you find yourself completely dependent on the one person you never expected to ever like, let alone care for. To the person that has always seemed to know you better than you know yourself.

"Are we playing spies?" Alia jumps at Marne's voice, putting a hand to her chest.

"Jesus, don't do that!" They laugh together, as if meeting for a regular social call. "I'm not spying! I'm just, observing. Waiting to see if they've added any surprises to our team."

"A-huh," Marne exhales a breath Alia didn't realise he was holding, sitting next to where Alia still perches. "And?"

"Either we're early or everyone else is late." She pauses. "Aside from the obvious."

"Well, let's go score some points with our leader. We should go say hi." Alia's heart quickens; her stomach tightens. It shouldn't be a big deal, yet it feels like one.

"Yeah. Um, okay then."

Marne leads the way from their hideout into the courtyard where Commander Dormer still stands alone. She smiles at their approach, just like she'd smile at anyone making their way towards her. Alia prays to herself that she didn't see her waiting alone. But like always, at the same time she hopes she did.

"Commander," Marne speaks first, now they're standing directly in front of her.

"Hello," she replies.

"Hi," Alia pipes up, her voice surging with a put-on kind of confidence.

"It's nice to finally meet you properly. I never got the privilege to attend any of your classes at the Academy." Commander Dormer laughs, brushing the odd loose strand of hair from her eyes. She folds her arms.

"I still hold weekly classes for anyone, well I did, Academy members or not, if you ever want to rectify that after all this has passed." They all choose to ignore the fact of how much and how quickly things are changing around them. "Although, you better be ready to work. I've been told on more than one occasion that my classes can be a little intense." Alia can't help but smile as Commander

Dormer winks at her, as if they share a secret. Like they don't already share so many. To their surprise, Marne simply laughs.

"I will definitely take you up on that. If we survive this."

Alia can feel the tone shift as everything suddenly gets serious. Like they've only just remembered why they're really here. As if any of them could ever really forget.

A ringing sound quickly disrupts the falling silence and Marne pulls out his phone before excusing himself from their company, leaving Alia and Commander Dormer alone.

Butterflies begin to fly within her again after realising this is the first time she and the commander have had a moment alone since her last day at the Academy.

She used to love these times. She cherished them. The moments where it would just be them and she could finally let herself be real and open. Alia would relax in her presence. She'd feel herself dissolving like she'd end up just a wet puddle of nothing for everyone else to walk in when the moment was over.

This time feels very much the same, but with a thin layer of something else stretching over the surface. Nerves? Worry? Or plain old simple fear that the person you used to look up to and trust the most will now look down on you differently because it's no longer their duty to care.

Although it feels like a lifetime of just smiling in a silence a lot more awkward than ones Alia is used to in her presence, she is relieved when the commander finally finds new words to say.

"It's great to see you again, Alia," Commander Dormer begins. "I'm glad to see you're doing well here."

"Well," Alia sighs. "I'm trying. Just like you taught me." Commander Dormer smiles, loosening her arms. Alia stands with one leg folded over the other, her hands holding each other as if mimicking what she imagines she'd do if there were two of her standing here instead of just her.

"Thank you for your letters. I'm sorry I never wrote back to you. I meant to talk to you when I came on my visit, but as you've probably heard, I had to cancel. Something, unavoidable came up. For that I apologise."

"You don't have to explain anything to me," Alia speaks, already feeling flustered like she's the one having to explain. "You can't plan for things you don't know will happen. And, you should never expect things to go exactly like you want them to."

"Are you quoting me?"

"Possibly." Even though they both laugh, Alia feels the need to quickly look away, like she's suddenly embarrassed.

After everything they shared for so many years, neither of them could ever have expected their next meeting to go quite like this one. To be wrapped in such strong cotton that they're both afraid of saying something that they will later regret. Neither of them wants to be the first one to pull at the first thread.

"Anyway, I'm so pleased to see you thriving here. The General must think a lot of you to assign you to this group." Alia smiles, feeling overjoyed from the sudden praise that she didn't know she needed so much until this moment.

"Well, I learnt from the best." They laugh together for a moment before another silence falls between them. However, this one feels a lot more comfortable and nostalgic, this they both feel together.

"Alia, I feel like I owe you another apology," Commander Dormer confesses, having looked down the slightest bit to reach Alia's eye line. Though Alia was a later bloomer and did most of her growing throughout her time at the Academy, she never did quite reach the same height as her commander.

"Seriously, you owe me nothing." Alia tries to laugh. "I'm always going to owe you, never the other way around."

"Just listen, Alia. I know I promised to come and see you after you left the Academy. And I know how much my promises meant to you. After all—"

"Why make one if you're only going to break it," Alia chants, her smile now smaller but still present.

"Exactly."

They hold the smile between them and begin to imagine that this could be another day at the Academy; Alia throwing punches at the hanging target while Commander Dormer carefully circles her, observing each of her movements and choices closely. Together, they can almost smell the sweaty chalk dust and old fraying fabric between them.

"I know this is all a great honour, but, why would the General ever pick me for this? I mean you and even Marne I understand. But me? I just, don't."

"She hasn't told me any of what went into the selection process so while I can't comment directly on her choices, I will say that you're still one of the most determined and gifted people I've ever had the privilege to teach. Never forget just how far you've come Alia. I certainly haven't."

Alia almost feels herself welling up although isn't exactly sure why. Yes, she's been known to get a little over emotional at some of what Commander Dormer has said to her over the years, but never like this. While of course she believes what says because she's Commander Dormer, deep down Alia still doesn't quite understand why anyone would have this much faith in her.

As if purposely trying to interrupt, Alia turns around at the noticeable sound of the approaching voices of the remaining commanders. If she were alone, she'd hold her eyes but instead, she just sighs, knowing that the moment has definitely passed.

"I'll let you get on, Commander. I, um, I'm glad—" she sighs again as her words fail her. Thinking of exactly what she wants to say on the spot has never been an easy task. "See you around."

"Chin up Alia. You're going to need to remember that." She nods.

"I will."

Alia's face falls as soon as she turns around, with the intention of walking away. But to her surprise, Commander Dormer doesn't let her step far before she puts a hand on her shoulder.

"Hey," she says, just before Alia turns around to look her in the eyes. "You've gone back to having two braids." Alia self-consciously puts a hand up to her hair as if to see if her two carefully woven braids are still secured in place. Of all the things for Commander Dormer to say, or even notice, that definitely wasn't what she was expecting.

"Um, yeah. It's weird but I could never quite do just the one. Always came out too loose or wonky."

"You've still got time to learn." She nods.

"Maybe."

Exchanging one last smile, Commander Dormer turns around and makes her way towards her fellow commanders who are currently lingering next to a tree at the far end of the paved surface.

Scanning the now livelier room, Alia is relieved to see Marne waiting for her, along with the girl from the Generals Office who she didn't even notice had arrived. Together, they sit on the edge of one of the wooden benches that could be easily mistaken for one stolen from an old-style school playground.

They appear to be deep in conversation. About the mission or their likely past Alia isn't sure. But whatever it's about, it looks important. So much though that Alia feels bad intruding.

Feeling the need to linger a little, it takes Alia a minute to feel like she can join them, sitting down next to the girl, happy to let them ignore her for a minute while she takes the time to steady her racing heart.

"Well," Marne finally speaks, turning his attention to Alia's glowing eyes, "now that looked intense." He laughs, as does the girl. Alia finds herself joining in but isn't completely comfortable about it.

"Um, that was not intense."

"Oh, not from where we were sitting," she adds. "I'm Lola by the way."

"Alia." She smiles, as people usually do for nothing more than common courtesy when you first meet someone.

For someone who can only be one, maybe two years older than Alia, Lola seems like someone who has just lived for so many more years. Quite what makes her see Lola in this way, Alia isn't sure.

However much like Marne, Lola also just looks like she's meant to be here. With equally, if not darker, skin to Marne's and matching thick black curls, Lola suits every part of her uniform more than Alia ever feels like she will. If they weren't about to head into battle, Alia would be excited to have the chance to see Lola, and Marne for that matter, in action.

"So then, what were you two talking about?" Although not intentional, Alia feels as if Marne is already pushing the subject. Like he knows it's something that Alia rather not discuss.

"Nothing special, honestly. Just about, you know, my brother and stuff. He's first year at the Academy so she knows more about him than anyone else. We don't really see each other around much anymore."

"Makes sense," Marne agrees. Lola simply nods.

"Although, I heard that Commander Dormer may not be keeping her status at the Academy much longer."

"What?"

"Oh, do tell," Lola urges, as if thrilled by the prospect of nothing less but meaningless gossip.

"Well, the way I hear it, the Academy's director isn't too thrilled by the fact that Commander Dormer took three totally unauthorised months off with no genuine explanation, one of which was during the week of the second year's end of year tests. Huge scandal, if that's the right word. I'm surprised you didn't already hear about it." Alia shakes her head.

"No. I mean, I knew she was out for a while, but I just assumed it was an Academy thing or something." She pauses, trying to connect this to anything that she remembers from her conversation literally minutes ago. "I hadn't heard anything."

"Oh, I assumed your brother might have told you. But then I guess he wouldn't have been there when it happened. And you would have just left."

"Yeah," Alia agrees, trying to shake it off and laugh with Marne and Lola while they wait for further instructions. "I guess so."

Now almost wanting to push Marne for further information, Alia has far too many questions on her lips when their attention is quickly diverted to the arrival of a new girl.

From her plain black clothing ensemble and timid expression, it's clear she's one of the chosen ones from the Academy. Although to look at, you'd wonder why. Alia always tries to never be one of those people that forms an opinion of someone just from looking at them. But sometimes, you just can't help it, you see someone and the thoughts just start rolling.

The girl, who names herself Cora, a second year Academy student who like Alia, by appearance seems to be a lot younger than she is. But even her young features don't take away from her shaking hands and quivering lip.

Of course as soon as she steps further into the Courtyard, the commanders all swarm around her, clearly trying to calm her obvious nerves and reassure her that she's here for a reason and that she'll be okay, no matter how much they can never really be sure of this.

As much as she knows she shouldn't, Alia flinches as she watches Commander Dormer put a hand on Cora's arm and rubs it until Cora's body finally starts to relax and her breathing becomes steady. She knows she's just doing it to help, she knows it's because she cares about making sure that everyone is okay, but Alia still can't stop herself from feeling a little bit jealous.

Trying to get back into the correct headspace, Alia turns her attention to Marne and Lola, taking a minute to close her eyes and remember what she's doing and what is really important.

"Hey, Alia," Marne says, looking towards her, sudden concern clear on his face.

"What?" She feels herself snapping towards him but knows full well that he's not the one she's angry at.

"Didn't you say your brothers at the Academy?"

"Yeah, so?"

"Well."

As Alia slowly turns around to look back towards the commanders, both her head and her body don't know what to do when she sees Eli shaking hands with each of the commanders.

Above anything else, it's clear he's excited. Overjoyed by the prospect of getting to come along and be involved in something real. Just like she does. If Alia wasn't so confused, she'd want to laugh. Laugh at how he clearly put his name down without talking to anyone about it and probably never thought he'd be selected. In that respect, he couldn't be more like Alia if he tried.

Standing up from the bench, Alia continues to stare until he finally meets her gaze. Even from the distance between them, Alia suddenly notices something unusual in her brother's eyes. Something that she's only seen a handful of times before, fear. Real, genuine fear. But fear for what? His life? Hers? The outcome of the pending war?

In this moment, all Alia knows for sure is that in a very short time, she and her brother will venture out and try and capture the single but most dangerous threat her world has faced in nearly fifty years. It's no longer just a question of can they do it, but can they do it while staying alive?

"Thank you all for coming," Commander Dormer begins as Alia, Marne and Lola leave their bench and join the rest of the group. Eli stands between Cora and Commander Thornbe, doing all he can not to look Alia in the eyes.

While still feeling uncomfortable about the whole situation, Alia knows that right in this moment, she has to keep her head on straight and think about what's really important, even if it's killing her inside. "As you all know, we have been tasked to try and capture the Royalist before they reach their intended destination in Aster."

"We won't try, we'll win," Marne pipes up, all attention suddenly falling on him. Commander Dormer beams.

"Now that's the attitude I like to hear." They exchange one last smile before her gaze drops to the left side of Marne and onto Alia. For a second, they simply stare at each other before both regaining their correct agenda. "I know the General has informed some of you but for those who are unaware, we will depart early tomorrow morning. Our first stop will be Lily and from there, we will follow the Royalist as more information comes in. We have people attempting to track her every move."

"Why waste time going to Lily when we could be chasing them from the beginning?" Eli says, all eyes and focus moving onto him. "Lily is a wasteland."

"And how would you know?" Alia finds herself saying before she can stop herself. Eli gives her a look which she is quick to ignore.

"In order to learn more about them, we're going to the prison." At this, no one speaks. No one dares.

As much as she knows they're going there to gather information, Alia can't help but be excited by the thought of getting to travel to a realm that has been abandoned for as long as she's been alive. Never mind the fact that she gets to go there with Commander Dormer and Eli at her side.

"Tonight, I give you the opportunities to say goodbye to your families and loved ones, who, I apologise, have already been told personally by the General at your involvement in this crisis."

Oh, shit.

"It will also give you the chance to rest up for the long journey ahead. I can't promise you it will be neither safe nor easy. But I can promise you that if we stick together, we will succeed. We will save not just our realm but all of them." From the long breath she takes and the smile on her face, Alia can tell that it's been a while since Commander Dormer's been able to give a speech like that.

"Now go, there is still a lot that needs to be planned. We will meet at the train station, 8am tomorrow morning. Dismissed."

Before anyone has the chance to say anything, Commander Dormer nods towards them all and turns fast on her heels towards the exit of the Courtyard. Commander Thornbe follows soon after along with Commander Peircly. Alia wouldn't be the slightest bit surprised if they'd gone to meet somewhere more private to discuss further strategies for the days ahead. It would almost be weird for them not to.

Lola and Marne also seem keen to escape this environment and go home to prepare. Bidding Alia a quick goodbye, they both walk away together before splitting into opposite directions.

Aside from Alia, only Eli and Cora remain, quietly chatting in a corner, a safe distance away as if making sure they aren't heard.

As much as she wants to confront Eli and tell him he can't go with them, she knows it's not the right thing to do. As much as she may hate it, he's here for a reason. He's always been a strong fighter, maybe that's why he was chosen. Or could it be simply for his vast potential? It could be anything; Alia knows this to be the truth.

In an ideal world, she'd like to think more than anything that it was Commander Dormer who recommended every Academy member here before the General signed off on it and she hand-picked Eli as an effective way to get to her. But she knows this will always just be a fantasy. The truth can hurt, but sometimes, it's an easier pain to face than living surrounded by fanciful thoughts that could be true in another life. But this is their life, their only life.

Swallowing all her initial outrage, Alia walks up to the remaining group of chatter and stops next to Eli. Leaning in so her mouth is inches from his ear, she whispers softly, "See you at dinner."

With nothing else to say, Alia makes her way towards the exit.

Ten

As if mirroring the start to their previous *family dinner*, all anyone can hear is the sound of cutlery scratching yet more plates full of home-cooked food. Like usual, Fiona and Arna are sat on one side of the table with Alia squashed conveniently between Abella and Eli on the other. She and Eli haven't said a word to each other since the group meeting and neither of them are keen to be the first to break the ice. Abella seems the happiest of everyone, as per usual, making Alia even more uncomfortable in this house, in this room, than ever before.

"So," Abella says, finally beginning a proper conversation. "Have you two started on wedding plans yet? I'm dying to tell you all my ideas!" She almost squeals with pure excitement. Alia and Eli remain neutral while Fiona beams back towards her. Arna stays unusually quiet, only breaking a small, almost unnatural smile.

"Well, we haven't really decided on anything yet. But we'd love to hear your ideas," she says, her voice unusually high, clearly trying to raise the dreary mood. She grabs Arna's hand tightly and continues to smile towards Fiona.

To anyone who doesn't know their family, they'd think Abella and Fiona were genetic relatives rather than through a pending marriage.

"Of course, we'd love to hear your ideas, Abella. How kind of you to want to help us," Arna finally speaks, her voice of a much lower and serious tone. "But I'm afraid we have rather more important matters to discuss."

Here we go, Alia thinks. Sitting up in her seat and putting down her fork, preparing for the panther to lurch towards her.

"Anything you'd like to tell me?" *In three, two, one...*

"Eli?" *Wait what?*

Alia and Eli simultaneously sit up, confused about the arising situation. As not only the elder sibling, but also the most experienced one of them going on the mission, Alia looks towards Arna, thoroughly confused as to why the blame isn't instantly being pelted onto her like in a normal situation. Eli sits up and looks towards Arna, an unusual fear blazing in his emerald eyes.

"Um, Mum, I don't see what the problem is here." If Eli's finally going to stand up to Arna and fight for something he really wants, this evening is going to turn out to be a very different one compared to how Alia was expecting it to go.

"Excuse me," she begins, her voice suddenly authoritative and deep within parent mode. "Let's just cut to it shall we? You're not going on this mission, Eli, it's too dangerous and you're too young to go. Enough said already."

"Mum, I'm eighteen! I'm out in the world and I was asked to go so I'm going!"

"You may be eighteen but you're still at the Academy, which means you're still learning. You can't decide to take on the world with this little training, Eli, you're not ready and that's final."

"Mum, please," Alia braves to speak. "He didn't choose this, at least completely, neither of us did. We were asked by the most prestigious Protector of our time to be part of a team that matters, the chance to do something great! You can't honestly be saying that he has to refuse this opportunity? He was clearly chosen for a reason."

"Just let your mum handle this, Alia," Fiona adds, her voice unnaturally calm.

"This has nothing to do with you." She snaps back more than she means to.

"Alia, please, you're not helping anyone," Arna says, her eyes now narrowing towards her. "I know you felt you could take on the world when you first started the Academy, but luckily, you learned early on that you still needed help. Now, I need Eli to learn this lesson too, and he will not do that if he goes with you so keep quiet!"

As much as she wants to continue to rattle the cage, she knows this is a fight that Eli has to win on his own. And if he fails and has to pull out, then she wouldn't have to worry about him on their journeys. In her eyes, this could be a win whichever way it falls.

"Mum, I can understand that you're upset but there's nothing you can do or say to change my mind. I want to go! I want to help and I want to be part of something real!"

"Eli, please, just listen to your mum, she's just trying to protect you," Abella tries to add, her also unnaturally calm voice posing more of a hindrance than help to the continual rising conflict.

"I don't need protecting!" Eli shouts, more into the air they're all suffocating within. "You may think I still do, but I don't! I know I still have a lot to learn, but I'm not going out there to face the Royalist alone. Commander Dormer, Commander Thornbe and Commander Peircly are going to be right there. So is Alia and loads of people. I'll be safe with them, Mum, so just let me go! You seriously can't think that you can protect me from the world forever?"

Arna says nothing. Everyone remains silent. Leaning forwards towards him, putting her hands together on top of the table, Arna narrows her eyes closely to Eli as if he were the only one in this room still breathing.

"Even though you're an adult, I'm still your mother and my word is final. I'm calling the General in the morning and telling her you're out. Apart from going to the Academy, I don't want you out of this house. I need to protect you until you're ready. You'll see I'm right eventually."

Shockingly, Eli says nothing. No one does. Seeing that he's close to breaking down in tears of pure fury, Alia sits up and looks towards Arna.

"Don't you feel like you should protect me too?" She pauses, coughing slightly as if to cover up her unusually calm and timid tone. She waits for an instant come back, but nothing comes. "I want to go and you know I will, but why shouldn't you try to stop me too? Yes, I may be older and have more experience than Eli. But I've never been out into the real world, as you call it, either. So, what's the difference?"

"You're asking me why I'm not forcing you to pull out too?" Alia nods, now feeling too nervous for a simple reply and wishes she'd never asked the question at all. "Honestly, I know you'd never listen to me so what's the point in fighting about it? As long as you've got your precious Commander by your side, then you certainly won't let me stop you. She'll keep you in line just fine and then return you back to me when you succeed. If, you succeed."

Feeling previously deeply buried anger towards everyone and everything erupt inside her, Alia shoots up from her seat and exits the room. She strides quickly towards the front door and slams it behind her.

Dropping onto one of the steps leading to the door, she feels tears welling up within her eyes. But she can't let them go, she can't let anything go. The day she cries in front of Arna is the day she really admits defeat. And that day is still a long way off.

Unsure about how much time passes before she hears any sound of human noise, Alia jumps slightly as the front door opens. Abella appears, her dress somehow creaseless and as perfect as ever. As perfect as she always appears to be. Alia would like to say that she's not at all jealous of Abella. Which is a lie. But feeling like she'd like to be Abella is also a lie.

Unsure of what exactly her feelings fall under, Alia is sure that they fall somewhere between the two.

Breathing in the slightly chilling night's air, Abella sits on a few steps above Alia. Taking a few minutes to look out into the night, they sit in silence for what feels more like an eternity.

"You shouldn't have walked out. You've just made things worse for Eli," Abella remarks, clearly wanting to cut right to the core of the problem.

"Well, Mum's already made it quite clear that he's not going, so, I don't see how I could have affected anything."

"Well, you did. You pissed her off even more, which she's now directing towards Eli. That clearly doesn't help him."

"Well, take that up with her then not me!" Alia feels herself shouting but instantly calms down her voice. "What's done is done and what's said is said, I have nothing more to say on the matter."

"Not even if it helps Eli?"

"Well, as you have so clearly pointed out, nothing I can say will help so what's the point in saying anything more?"

"Good God, Alia, are you really that thick?" Abella is shouting now, a rare thing for her to force her voice to do. At least in this household. "Mum is just scared, for both of you. She knows that Commander Dormer will be there to protect you, but what about Eli? He'll have no one to protect him when things start turning to shit because he wasn't ready!"

"I'll be there for him!" A short silence whirls between them. "So will all the commanders and the rest of the group. Plus, each realm is going to be crawling with Force members, we'll be fine!" Abella huffs, clearly meaning to be mocking.

"You say that now, but when have you ever been there for anyone? Really?" Alia feels her body tightening as she senses where this conversation is going. "What about when Dad left? You did nothing for anyone. Just crawled away into your little training room hole, totally on your own. Why would now be any different?"

"How are those two things even linked?" She feels her voice raising but can't seem to soften it. "Dad didn't leave, Mum let him walk away so she could get a shiny new partner that wouldn't screw up as much as him."

"At least you admit he was a screw up."

"Like Fiona isn't?" Abella huffs and stands up defensively. Alia does the same.

"Why do you always have to make everything about Fiona? She makes Mum happy, that should be more than enough for you!"

"It would be, if I thought she was right for Mum, but she isn't and never will be! She's not as screechy clean as she makes herself out to be, but you're just too blind to see it."

"Oh, like everyone you care about aren't exactly the same?" she challenges, causing Alia to huff into the air this time.

"Just stop please, I can't take this anymore. You'll never understand just like they won't, like Mum won't."

"Maybe she would if you'd ever try to open up and explain things properly without getting all worked up."

Feeling the need to just storm off back home just to make a point, Alia goes to turn on her heels but stops when the front door flies open.

Eli takes long quick steps away from the house and doesn't even stop to say goodbye to either Abella or Alia. Watching him run into the night, Alia laughs to herself and smiles at Abella.

"There are just some things you can't fix." She pauses, walking down a few steps before turning back towards her sister. "Enjoy the rest of your night, tell them I say goodbye."

"I hope you lose out there," she remarks, making Alia stop dead in her walk away. "I hope you lose so that people who deserve to win do. You can't remain this stubborn forever, you'll never get anywhere out there and you'll never catch that Royalist. Forget Eli, you are way beyond ready for that. Your commander at your side or not." Feeling the need to laugh more than anything, Alia does as she turns away once again.

"Oh yeah? Watch me."

Eleven

After the conflicting events of the previous evening, Alia won't be the least bit surprised if her mum had managed to track Eli down and imprison him in his room until not only their team leaves, but the overall threat of the Royalist has passed.

While unusually trying to avoid looking at it from her mother's point of view, she can see exactly why she'd do it, but it doesn't make it anymore right. She has to remember that Eli isn't a child anymore and while he's still learning, he's also old enough to make his own decisions. She needs to let him go, just like she let Alia. Even if it was long before she should have.

Now approaching the entrance to the station, Alia stiffens at the tapping of approaching footsteps. Someone is running towards her. Expecting it to be Marne or even Lola, she prepares to give them a traditional but nervous hello until turning around to see the unexpected.

"Eli?" she says, her voice small as if she can't believe she said anything at all. Alia stops walking and Eli eventually manages to catch up to her. Leaning down for a moment to catch his breath, Eli stands up straight and beams towards her.

"Are we late?"

"So, you're finally going to disobey direct orders from the commander of our house?" Neither of them can help but smile towards one another. "And nice uniform by the way." She laughs, pointing towards Eli's black Bureau uniform that would be identical to hers if it weren't for his missing embroidery, just like hers on her first day. As much as Alia doesn't want to admit it, it suits him. Suits him more than it has yet suited her.

"Thanks. I guess they thought it important that we all look the same. Well, at least close enough."

"Probably." They laugh again. "Anyway, um, yeah, she needs to see that I can do this, that I want to do it. She has to let me go sometime."

"Well, I never thought I'd see this day." She smiles again. "But I hope you're not here simply to just piss Mum off? Saying you wanted to come was clearly enough to do that."

"Of course not," Eli argues, his face no longer containing a smile. "You know I wanted to be a part of this whether Mum agreed or not. It's a huge honour to even be considered let alone chosen for this. I'm here for the long run, and I'm here to help."

"Glad to hear it," another voice says coming from behind them. They turn to see Commander Dormer approaching them. Eli instantly looks towards Alia who doesn't take her eyes off the approaching Commander. "Good to see you both here." She smiles towards them, now standing slightly behind them. Eli nods but can't help smile brightly back. "Now, we have a lot of work to do. Let's go and find the others." With that, Alia and Eli follow Commander Dormer together as they're sure to do a lot of in the coming weeks.

***

With only a few brief words spoken at their first official gathering, Alia soon finds herself on the first part of their journey. Straight out of Calla to their closest neighbouring realm; Lily.

Except for those who are either stationed there or are a part of the Council, barely anyone outside of the selected few has ever stepped a foot into Lily's realm since the Royalist war. Suffering the most damage out of them all, it was long ago deemed uninhabitable and only fit for one new purpose, to serve as a prison itself to the last living Royalists. They've each heard rumours about the extensive damage that's never been repaired, but none of them can quite imagine how it will be.

Alia sits along with Lola and Marne, at the back of their train carriage, watching the landscapes and buildings zip past them quicker every passing second – almost as if they were flying.

While trains are rarely used aside from food transportation and a quick means of transport for those with a high enough clearance, it's in moments like this where everyone is thankful for their invention and smooth running.

Although hardly used by actual passengers, Alia marvels at all the little details put into clearly making someone's journey's as comfortable as they can. There are rows of soft cushioned seats, with a layer of soft carpet concealing the rattling metal floor. Although there's nothing to cover the open steel ceiling that arches over them.

This is nearly all of their first times sitting on something moving this fast and experiencing their surroundings in a whole new way. Alia feels almost weightless, as if she could really take off and find her place up there in the sky.

Commander Thornbe sits alone in the middle of the carriage clutching his stomach. Of all the people enclosed within the small metal contraption, no one would have guessed that it would be him to be having trouble with the rapid vibration and buzz beneath them.

Eli and Cora sit together quietly talking as if they were anywhere else and weren't moving at all. Alia finds it fascinating how one new mode of transport can affect every single person in completely different ways.

Although surprised at first that Eli chose to sit with Cora over her, especially after everything that happened the previous night, the more he watches them so relaxed just sitting there and talking, the more she seems to understand.

Commander Peircly chose to take the driver seat and remains closed off from everyone else. At the very front of the carriage, Commander Dormer sits very poised but alone as she watches the hills and the rocks pass her by.

As the only one who has ever been on a train before, aside from Commander Peircly, and also to Lily before, Alia can only wonder how she must be feeling to go back to a place that was once seen as a new beginning, not a new threat. And especially, not another graveyard.

Twelve

Stepping off the carriage, no one can quite believe the desolate landscape that now surrounds them. Alia can think of no better way to describe it than the remains of a city left in the middle of an undisturbed desert. Everything seems as if it had been untouched for so long and in many ways, that's exactly how it has been. Or at least, was.

The ground beneath them is an odd mixture of rubble, dust and rocks, bathed within a sand like sheet that in a certain light seems to glisten as if it were something solid. Although the realm was destroyed back when her mother was only a young child, Alia has grown up with stories of how Lily used to be the most magical realm, in every possible way.

The stories go that part of the grass used to sprout pink in the summer season, echoing the flowers that earnt Lily its name all those years ago. The resonates of the founding flower stretching across to the bulky trees. During every season, a single leaf of the blossom shade would develop against the regular leaves of the changing seasons.

But it was the roots of the trees that everyone used to pay attention to. Growing higher above the surface and a lot larger than they should have been, the rest of the roots used to burrow deep beneath the earth and sprout again at the very edge of the realm, signifying their connection between Lily and the rest of the world that lies beyond Lexia, which is in itself, a whole other kind of story.

Back at the Academy, Alia remembers countless elders coming and giving talks about the importance of their roles, yet each one of them always ended up getting side tracked by questions of Lily. Some would talk of the glistening stones that shone when the sky grew dark while others would go on about the fact that although the seasons changed, as they did in every realm, Lily remained a cool but comfortable temperature all year round, as if the air in many ways remained frozen in a perfect minute.

If all the stories she ever heard were really true, Alia almost feels sick at the sight of what this land has become. All the grass has burnt away, leaving a dry earth that was scorched beyond repair. Nothing can grow here anymore, only fade away as if it were never there at all.

Even the trees have all withered away now. Each one nothing more but stumps of aging wood left to grow old amongst the abandoned stones of the structures that still resemble what used to be buildings.

Commander Peircly is the last to exit the carriage, sending it off down the tracks when everyone has their feet safely on the ground, no matter how unsafe the ground itself may seem. The commanders quickly disperse into all directions with Cora and Eli quick to follow them. Lola and Marne both stick together as they have a short wander away from everyone else. Stepping away from the tracks, Alia reaches down and grasps a handful of sand, her hand tingling as the grains trickle through her fingers. Feeling it all slip away, Alia looks up and tries to take in everything she can see as well as everything she can imagine people used to see.

"Be careful what you touch." Commander Dormer speaks, suddenly appearing at her side. Alia laughs, brushing the lingering sand off her hands as the rest of her body involuntarily tenses.

"Why is there so much sand?" Commander Dormer shrugs, bending down herself and lightly grazing her fingertips over the smooth coating.

"This land has been untouched since the war. It could have blown in from anywhere." She smiles, returning to her feet as Commander Peircly joins them, drawing in all of Commander Dormer's attention.

"No time for sightseeing, we shouldn't be here any longer than necessary. The Royalist might still be here."

"I doubt it." Lola says, suddenly appearing along with Marne to join the conversation. Command Thornbe then approaches with Eli and Cora and all of a sudden, they all seem to be huddled in a circle. "If I were the Royalist, I wouldn't stick around here when I suddenly had the freedom to go anywhere." Alia nods, knowing if it were her, she'd probably wouldn't stick around either.

"Even so, let's not hang around to find out." Commander Dormer continues, taking a minute to straighten her jacket and secure the box and pouch of arrows across her back. "Everyone, stay close."

***

Even from a distance, the Royalist prison isn't exactly what Alia imagined it to be. She envisioned it to be more like a traditional prison, with barred windows and tall stone towers, similar to the confinement chambers they have in each realm. Whereas in reality, she thought it looked more like an abandoned bomb shelter. Built-sideways and down rather than up, with rounded outside walls and little windows that seem more like ones you'd find on a small house.

Yet the closer they get to it, something else about it just seems, odd. Alia tries to tell herself it's just the light, the way the sun rays are skirting over the sand that acts as a type of blanket across the broken roof. But when the brightness of the natural warmth is covered by one of the three moons that can usually be seen around this time, the shimmering doesn't fade, it just dulls.

A group of Force members suddenly emerge from the other side of the prison, guns and arrows pointed until they can see that it's just Commander Dormer.

Getting a closer look at them, Alia can see that though dressed the same as the Force members back at the Bureau, this particular group have a green sown flower, a Lily, on the left arm of their uniforms. They are the new sole Protectors of Lily, even if there is no one actually left apart from themselves for them to try and keep alive. Now almost directly in front of the prison, the Lily Force, as Alia has now named them, keeps a slight distance from her own group gathered together behind Commander Dormer, who slowly steps forwards, leading one of them to do the same.

"Captain Danver, pleasure to see you again."

"And you, Commander." The two smile, shaking hands as if this were a kind of formal gathering.

Her hands down at her sides, Alia's eyes and attention slides between the commander and the prison. Now close enough to really look at it, she pays close attention to the shimmer that seems to be present all around the prison. Almost like a type of force field, seemingly made from dust, sand and sunlight. All totally impossible, yet something she's witnessing first hand.

"Everyone spread out, take a good look at it." Commander Dormer instructs with everyone getting to it right away.

Marne happily skips towards the building, climbing straight up on the remaining stones as if it were a playground attraction. Eli and Cora mimic him, standing tall upon the structure and looking out at the desolate surroundings that only seem worse when compared to something that used to hold so much life.

The other commanders stand with Commander Dormer, already deep in conversation with Captain Danver and his team. Alia approaches the building with caution, reaching out at the flying dust that skirts around her fingers with no fear of falling. Unable to understand it, Alia finds herself smiling.

"I wouldn't stay in that thing for too long." Lola says, joining Alia under the stagnant grains. "It's magic, or sorts at least."

"How do you know?" Lola shrugs, laughing like she was a giddy child who doesn't want to let go of something beautiful.

"I've heard about it. My grandparents were from Lily. They worked on stuff like this before the war."

"For real?" Lola nods, still caught up in what surrounds them.

"Yeah. For a long time, it was their greatest joy."

"I can see why." The two laugh and practically dance under the rays until a loud whistle brings them back the task in hand.

Looking over, they see everyone, including Lily's Force members, all gathered together by the entrance of the prison. Both sad to leave the magic behind, the two pull themselves away and join their team.

Commander Peircly directs everyone's attention towards the back of the building where the largest hole has been made. Everyone watches as he traces the surfaces, moving his fingers in and out of the stone.

"The only concrete thing we know is that the Royalist broke out from the inside. No one got her out, she did it all herself."

"Wait, it's a girl?" Cora frowns.

"According to our records, there was one female missing after we identified the other bodies. So yes, we have concluded that the missing Royalist is a she—" Captain Danver cuts in before quickly stepping back again.

"Never mind her gender. She could have got someone to help her. There's no way of knowing for sure." Marne then speaks, clearly so sure of what he believes could have happened. "Could she have convinced someone to help her?"

"Impossible. Everyone here was handpicked and loyal to their positions." Captain Danver jumps in yet again, quick to defend the lives of all that were lost.

"It's unlikely, but not impossible." Commander Dormer comments. "We know all the Royalists inside still had magic, that's a fact we can never change. But as to how much or how they could use it, we can't be certain of."

Signalling his men to move out, Captain Danver whispers something into Commander Dormers ear, causing her to nod but say nothing in return as he then follows some of his people away from the building while a few hang around before going inside. Commander Dormer then follows them in, everyone else close behind her.

"Did any of you imagine it differently?" Eli pipes up this time, his eyes moving quickly up and down. The building "Like, taller? With bars and stuff."

"That wouldn't have been as effective," Commander Peircly says, "This was constructed to the exact specifications that were designed from the research that was conducted and gathered for years about every weakness the Royalists had. From the material used to the way it was built. It was marketed to be indestructible."

"Nothing's ever indestructible," Alia says, not realising she's spoken until it's too late. Commander Peircly simply laughs. Alia stiffens at his gaze.

"Agreed." He pauses, straightening up and moving to the other side of the main room they stand in. "But it's still more impressive up close."

He leads the way inside the prison. Alia runs her hand across the remaining rough walls, still not quite believing that the Royalists spent their every second here for so long.

They soon enter into a large room, filled with nothing but several beds and a table, each piece clearly made from cheap but solid materials. Commander Dormer and Commander Thornbe stand in one corner, talking to two of the remaining people from Lily's Force. Alia keeps her focus on her surroundings and marvels a little at the detail and effort put into something so important by so many to construct all of this in the first place. To have it all ready and waiting in place for so long. Back then, it really was as simple as hiding a trap in plain sight.

Eli and Cora, suddenly emerge through the door, meaning that everyone from their group is now present along with those from Lily's force.

Considering how cramped it suddenly feels with the majority of them now inside the one room, Alia starts to wonder how it must have been for the Royalists to have been trapped all together like this so long. They could barely move without bumping into each other, god knows what it was like to actually live like that, family or not.

"So, they were all in here together, for all that time? Was that even safe?" Lola asks.

"Completely," one of Lily's Force says, tracing her fingers over the layered dust on the wooden table. "While we wanted them to be punished, not all of us believe in suffering. Living out their long lives here, in this room, seemed punishment enough. It didn't seem right to deny them being together through their final years, no matter how long. They were family after all." Alia finds herself smiling, taking a close look at everything in the room.

"At least we have humanity." Although she whispers this more to herself than saying it as a contribution, she spies a smile creeping across Commander Dormer's face, her eyes clearly narrowing on Alia for a second.

"There were hatches in several walls and we had cameras with audio on them twenty-four hours a day. It's hard to imagine now, but the system did work very well for a long time," another member Lily's Force says, his long red beard getting Alia's attention more than his words. It's rare to know or even see a red headed Protector these days. A simple fact that everyone, including Alia, always seems to just brush over.

It became sort of an old wives' tale that people born with red hair were more capable of harnessing more advanced types of magic and all emigrated to Lily at some point in their lives. Although not believing a word of it and thinking of it as nothing more than an old idea with no proof attached, Alia still had to look at someone twice if they possessed such a unique feature, Lady Dany included.

"It looks like a fool proof system," Commander Dormer speaks, walking around the room once more before stopping in front of him, her face clearly hardening. "So, what happened?" She folds her arms and looks him clearly in the eyes. Alia finds it almost comical that he clearly winces.

"Well, um—"

"They were given their evening meal as normal. Everything was normal, from what the people could tell." the woman takes over, standing head on with Commander Dormer. "And then, all the cameras suddenly went down. The power was failing; the doors to the room became locked from the inside. You name it, it happened. And then, it was like a massive surge of energy erupted and everything shattered. By the time out team managed to get here, every Royalist bar one was dead, along with all our people stationed across the entire realm." Everyone falls silent at the tragic end that they all knew was coming.

"Wow, that's one hell of an explosion." Marne says while everyone else remains quiet for far longer than they should.

"So, do you have anything else to show us?" Commander Dormer says. Almost instantly, the female Lily Force member, who hasn't mentioned her name, nods and exits the prison, not even indicating that everyone should follow, they just do.

She leads them to a small building far enough away from the prison for it not to be seen easily yet still close enough for them to move between the two quickly if necessary.

Going around to the side of what can only be described as a box-like building, constructed mostly of bricks, she takes them into a cold room.

The whole room is very clinical and clean, but not in the same way that the Bureau is. It's obvious to Alia that what they're standing in isn't like any kind of room they have at the Bureau. This, is a morgue.

"Here." The woman pulls on a handle, one of many that litters a single wall. In pulling it she exposes a large draw with a body in it.

Everyone apart from the commanders and Force members look away, making it obvious who has and hasn't ever seen a body before.

Alia and Lola are first to look back and take a proper look at the shell that used to hold life. Looking at a real body is such an odd experience.

Studying her, at least she assumes it's a her from the long grey hair and in certain areas, slightly rounded body, Alia finds it almost unbelievable to think that not long ago, this woman was alive. She was walking around, probably talking and maybe even laughing. She was a person with breath in her lungs and magic in her veins. Above all the wrong she did, at the end of the day, she was still human. She was still one of them.

Although feeling suddenly nauseous, Alia finds that she can't look away. Her eyes remain transfixed as Marne, Eli and Cora all can only manage a quick glance before having to look away again, each make a kind of disgusted noise as they do.

"This was one of the bodies we recovered after the break out." The woman goes on.

"What happened to her?" Commander Dormer's voice is suddenly soft, like she's afraid to speak in anything more than a slightly hushed tone in respect for the dead, no matter who they were.

"We're still trying to work that out." The woman takes a breath. "Apart from her obvious cuts and bruises from the explosion itself, there's nothing about her body that explains her death." At this, everyone finds themselves frowning. "It still doesn't make much sense but from all the tests conducted so far, on every Royalist not just this one, it was like all the life was sucked out of their bodies leaving nothing but the empty shell."

"But that's impossible, surely," Alia says, caught between still being confused but also being rather amazed. "Even if they had magic, surely, that just couldn't happen." The woman shrugs, slowly pushing the woman back into what Alia can only presume is some type of freezer.

"The whole thing is still a mystery." She pauses. "We were measuring their heart rates, blood pressure; you name it, every minute of every day. Some were healthier than others but that's just age. And then suddenly, it was like all their life had been sucked out of them. Everything they had, gone. Finished."

"So, maybe the Royalist, what, took it? The living one I mean. Maybe that's how she escaped. How she got powerful enough to escape." Eli suggests.

"That seems to be the on-going theory." Commander Thornbe answers, clearly wanting to seem as if he knows more about it all than he actually does.

"What about the data records? Of their health and the camera footage?" Commander Dormer asks, her arms now folded but her face unchanged. The woman shrugs, clearly feeling a little defeated by this point.

"Gone. All of it. Lost in the power failure. Almost like it was planned." Commander Dormer sighs before turning back to everyone looking at her expectantly. Everyone including Alia.

Taking a long breath, Commander Dormer politely nods towards the woman and leads the way out of the little brick box.

"Thank you." Commander Peircly says once they're all out of the building. He smiles and shakes the woman's hand, in the same formal manor as the exchange between Commander Dormer and Captain Danver had been upon their arrival.

"I know it's not much to go on, but I think there's still more to find. I suggest we set up camp here tonight and gather more information before moving out first thing in the morning. Any questions?" Commander Dormer looks around at each member of their group in turn.

"But are you sure it's safe to stay? I thought you didn't want us to hang around."

"We don't. But, it's necessary. Remember, you all knew the risks signing up to this." Commander Thornbe's voice is strict, like he was giving them a warning not to directly question them.

"So where will we go in the morning? Straight to Aster?" Cora asks.

"Most likely. But running to Aster could be one great diversion." She pauses, taking a quick look up at the changing sky. "This Royalist is smart and god knows just how powerful. With any luck, she left something behind that will give us a clue to her next move. Everyone has to slip up sometime." She pauses, as if thinking about what exactly to say next. "Now go. Gather wood and sticks and anything useful. And always keep your eyes open, you never know what you might find."

Everyone gives her a nod of understanding and parts ways. Marne and Lola quickly jog in the direction of a collection of trees while Alia hangs back and wanders once again towards the prison.

Sitting on one of the rounded walls, she clears the dust from the bumpy shell and lets her mind begin to question what really happened and where the Royalist could be right now.

That is, if they're even still alive.

***

As the night draws in quicker than any of them anticipated, Alia sits on a log around a burning campfire along with everyone aside from the commanders.

For being a team assembled by the General, Alia would have thought that they'd discuss more details about the mission together rather than just the commanders talking amongst themselves and only sharing details that they deem necessary.

Alia knows she shouldn't be watching them. She shouldn't be interested in all their little movements and shuffles on the rocks they perch on only short distance away.

"What you looking at?" Eli says, breaking the silence around them and sitting beside her.

Even though they are now on the same team, there still remains a small divide between Bureau and Academy members with Alia and Eli being the only ones to occasionally bridge the gap. Cora sits alone, clearly happy keeping to herself, on one side of the campfire while Marne and Lola sit on the other, leaving Alia and Eli now in the middle.

"Nothing." She pauses, finally moving her eyes away from the commanders to Eli. "Why are they always talking in secret? Aren't we all supposed to be a team?" Eli shrugs, clearly not bothered by their lack of engagement.

"Who cares. They'll tell us if it's important. Plus, even though we are a team, they'll always be a higher rank than us. They're just used to taking the lead, knowing stuff first."

"I guess so," Alia replies, sighing while taking another quick glance in their direction. "I just wish they trusted us more. We're all meant to be here for a reason." Eli laughs, looking between the stars above and Alia's confused glance.

"Come on, Alia, not everyone has the same level of trust that you have with Commander Dormer. The rest of us have to earn it. Especially me and Cora, this is all totally new ground for us. Besides, the other commanders are probably still testing the waters. They'll tell us when they think they can trust us."

"Why do you always have to bring up Commander Dormer? Why can't we just have a normal conversation?" Eli laughs again, as if unfazed with her agitated tone.

"Because you never shut up about her and your time at the Academy!" He says, his voice a little too loud for comfort. "How much she taught you, how great it was and how much you miss it, like we get it."

"I do not!" She tries to keep her own voice to a steady level. So far, no one has given them a second glance. "Just because I mention her in passing conversation doesn't mean anything. And yeah, I miss the Academy, so what? I'm allowed to say that aren't I? To feel that? It was a big part of my life for three years where I literally did learn everything I needed to."

"Yeah, but I wouldn't keep going on about it. It's weird. You've left, it's in the past. Why go back when you're now somewhere you've trained to be your whole life?"

"And why don't you get over yourself and grow up." Alia stands up abruptly, this time attracting everyone's attention, including Commander Dormer's from the rocks she still sits on. "I'm going to go and get some more firewood," she says, starting to walk in the direction of the woods which is a short distance to her left. Eli takes her arm, although not forcefully.

"No, I'll go. I need a walk," he says through short repeated breaths. Alia looks him up and down. "What?" He sighs in a clearly overdramatic way. "I'm grown up enough to go on my own, aren't I?"

Alia rolls her eyes as she watches him practically storm away into the night.

It's only when watching him walk away that Alia realises the truth to a lot of what he said, no matter how hard it is for her to admit. She knows she needs to let go of the Academy. She knows she needs to let go of everything she loved then and focus on the now, especially given where they currently are and everything they have to do. But as with anything, thinking about moving on and actually doing it are two very different things.

As if deciding now would be the perfect time to re-join the group, the commanders each leave the rocks and find an empty spot around the bright spitting fire.

Commander Thornbe and Commander Peircly both sit between Cora and Marne, unknowingly making the gap between the two groups bigger than before.

Instead of following the others, Commander Dormer makes her way towards Alia, who still remains standing just outside of the circle, her arms folded and face hardened.

"What was all that about?" Commander Dormer asks, now standing directly in front of Alia.

"Nothing, just, normal sibling stuff." She tries to laugh but is clearly very unconvinced. "It's just, complicated." She sighs, turning around, staring at everything directly in her eye line. "Why is everything always so complicated?" This time Commander Dormer laughs.

"Because that's life. The easy bit is over, now the real hard work begins."

They laugh together quietly, taking a minute to admire the shining sky above them.

Out of all the realms, Lily always did have the best view at night. Fewer clouds meaning more starry nights. Just another thing that was lost before people like Alia ever had the chance to appreciate it. Looking up at it now, Alia can almost imagine what it was like before. Although she can never know for sure, she's heard plenty of others say that when magic was around, certain starts used to glisten all night long and become fixed points in the sky, no matter what direction you're looking up from.

Commander Dormer suddenly sighs, her eyes skirting between the sky and everyone else sitting down.

"I think it's time we all get some sleep. Don't worry, I'll wait up for Eli. I'm sure he won't be long."

"I wouldn't count on it." Alia huffs. "There were nights where he'd be about walking for hours. Just helps him clear his head I guess."

"We all have different methods of keeping it together. Or at least trying to. As long as they work, and don't hurt anyone, there's no harm in it." Alia nods.

"Yeah, I guess so." Smiling, Command Dormer lightly brushes Alia's shoulders before steering her back in the direction of the campfire.

"Lights out people. I need everyone awake and raring to go as soon as the sun comes up."

To Alia's surprise, no one says a word. Everyone simply gets up and heads towards their sleeping spots, taking off their relevant layers and burying themselves beneath their blankets.

When laying down on the hard ground beneath her own blanket, Alia takes in a long breath, closing her eyes and then opening them to the blissful sky above. Putting her hands together, she continues to stare up.

"It's never been easy," she whispers, smiling at the shiny things that meet her eyes until they're too heavy to keep open.

Thirteen

Alia awakes to the smell of dried out smoke being wafted around them by the oddly nice warm morning breeze. Yet even though she's far from cold, Alia still shivers a little, sitting up and pulling her blanket tighter around her shoulders before putting her jacket back on.

Around she sees nearly everyone still quietly sleeping. Commander Peircly and Commander Dormer appear to be the only ones gone from their beds. Gone where exactly, she isn't sure. She nearly laughs at how loudly Commander Thornbe still lays there snoring.

How hasn't he woken everyone else up? she thinks, concealing her laugh with her blanket.

Her sleepy eyes then travel to Eli, lying peacefully not far from her spot. She hasn't watched him, or anyone for that matter, sleep in the longest time. Not that she misses it, or ever made a habit of watching people sleep, but she's almost found the strangest comfort in being able to see people when they're at their most peaceful with still the ability for them to wake when they need to.

In the distance, she spies Commander Dormer and Commander Peircly running towards the sleeping recruits, their eyes amidst with worry and urgency. Something's happened.

Something bad.

"Get up! Everyone! Now!"

"Wakey-wakey people!" the commanders shout as they approach. One by one, everyone wakes and stands to attention, waiting for further instructions. Commander Peircly gathers around in a small circle, as if afraid they could be easily overheard. But he isn't the one to speak.

"Our people have just informed me that there's been a sighting. Someone has described a weak looking woman covered in a grey cloak lurking on the outskirts of Anemone," Commander Dormer says, her words rushed even in her quiet tone.

"Damn, she got there quickly," Lola says, taking it in as everyone is clearly trying to do.

"We search every train that comes into and leaves each realm and she's likely to know this so it makes sense that she'll be walking, taking public roads and footpaths. If this is the case, then everyone in all the realms is now at great risk. Especially, those in Anemone."

"Can't we do something from here like right now? Evacuate the realm or something? Make sure everyone gets out safely." Cora asks, her innocence suddenly so pure.

"It's too risky. The second she sees anyone acting strangely, she'll know we know. And when that happens, we don't know what she'll do," Commander Thornbe replies, his voice hoarse and scratchy. Clearly not a morning person.

"She's been locked up and living in a cave for god knows how long. How will she know what's normal?" Marne contributes. *Good point,* Alia thinks to herself while trying to figure out what she can contribute that will be useful.

"She's a highly intelligent individual who also has magic. A deadly combination. For now, it's best to play it safe and really try and learn how powerful she is before doing anything like an evacuation."

"Lady Talia and her advisors, as well as the General, have been notified of the development. We've instructed her to warn her people to look out for any odd behaviour or occurrences that they might see. For smart people, they don't question a lot of what they're told when it comes to things like that."

"You mean, they still don't know what's really going on?" *Was that a good enough question?*

"No," Commander Dormer answers. "The Council voted that as of right now, everything is still on a need-to-know basis. Everyone will be told at the appropriate time, not before."

Everyone looks around at each other, fear present in each and every one of their eyes. They were really doing this, they were really chasing after the Royalists. And they were doing it now.

As if on cue, a small automatic food carriage begins making its way towards them on the tracks. It's wooden material instead of metal and far smaller than their train carriage was. As much as she shouldn't have thought about it, having never actually seen one, Alia presumed that the food carriages would be like a copy of the train carriages. But apparently not.

This carriage it's also moving a lot slower, its steady movements makes it seem like more of a child's toy than an actual machine that so many depend upon each day.

Commander Dormer smiles.

"That's our ride. We don't want to be seen by too many people if we can help it. Best to keep out of prying eyes."

"But isn't it a bit, like small?"

"And slow," Marne and Lola interject, clearly not as appealed as the commanders are to their lift.

Eli simply laughs along with Cora who also seems more confused than anything. "We could walk there faster than that thing."

"Whether you like it or not we're taking it. Get ready to jump on or you'll be left behind," Commander Dormer says, quickly gathering her things as the carriage approaches. Everyone soon follows in her lead, preparing to jump aboard.

With a short but powerful run against the tracks, they all land on their feet inside the only part of the carriage that isn't taken up with food and medical supplies.

Everyone staggers for a minute as Commander Thornbe pulls the previously open door shut. Marne grabs an apple from the top of a large food stack and throws it in the air, catching it happily.

"At least we have breakfast." Everyone seems to laugh, now regaining their balance; they each divide up into the carriage and sit down, knowing of the long journey ahead of them. At least, everyone aside from Eli.

Keeping a relatively straight face, he moves to an unoccupied part of the carriage and sits alone, staring through the small cracks in the ancient wooded structure, watching the landscape rush him by, much like he did when they sat in the train carriage.

Yet this time, his eyes seem to have a purpose. A true meaning. Almost as if he's looking for someone, or something. And whatever it is, it's out there, somewhere.

Fourteen

The majority of their journey has been a slow, but ultimately quiet one. Some have occasionally whispered to each other while others like Alia have kept to themselves for the entirety of the ride.

Now used to the feeling of the wooden carriage being propelled at one constant motion, Alia finds herself lost within her thoughts of what might be, instead of what is. Over the years she's found that in moments of quiet, if she thinks about everything that could happen, she'll be less surprised if one of her outcomes actually comes true.

"I thought we were going for, you know, the subtle approach." Alia blinks at Marne's voice. He peers through one of the bigger gaps in the rattling wood.

Even through the smallest cracks, they can all see the food cart approaching the entrance to Anemone's inner city, rather than the little dusty storage hut they're usually sent to.

"I think they're expecting us." Commander Thornbe says, as the cart very slightly begins to slow.

It isn't long before the movement of the wheels completely stops and the shapes of stationary bodies become clearer through the wooden shell. Opening the main compartment door, Alia can see that while they're not at the usually loading bay, they have stopped within some kind of short tunnel that both echoes every small sound while also letting in the light of the morning from all directions. The commanders, as usual, are the first to get out and gaze upon the new and familiar faces that stand before them.

"Good morning, Commanders, and everyone." Lady Talia's voice is on the surface, as gentle as the smile she bears to them all. But it only takes one look at the four Guards positioned behind her to know that she is here for far more than a casual greeting.

"Lady Talia." Commander Dormer nods politely before closing the carriage door. "Nice to see you arrived back safely, and oddly fast might I add." Lady Talia laughs, her voice bouncing against each rounded tunnel wall.

"Express transport courtesy of the General."

"Of course." She pauses as each of the commanders instinctively all very carefully move their hands towards their weapons. Alia tries to keep her eyes up, not wanting to draw any unnecessary attention to anyone. "I take it that you know why we're here?"

"Of course." Lady Talia replies, almost mimicking Commander Dormer's previous words. "The vote to create your little group to hunt down the Royalist was unanimous by the Council. We all felt it was the best course of action to take."

The way she stands, the way she talks, it's like Alia can just see the word privilege seeping from every part of her well poised body. While Alia will always commend Lady Talia for not being raised to rule, but fighting to earn it, it doesn't mean that now she has it, she won't turn into a version of all the previous leaders Talia's generation fought to be rid of.

Clearly questioning something about her manor as well, Commander Dormer shifts her weight between her feet, like she's ready to run, and her eyes skirt across every Guard distinctly waiting for a fight.

Although originating in Calla, it's obvious that every Guard has been in Anemone far too long. When leaving the Academy, Alia never once considered not going onto the Bureau and going into a line of Personal Protection assignments instead. While she's sure it would be considered a great honour to have such an important person's life in your hands, she always questioned whether her heart would really be in it if she took on a task of protecting someone that she has very little care to actually protect. While she knows if she had to, she'd just do it as it would be her job, but Alia would much rather have to earn a position that means something to her. Even if means going about everything the long way around.

"We also feel the same." Commander Dormer eventually continues. "And we will try and make our presence here as undisruptive as possible. We wouldn't want to give anyone any cause to panic."

"On the contrary, Commander. We've just received news that The Beguile Clowns have just come to town."

Everyone, aside from the commanders, lets out a little shriek of excitement, which is quickly put out with one stern look from Commander Peircly.

The Beguile Clowns. Just the name is enough to get anyone a little giddy. While it's not uncommon for people to decide, when the time comes, to leave their realm for another in pursuit of what they really want to do, it is unusual to leave and choose to not belong to any realm at all.

Each realm is in charge of something; Calla is Protection, Anemone is Technology, Orchid is Food and Aster is Intelligence. Everyone has a part to play in keeping everything running smoothly. Everything works and most of the time, it works well. But there are always those who have to say no.

To those who decide the structured realm life isn't for them, well, they literally run away and join the travelling circus. Or as they liked to be called, The Beguile Clowns.

"Does that mean we can go and see the Circus?" Marne says, his tone directly caught between being mocking and genuinely serious. While the commanders huff, Lady Talia laughs.

"Actually, I was informed to come here and tell you myself that there has been a sighting, near where the Circus is setting up. It seems the most logical place to look for her."

"Sweet." Marne laughs and shares an odd look with Talia.

Alia rolls her eyes but also tries not to smile at the thought of getting to go. Glancing quickly over at Eli, she sees him trying not to make it obvious that he's doing the same thing.

"It isn't the worst idea in the world." Commander Dormer says, almost smiling herself.

"Good." Lady Talia smiles, somehow even wider. "I will let my people take you there personally. At least with all the excitement, a few extra uniformed officials won't turn too many heads."

"Let's hope not." Lady Talia and Commander Dormer give each other one last nod before the Guards all turn around and start walking in the direction they all then follow.

Hands now off their weapons, Commander Thornbe and Commander Peircly take the lead behind the Anemone Guards with everyone else trailing behind. Alia tries her best not to look but in the end gives in and steals a glimpse behind them. Sure enough, Lady Talia remains still, her eyes solely on them. Her long reaching smile now replaced with something else, something Alia doesn't recognise. Something she wants to know more about.

"Head forwards." Commander Dormer whispers, her hand briefly moving Alia's head. "It's not polite to stare."

"I wasn't staring." Alia replies, her voice just as hushed. "Do you really think the Royalist is at the Circus? Or will be?" Commander Dormer shrugs.

"Only one way to find out I guess." Alia nods as they both keep their focus forwards, making sure not to fall behind the rest of the group.

***

The route to the Circus is far from a glamourous one. Alia thinks it's as though the Anemone Guards deliberately led them down all the dingy back alleys rather than letting them soak up the sites of the realm.

It's rare that anyone really gets to travel between realms, unless you're either on the Council or are travelling to see family who you've moved away from, much like Abella's visit for their dinner just before they left.

Alia always liked to think that travel was another reason she always wanted to join the Force. Getting the chance to see the world while doing your duty and protecting the innocents of each and every realm. What more could Alia ever hope to achieve in her life?

"Is that it?" Cora says, pointing to the top of a large pointed tent that can clearly be seen from miles away, which Alia believes was probably the whole point of it. Attracting people from far and wide to all come together and enjoy the same performance.

"Yes, I believe it is." Commander Dormer agrees.

As they move closer, Ali can't help but let out a little excited but quiet squeal. Clearly hearing it, Commander Dormer laughs, looking towards her.

"Don't get too excited. We may not even be able to stay for the show." Alia sighs.

"I know, but I can't help it. I've never actually been to the circus."

"What?" This time it's Commander Dormer who fails to conceal her shock. "Who has never been to the circus?"

"Me, apparently." Alia laughs. "The only time it was in Calla when everyone in the house was free to go just happened to be the time that I caught the flu and didn't leave the house for a week."

"Oh, bad luck there."

"Don't remind me." Alia smiles, happier than she should be at the lightness and ease of their conversation. "Mum always promised we'd go again when it came back. Then when it finally did, I dunno. There was just, too much else going on. And, we never went." Commander Dormer walks silently for a minute, her eyes moving between the path in front and Alia who still walks besides her.

"Well, if it will help you stay focused on actually staying alive. How about I promise to take you if we survive this?" An even wider smile stretches across Alia's face.

"Is that a bribe Commander? Surely you're not allowed to bribe me to do well?" They both laugh, this time loud enough to cause a few heads to look towards them. At the input of other eyes, they both find themselves looking down for a minute.

"It's not a bribe, it's just encouragement." Alia nods.

"I think that's something I can get behind." Commander Dormer nods in return.

"Glad to hear it." They continue laughing until they approach the designated pebbled path leading towards the large tent.

The guards bring them right up to the entrance and allow everyone to gaze up before attempting to speak.

"Wow," Alia whispers, smiling as her eyes dance around every point of the tent, taking note of everything from the elegant lettering and drawings of the performers to the bold red background and black poles which seem to be the only things holding it up.

Clearly thinking they don't need to address everyone directly; the Anemone guards quietly say something to Commander Thornbe before moving past everyone in the direction that they came from. They move in such a stiff and structured fashion that Alia wouldn't be surprised if it ever came out that they were part machine, no matter how futuristic that idea currently is.

"Okay everyone, listen up."

Even though it's Commander Thornbe who speaks and will be taking the lead on this, Alia still commends him on giving Commander Dormer a look before saying anymore, as if asking her if it's okay to do so. In many short years, how times have changed.

"We don't know if she's here, or may have been here, but it's your objective to find out without asking people directly." Marne frowns.

"So, you want us to indirectly ask these Circus people if they've seen anything odd in the past, what twenty-four hours? All without making them suspect that anything is wrong?" Commander Thornbe nods.

"What? Not up to the challenge?"

"Always! Let's do this." Marne laughs, bouncing up and down, clearly raring to go.

"Good. I want everyone to split up to cover more ground. We need to meet back here by sunset at the very latest. Understood?"

"Yes." Everyone chants together, already splitting off and in some cases, bolting through the entrance.

Alia decides to take a slow wander inside, soaking up everything she can see.

Although just setting up, Alia smiles widely at everything going on around her. There are people on the trapeze practicing their routine, juggling acts littering the main sandy circle floor in the middle of the room and various other people just walking around.

Everyone is wearing combinations of fabrics that Alia has never seen before. There's no structure here, no routine, no right or wrong way of doing things. Here, everyone seems, well, free.

And it's amazing.

"Can I help you?" A guy says, suddenly appearing at her side.

"Um, hi." She responds, suddenly feeling very awkward.

Turning to face him, Alia studies the guy, trying to place him among all the acts that she's both seen practising and also knows about.

From his toned and clearly strong body, covered mostly by an odd thin black material which conceals his rather pale skin up to his shoulders, leaving his arms and neck open and exposed. A random star pattern is all over the black fabric and Alia can only imagine how much it must shine under the bright stage lights.

Maybe he's a juggler or one of the people who swings from the ceiling using ropes that always look like they're going to snap.

No matter what he does, the Circus guy reminds her a lot of Emmett, so much so that once she realises, Alia can't un-see it. He has that classic *fall for me* look that she imagines will only help draw in more crowds of giggly young girls who all want to experience that forbidden love story.

"I'm Kole, with a K. I'm one of the tumblers here."

Huh, a tumbler. I was close enough.

"Hi, Kole with K. Nice to meet you." Alia holds out her hand. Smirking, he takes it. Alia fights every urge she has to bite her lip and run away. This is all just a part of her job now. "I'm—" She instantly hesitates.

Am I even allowed to tell him my name?

"I'm, um, here to make sure that, um, everything is okay." He raises an eyebrow, indicating that he clearly doesn't believe her. Yet, he doesn't walk away.

"Well, as you can see, so far so good." Alia nods.

"Good." While neither of them talk for a minute, with everyone else still busy around them, they are far from standing in silence.

"Was that all?"

"Um." She takes a breath, considering how much she's really allowed to say outright and how much she has to try and phrase in a particular manner. "Actually, I'm enquiring as to if you've seen or heard anything, um, unusual, in the past day or so." He laughs, probably more than he should, at her question.

"Anything unusual or strange." He puts a hand to his chin, as if over exaggerating the fact that he's thinking about it. "Well, some people would say that's us all over. Us Circus people, I mean."

"I think you're amazing. All of you," Alia says before she can stop herself.

"Oh yeah," he says, in that smooth kind of way with eyes that some would look into and just melt. But not Alia, mission or not. "You like us Circus lot do you?" She smiles.

"What's not to like?" He laughs again, taking a small step towards me.

"Walk with me? I'll see what I can remember." She nods, letting him lead the way through the tent.

They walk through the centre of what will clearly be the stage before exiting through the back. Alia expects it to lead them outside but instead, it takes them to another part of the tent. They brush past large mirrors and an array of costumes. Alia has never seen so much colour in one place, let alone across a single rack of clothing.

Several people give them a peculiar look as they pass but no one stops to comment. Alia is sure that they must be used to seeing people like her around from time to time.

"So, you like the Circus?" Kole asks, taking the time to study Alia's face while not letting them drift off course.

"I mean who doesn't?" She smiles, still not believing she's here, let alone here in Anemone.

"Oh, there are some. We always get at least one thing thrown at us from the audience during a show."

"Seriously?" Kole shrugs.

"Goes with the job I guess. Not everyone understands that we don't all do what we do out of choice."

"In what way?" Kole remains quiet as he brings her through another door, this one actually leading them outside.

Although the sky is still bright with the light of the day, there is a certain shadow to it, like the night is already drawing in but only in one particular section.

Kole motions for her to stay close, weaving between people as he brings them to another tent. Although small to look at, when venturing inside, Alia believes it to be anything but.

With no windows of anywhere for light to get in, the room is lit by hanging fires, each one secured to the rounding walls of the red tent. While to look at she doesn't believe it to be a safe place to have a fire, she also knows it isn't her place to comment.

The flames each look down and illuminate a white padded mat that takes up the majority of the circular Earth the tent is pegged into.

Alia lingers at the side while Kole moves to the middle, bouncing a little on the white mat.

"Go on then. Show me what you've got."

Kole laughs as he positions himself at one end of the mat. Giving it a short run, Kole practically flies into the air, successfully pulling it of an impressive combination of turns and flips until he lands with his feet on the ground as if it was nothing. Alia claps, a real, genuine smile on her face.

"Wow," she begins. "Bravo sir." He returns her smile with a simple backflip and a bow. "I can see why audiences like you, at least most of them from what you say."

"Well, I guess some of us are just born for this." He laughs, motioning Alia to join him on the mat. Without much hesitation, she does and they sit.

"So, you wanted to know about anything odd and unusual."

"I did. But more in the traditional sense."

"And why are you so interested?"

"Um." She pauses, not quite sure what to tell him as for some reason, she doesn't want to have to lie.

"Let me guess, you've been instructed to ask me, but not in the way that I actually know what's going on?" She frowns, suddenly nervous that she's already said too much. At her face, Kole finds himself laughing once again.

"Don't worry, you haven't betrayed your code or whatever." He continues to laugh alone while Alia remains more confused than ever. "I'm Calla, born and raised. Or at least I was."

"Seriously?" Alia gasps, both from shock and relief.

"Oh yeah. I trained at the Academy for a year before I decided enough was enough. I still remember a fair bit from my time there through."

"Huh, wow." Alia laughs, looking between the blazing warmth above and Kole's glistening eyes.

"What?" He nudges her, moving a little closer. Alia tenses but doesn't attempt to move away.

"I dunno, just, I guess I never really thought about it. Where all of you come from. It's not like you're born into the circus."

"It does happen but, no. Usually, we do all have to come from somewhere. And currently, we're from all over."

"Why did you choose to leave? What didn't you like about the Academy?" Kole shrugs, leaning back on his hands.

"There wasn't anything particularly bad about it. I guess it just wasn't for me." He pauses. "I was never one for order and rankings. I like to entertain people, I like to make them smile." Not sure whether she does it out of choice or because he said it, Alia finds herself smiling. "See right there! Just like that." They laugh at his sudden excitement. "The joy you can bring to someone just by pulling off a few tricks that would otherwise be seen as impossible. At least, with magic gone." Alia nods.

"I bet there's no other feeling like it." Kole shakes his head.

"So far, nothing even comes close to it."

They continue to laugh as Kole again moves closer, bridging the gap between them so much that soon enough, Alia can feel his breath on her neck. The warmth of another body that's equally comforting yet some reason, very unsettling. Bringing one of his hands to her cheek, her leans in as if he's about to kiss her.

Heart racing and sudden confusion in her head, Alia moves away seconds before his lips would have touched hers. Alia instantly gets to her feet and moves a little away from Kole, desperately trying to regain her objective without things becoming extremely awkward.

"Um." She sighs, closing her eyes with her back to him. Slightly shaking her head, she takes a breath before looking back and focusing in on his eyes. "So, since you know how I work, I guess I can just come out with it." She pauses again, her footing suddenly uneasy on the firm but slightly sinking mat. "We're looking for a woman. Quite elderly, we think. She was seen walking around near here covered by a grey cloak. We're just, enquiring if anyone has seen her."

Alia is relieved when Kole also gets to his feet but doesn't attempt to approach her or leave the tent. He remains still, his eyes transfixed on her.

"I mean I can't talk on behalf of everyone but I can honestly tell you that I haven't seen her. But I'll be sure to take a detailed look at the audience tonight."

"Thank you." Alia smiles, although this time it feels a lot more forced and barely real.

"You will stay for the show tonight, won't you?" Alia can't help but bite her lip this time, causing Kole to sigh.

"You're not Anemone based, are you?"

"No. We might be moving on before then."

"We?"

"Yeah. I'm not here alone, there's a few of us looking for her." Kole nods.

"Must be an important woman."

"Of sorts."

"Is she dangerous?"

"We don't know." Alia responds, a little too quickly. "But if you do see her, don't approach her whatever you do." Kole nods again.

"I promise."

Both feeling like there's nothing more to say, they stand in silence until Kole crosses the tent towards the only available door.

"I'll, walk you out."

"Thank you." Alia smiles, swiftly overcome by a new sense of guilt. Guilt that she couldn't tell him more, couldn't even tell him her name. And guilt that she didn't kiss him. Not because she's working and she knows she shouldn't but because, she just didn't want to. She didn't want to make him think that they could have had something that wasn't going to happen, even if it was only for one night.

They walk in silence back to the entrance of the main tent where Marne is already waiting, along with Commander Dormer and Commander Thornbe. Everyone's eyes fall to her as they see her approach with Kole at her side. Before getting too close, Alia stops and turns to Kole.

"Thank you, for all your help. And your tricks, they were amazing really." He laughs, as if forgetting a lot of what they've just been talking about. "I can see that you made the right decision. This is certainly the life for you." He smiles, suddenly very smug.

"I like to think I chose well." She smiles, ready to leave him now. But before she can, he puts a hand on her arm. Even from this distance, Alia can feel Commander Dormer's eyes in particular focused on her every move. "You could have this life too you know. You could stay." At this, Alia laughs harder than she has all day.

"Now that, is crazy."

"Why? You feel trapped I can see it in your eyes. You don't want it as much as you think you do, as much as you've been trained to think. You want freedom, I can give you that." Sighing, Alia takes a brief glance over her shoulder at both the commanders and Marne. It doesn't take long for her to remember that she can't afford to get distracted or forget what, and who, is really important.

"I'm happy where I am, thank you very much. Besides, you don't even know me." Although firm, she makes sure to say it in such a way that Kole will not be offended. "But thank you for the offer. I, I'll do my best to hang around. Make sure I come and see the show."

"I'll look out for you, stranger." With that, he smiles and vanishes back inside the tent.

Feeling a new sense of warmth and giddiness, Alia glides back to where everyone else is standing and tries not to smile as wide as she knows she still is.

Marne is quick to approach her while Commander Dormer makes it known that she's too busy talking with Commander Thornbe to ask her questions.

"That looked rather cosy. You move quickly Alia, I never expected that of you, I'm impressed."

"Oh, shut up!" Alia laughs, pushing Marne as he playfully tries to get a little too close. "He was nice and he was helpful, end of."

"Yeah right. Have you seen his face? And under that uniform well—"

"Seriously, just stop!" Although they both laugh about it, Alia feels herself getting slightly defensive.

There was nothing to tell, but even if there was, why should she have to tell him about it? Yes, they're friends but it's not like they're exactly close.

"Anyway," Alia takes a breath, making sure she feels calm enough to continue the conversation. "How did you get on, any luck?" Marne shrugs, dragging his feet across the stones that cover the ground they stand on.

"Nothing really. Nothing helpful." Alia nods, hoping that will signify the end of the conversation. "The commanders think we should hang around though. Apparently, someone saw someone who could be her, heading this way not long ago. There's every chance that she could end up here by tonight."

Knowing that they now get to stay, Alia is both happy and nervous. Happy that she finally gets to see the Circus, but nervous that she has to once again look Kole in the eyes. Happy that they're in with a possible chance of intercepting her before anyone gets hurt, yet nervous of everything that would happen if she were to come here. No matter what way she looks at it, Alia can't seem to settle on any future outcome which won't result in someone, somewhere, being unhappy.

***

Minutes before the evening performance is about to start, a part of Alia has never felt so alive.

She never imagined you could fit this many people inside a single confined space. Every seat is filled and everyone is clearly excited.

Looking at everyone, for once all in very casual dress, Alia finds it odd that right now, she'd not be able to pick out a Guard from travelling food worker. Once out of uniform, everyone just seems to mould together, still different but yet, the same. How easy it would be for the Royalist to be here, blending in as if she were any other member of the realm.

Alia stands at the very edge of the tent, along with everyone aside from Commander Peircly who is taking his shift to observe anything that might happen outside. While they're allowed to watch the show, they also have to remain vigilant and alert at all times.

Soon enough, the lights begin to dim, causing a new wave of excited squeals from practically every audience member. Alia feels her heart quicken, both at the fact that the show is about to begin and that she knows that if anything were to happen, it would be now or very soon.

Almost as soon as the first act takes the stage, Commander Dormer quietly excuses herself outside. Alia knows her movements are none of her concern. She knows she needs to stay focused and watch the room as if her life depended on it. Yet, she finds herself following the commander before she can talk herself out of it.

The night outside is quiet and still. The sky above is a coal black, full of both stars and mild clouds, along with a moon. You can only see one of the three moons from Anemone and tonight, it appears to be almost as bright as the sun shone during the day.

Two fires burning on the ends of tall wooden sticks are placed on either side of the Circus' entrance, like an indication for anyone late to just head on in.

At the end of the pathway, right next to the flames, Commander Peircly stands, his eyes gazing out into the night.

Lingering by the entrance to the tent, Alia watches as Commander Dormer clearly relieves him, taking his place as he starts to walk back towards her.

She doesn't know why, but Alia feels the need to not be seen. Bouncing down another side of the tent, she makes sure that Commander Peircly is safely back inside before she attempts to move towards Commander Dormer.

With each step, Alia knows that she should just leave her alone and go and enjoy the show. But she doesn't want to. With all the confusion with Kole and tension surrounding the evening, Alia wants nothing more than to curl up and wait for everything to just become clear and simple. Commander Dormer always had a knack for making that happen.

"Commander."

"Oh," Commander Dormer gasps, briefly putting a hand to her chest. "Alia, don't do that." She laughs, indicating for Alia to join her. Together, they perch on a small step, separating the stony path from the plain concrete of the rest of the street.

"I didn't mean to make you jump." They both laugh, although the echo of their voices quickly evaporates into the night.

"You should go back inside, enjoy the show! You always said you wanted to see the Circus."

"I know, but," Alia stops, finding herself sighing more for effect than how she actually feels. "They'll be other times and, I honestly wasn't feeling it." Commander Dormer raises an eyebrow.

"Oh yeah. Doesn't have anything to do with the fine young acrobat I saw you with earlier." Although annoyed that someone else has brought up Kole, she knows she's far less annoyed simply because that person is Commander Dormer.

"Oh please, don't you start too." Alia practically whines, putting her head in her hands while the commander laughs. "I can swear on anybody's lives that it really wasn't like that. Besides, he's a tumbler, they're very different to acrobats." The commander laughs again.

"Okay, alright fine. But still, he seemed nice. I'm glad I can count on you to be professional though."

"It's not, just that." The commander frowns, full attention on Alia. "I don't really know how to explain it, but, it's like, I dunno, I'm wired wrong. Like there are all these people around that I should like but don't."

"You mean, you'd like him more if he was a, a girl?"

"No," Alia sighs, for real this time. "I wouldn't like him even if he was some, one of a kind talking frog. Or, something like that." Commander Dormer smiles. "It would be something if you ever discovered a talking frog."

"You know what I mean." For once, Alia's tone is stern, trying everything she can to make the commander take her seriously.

"Where's all this come from Alia? With everything else we're dealing with, why are you stressing about this now?" Alia shrugs.

"I dunno." Commander Dormer nudges her.

"Tell me." Alia shakes her head until the commander nudges her again.

"He asked me to come and join the circus."

"What?" Commander Dormer can't stop herself from laughing.

"Why is that so funny? It was a nice offer, okay. The Circus seems like an exciting place."

"Yet you're still out here with me when you could be inside enjoying the show."

"As I said, I just wasn't feeling it. Besides, I never would have taken him up on it."

"No?" Alia shakes her head.

"Of course not. I may not have found my home yet, but I think I'm on a pretty good track to."

"That's my girl." Alia smiles, feeling a sudden warmth at Commander Dormer's words.

For a minute, Alia can almost forget where she is and everything just felt right and comfortable. A feeling that she knows she'd do anything to hold onto, even if holding onto it is exactly how she lost it the first time.

"Are you okay though?" Alia finally asks, as if suddenly remembering her true purpose for following her out here. Smiling the commander reaches out and grabs one of Alia's hands.

"I'm always okay." This time, it's Alia who raises an eyebrow.

"Is it bad I don't believe you?" They're both about to laugh when suddenly, they hear a scream.

Alia never liked to believe that certain screams are literally ear piercing. Like you can feel their fear, simply through the shrill in their voice.

She and the commander both get to their feet as the first few people begin to run away from the tent. As hard as they try to fight their way through the racing crowds, too many people are coming out two quickly and both Alia and Commander Dormer find themselves getting lost within the sea of frightened faces.

It's only when they manage to get to the front, where they're greeted by the rest of their group, that sparks begin to fly seconds before the whole tent goes up in flames.

Fifteen

The screams, the smoke, the deaths…

Alia's eyes are closed, trying to piece together everything that happened from the minute the Circus tent caught fire to right now, as they ride yet another carriage towards their next destination.

Whether it's the shock or just pure confusion as to how everything went so wrong so quickly, Alia can only manage to piece together bits of what happened, each appearing as flashes behind her eyes.

As soon as the tent went up, Anemone Protectors quickly took over, leaving them all to be vacated as if they were normal civilians. Alia remembers looking back several times at the tent, now glowing for all the wrong reasons. She thinks about Kole and how she wishes she'd see it all coming so she would have been able to get him out in time. Maybe she would have, if she hadn't had followed the commander outside. But then again, if she'd chosen to stay, she may not be here right now.

Among all the questions that no one will yet be able to answer, they received their orders to move onto Orchid after a possible sighting of someone running away from the tent. They could just have been a regular Anemone resident, their clothes possibly singed and blackened from the flames and soot that was blown across areas far away from the actual fire. They could be the most unimportant person. But then again, they could also be the Royalist.

Each of them is happy to be sitting within the four walls of enough food cart that seemingly bigger than the one they travelled in before, probably due to the fact that this one is completely empty.

All reflecting on everything that happened, everyone in the cart sits several feet away from each other, meaning that no one is close enough to another to cause any problems and there isn't a space in the cart that isn't being used. After several hours of travelling in silence, Cora is the first to do something very unexpected but then thinking about it more, totally normal.

She calls her family.

Clearly being careful not to tell them anything that will put them in danger, Cora skirts around their near-death experience and tells them that she loves and misses them very much. Soon enough, majority of their group are doing the same thing. Even Eli is at least texting someone who Alia presumes to be their mum.

The more she thinks about it, the more she knows she should probably do the same thing. Yet, she doesn't want to. She doesn't want to have to have the awkward conversation of declaring love and feelings just because she feels it's the last time she can. She wants to be able to do all that on her own terms when all of this is finally over, no matter what the world will be like when that time comes.

As expected, even when a new dawn breaks through the splintering wood, no one utters a word.

A part of Alia feels like she should at least try and talk to Eli. Try and be there for him in the sisterly type of way, as if finally trying to succeed in the role she's always struggled to fulfil. Yet looking at him, sitting comfortably besides Cora, clearly in the middle of trying to process everything in his own way, it's like she can't bear to disturb him in case she makes everything worse. So remains as she is, a safe distance away.

Marne and Lola remain almost nauseatingly close not far from Eli and Cora. Marne sits with his arm around Lola, holding her close like he's afraid something else could happen at any moment to take her away. Although unlikely, they know far too well that at this point, anything could happen.

With everything that's happened, Alia finds that she's kicking herself more at the fact that she can't stop thinking about Kole. Thinking about how she should have saved him, how he deserved better, and how much she wish she'd let him kiss her just so she knew what it would be like. Although she swore she'd never do anything even remotely intimate with anyone until it felt right, looking back now, maybe she would have had a change of heart after it had actually happened. Only now, there's no way she'll ever know.

Forgetting everything within her is connected in some way, it takes Alia longer than it should to realise that she's crying, or at least trying to. Even though she's silent, so to look at from any other angle than head on, you'd never have known.

But Commander Dormer sees.

Wiping her eyes, still not completely sure whether she's wiping away real or attempted tears, Alia finds herself staring towards the commander at the exact moment that her eyes are also on Alia. They share one of their many, and usually awkward, *see me* looks before Commander Dormer moves her head in a way that Alia believes, she's asking her to join her.

For once, Alia doesn't even think before shaking her head and looking away in the other direction. Even though there is nothing more she wants than to crawl into Commander Dormer's arms and let her hold her until she waits for the first layer of guilt to slowly wash away, she remains strong and stays where she is.

Alia knows that there will come a time where she won't have the option to hide away when things get difficult. She thought this time was when she left the Academy. But here is still, still wrestling with the same temptations over and over again. But this time, she can't allow herself to give in.

It isn't until the sun reaches its point that the cart comes to a jolting stop. They sit and listen for a minute before anyone tries to move. It's quiet, almost too quiet.

Still being the one closest to the door, Commander Thornbe gets to his feet and slowly pushes it open, revealing them to be in Orchid's Cart Shelter, surrounded by several other carts identical to the one they sit in. From the little she can see, the whole place is like an old wooden shack, appearing to be so rickety that a strong enough gust of wind could be enough to knock it over.

"Since it's quiet, we may as well talk here." Command Thornbe begins, his voice a dull whisper despite the fact though he says they're alone. Closing the door, he encourages everyone to move a little closer.

"Now we—"

"What is the point in all this, seriously?" Alia speaks, her voice strained and choked, like all her built up nerves and worries are now manifesting within a strange type of roughness, anger. Shame. "This is just going to be another pointless goose chase. We'll get a lead, she'll find out and do something and move on with us unable to do anything but trial behind like another pointless afterthought." She pauses, knowing if she were in another other situation, she would have walked away by now. "Why don't we just skip ahead to Aster? I mean but being here, she's close enough already so why don't we go somewhere we can actually do some good?"

The silence that follows is more like a tension, like Alia has just said what everyone has been thinking but would never dare to say out loud. As much as she thought she'd regret it, she doesn't.

"Now, you listen here." Commander Peircly, stands, cowering over her as if attempting to be both commanding and intimidating. Neither of which are working as far as Alia's concerned. "You have absolutely no right to contradict anything that we have been ordered to do!" He shouts like she imagines him doing if he were back in Lily with his team, his real team, the one who clearly never argued with him. "It is a privilege to be here. A damn right privilege that you—"

"But she's right though." Marne says, stepping forwards slightly as if to further make his point. "We're not getting anywhere with this, at all. It's like she knows we're on to her but can't do anything. She's playing with us and you know it, all of you." He narrows his eyes towards each of the commanders. "She's too strong for any of us to handle."

Behind them, Alia feels Eli tense, as to why exactly she can't be sure but quickly puts it down to having to witness yet another argument that she of course had to orchestrate.

Laughing more out of fury than pity, Marne goes for the door and jumps out of the cart, swiftly followed by each of the commanders. He doesn't get far before Commander Peircly catches up with him, grabbing Marne's pistole from his pocket and holding it high in the air.

"You stupid boy." The commander practically spits. "You gave your life your realm the second you stepped foot into the Academy on your first day. You had so much promise. And now." He laughs, keeping the pistole out of reach. "You're going to give up because you think we're doing it wrong?"

"I'm not giving up, that's not what I meant. I just think that—"

"Whatever you think is of no concern to us anymore. You're out."

A series of gasps and confusion stares radiate between everyone. Alia steps off the cart but keeps her distance while Lola, Eli and Cora remain inside but huddled by the door.

"You can't do that. I was chosen for this. I—"

"You were a volunteer that turned into an easy number, no more." Commander Peircly laughs, like he's making it obvious that none of them know as much as they think they do. "You aren't important enough that you can't be replaced. And, as you've made so very clear, you're just not up this. So go, you're done."

Finally lowering his arm, Commander Peircly keeps a hold of Marne's pistol and storms in the direction of what must be the town centre. He doesn't look back, at any of them, even the other Commander's.

"You can't just kick me out like that! What am I supposed to do now? Walk back?" Marne shouts towards Commander Peircly who still doesn't look back.

In the silence of realising what he's actually done, Marne kicks at the ground as he exhales in pure rage. If it weren't for him having an audience, Alia is sure that he'd be screaming right now.

When Marne finally stops and Commander Peircly is so far ahead you wouldn't know it was him if you weren't looking hard enough, both remaining commanders share brief quiet words before turning around to everyone remaining.

"You have ten minutes to make your way to the main square, or you're all out." Commander Dormer is the one to speak, her voice harder than Alia has heard it in a long time.

Fear of ending up just like Marne clearly kicking in, Cora bounds out of the cart and walks so fast she's almost running in the same direction that Commander Peircly went. Eli is then close to follow, practically glaring at Alia as he moves past her. Commander Thornbe takes his place behind them, aware that unless they've studied the maps of the realms enough, they won't know what direction to go in.

It's of no surprise that when leaving the cart, Lola heads straight towards Marne, who now sits on a barrel with his head in his hands.

If knowing that it wasn't all her fault, Alia would have gone over to him too. But aside from the fact that she knows she won't be able to look him in the eyes, she knows that she's probably the last person he wants to see right now. Lola will console him just fine on her own. Maybe she'll even leave and go back to Calla with him. If they are as cosy as they seem, it wouldn't surprise Alia in the slightest.

Knowing she has to carry on, even if right now it's more just so she can keep an eye on her brother, Alia finds the courage to move her feet one after the other until she's walking on the same stony path.

"In future, you should be more careful what you say out loud." Commander Dormer says as she walks side by side with Alia, easily matching her quickening pace.

"I'm always careful." Alia bites back, harder than was intending.

"I know. So what happened?" Alia sighs, knowing the last thing she wants to do right now is recount and analyse yet another mistake that she'd just rather forget.

"I dunno. I'd rather not think about it right now."

"Well, tough." The hold she suddenly has on Alia's arm is as hard as the anger in her voice.

At her touch, Alia's feet stop and her breath quickens. She's then gently pushed against one of the walls of the thin alleyway they've reached. If it had been anyone but Commander Dormer right now, Alia would be afraid. But she's not, at least not yet.

"I understand you're concerned and hurting, but don't go about it like this."

"Go about what? I was just standing up for myself, like you taught me!" She doesn't mean to shout, letting her words bounce between the dingy walls. Commander Dormer then moves her other hand to Alia's chin, holding it as if to make sure she won't be able to interrupt her.

"I never taught you to disrespect your fellow Protectors, let alone Commanding Officers. If you have a problem, yes voice it but never like that. Never make them feel like fools or look what happens. Yes, Marne should have known better but so should you." With every word her voice gets quieter, and her hold on Alia somehow seems to get tighter until she releases her hand from her jaw.

"Then why didn't you kick me out too?" Alia doesn't even attempt to look away and knows that she doesn't want to either.

Looking into her eyes, which shine a very similar hazel to Alia's, she holds her breath, waiting for her to say something, anything. Alia has never wanted and not wanted an answer so much, she feels herself counting down the seconds until Commander Dormer opens her mouth. But instead of speaking, she takes a breath and moves away from Alia, breaking the connection without any hesitation.

Knowing she's clearly not going to get any type of answer out of her, Alia is left to do nothing but watch the commander walk away. She knows she could shout, she could even run after her, but nothing she can do will make anything right. When she feels there's enough distance between them, Alia starts to follow her through the rest of the alleyway, taking the place of her shadow as she knows she's done far too many times before.

It's only when now walking alone that Alia starts to think more into exactly what Marne was trying to say.

She's playing with us.

While that alone is obvious. In her own way, the Royalist is playing with everyone. Treating everyone like puppets in her play to win the magic and change everything.

While she knows Marne only got involved because he saw it as has an opportunity to be heard, it does make her question why he mentioned the Royalist at all and if maybe, he knows more than he should. Maybe, she's playing with him more than anyone else and he's the reason why she always seems to be able to slip away. But now with him gone, could they be in with a chance? Or instead, will she start playing with someone else?

***

They reach the town centre with a lot more ease than any of them were expecting to. They gather almost dead in the centre, standing around a large circular fountain, decorated in such detail, it was like a work of art in itself. Drawings and patterns enrich the grey stone as if trying to tell a story.

It's no surprise to any of them when Lola appears, teary eyed with an angry stare but above all, she was there. She chose to stay.

Although trying not to make it known, Alia does her best to keep her distance from Commander Dormer. They stand on opposite sides of the fountain, Alia not daring to raise her eyes in her direction while the commander only looks at her when clearly observing everyone in turn.

As soon as the commander begins to speak, Alia finds herself zoning out, whether too enthralled by their new surroundings or just as a way to spite her, she can't be sure. As much as she knows she shouldn't be so childish and just let go of everything that happened, she can't.

Looking out at the town, everyone dressed so brightly with such cheer in their smiles, Alia wonders what it would have been like to grow up in a place

109

like this. No strict regulations, no uniforms, no clear pathway of where their lives should take them. If she weren't so confused about everything else, she'd be far more jealous about the life she could have had in a place like this. How different things could be.

"So, remember, subtlety is key." Commander Dormer says as Alia finally tunes back in. "We'll cover the large crowds while the rest of you split off and find out what you can." Everyone nods and mumbles but doesn't say anything more. With that, Commander Dormer nods at them and quickly walks away with the other two Commander's close behind her.

"Hey," Eli springs up in front of her before she has a chance to say or do anything.

"Um, hi. I'm surprised you're talking to me." Alia keeps her voice low. Deciding to just get a way for a while, no matter what Commander Dormer has told them to do, Alia begins to walk in another direction with Eli now not far behind.

"Of course I am." He continues, suddenly a lot less bouncy. "I've never seen you speak like that to anyone who isn't mum. Let alone the fact that she is our leading Commander!" It only takes Eli to laugh at this for Alia to smile, just a little. "But I know what it takes for you to break like that. I'm, I'm sorry about the fire and everything that happened at the Circus."

"What do you have to be sorry about? You didn't start it, did you?"

"No of course not." He laughs again, alone this time. "I just mean, I know you and, you would have felt like it was your fault for not seeing something that could have stopped it and saved your Circus boy."

"He wasn't my circus boy!" Alia shouts before she can help herself, causing several passing eyes to look over at them and stare. She sighs, moving them over to the side of the path. "I'm sorry, I didn't mean to—"

"It's okay, I get it." She sighs again, folding her arms. "You can the commander not talking right now?" Bowing her head, Alia shakes it from side to side.

"I'd rather not talk about it, Eli. But let's just say, if I put another foot wrong then I'll be out too." He nods this time, knowing not to press the matter further.

"Well then, we better get to it. Get you back in the commander's good books." Alia huffs with a smile but doesn't disagree.

"Okay then, what's your plan?"

Something about this realm must clearly agree with Eli. Within the hour, he's managed to find them both spare clothing to wear on top of their uniforms, greatly helping with the whole subtlety act, and is leading her down the streets like he owns them.

The more they walk and the more they see, the more Alia is convinced that there's nothing standard and orderly about this realm.

Everything, from the slightly off centred buildings to the mismatched cobbles that cover the ground, seems random but also like it fits.

They pass several large fields with each one seeming busier than the first. The distribution of food to each realm is something that you don't usually think about unless you see it happen. Now that Alia's seen it, she feels she should regard them all a lot higher compared to how she did before.

As amazing as it all is to see and although they're just visiting, Alia feels more out of place here than she has in any other realm so far. Eli however appears to be flourishing.

Taking the time to look at everybody individually passing them, from their stature to facial expression and manner, he gradually interacts with more and more people. Casually asking them questions that may seem normal to some but cause panic to those who know more than they say. Not that they've found anyone yet, but it's the best Alia has seen him in a long time. Almost like he's found somewhere he feels really comfortable. Somewhere he belongs.

Gradually, they reach the point in day where the sun begins to fall and shadows appear before them, signifying they're almost out of time.

Alia sits on a part of a long brick-built wall, her eyes moving between the busy harbour behind them, the sounds of boats echoing through the otherwise silent air, and the thousands of thin sand grains being picked up by the wind and crashing against the wall, as if mimicking small dust clouds. Almost as if, they were sitting in the middle of a desert rather than next to a pool of light blue water.

Eli lies next to her, one leg bent while the other swings backwards and forwards in front of the wall. One hand covers his eyes from the minorly glaring sun, as if he was on holiday rather than in the middle of a looming war.

Sighing, Alia finally gets to her feet, continually looking around at the few people still passing them, each going about their individual business.

"I guess we better get back. She's probably long gone by now. Unless she's watching us."

"We can't give up now," Eli replies, getting to his feet quicker than she expected him to move. "We still have a few hours, there could still be hope."

"Eli, give it up." Alia almost laughs as she turns to him. "I know you want something to prove yourself, believe me, I'm in the same boat right now, if not more so. But you can't force something that isn't possible." Eli laughs in response, taking her by the hand.

"Always the pessimist. But it's worth another quick scout." They smile as he begins to pull her away from the crashing waters behind them and towards the quieter, still busy inner city. He eventually lets go. Alia continues to smile, more at his enthusiasm than anything else. She is still very much in disbelief that he's able to remain so cheery and optimistic after everything that's already happened.

Eli leads them in and out the fading crowds, winding through people at small stalls and others simply walking. Even though they're only visitors within Anemone, Alia begins to wonder through each passing second where exactly Eli is taking them and how he seems to know his way around so well.

Eventually, he stops them outside a large modern house, clearly built after the Royalist war. Its newly painted exterior opposing the old and warn chipped cobble stone walkway. The street alone screams high status and power. Not a very likely place someone on the run would ever think to go.

"Eli, what is this?" Alia asks turning towards him, all the joy and wonder completely gone from her face. Eli tries to keep a positive smile, but the clear previous excitement is now under the surface of his nervous eyes.

"Before you storm off or cause another scene. Just, hear me out."

"What the hell have you done, Eli? Where are we?"

"Don't shout!" He pauses. "The last thing we need is people paying us any unneeded attention. You did that enough this morning." His voice becomes almost a whisper the more he continues to speak. "I've come to see Dad." Alia can feel her eyes stereotypically widening.

"Excuse me. He—"

"Yeah, I know. He's a dick. He's a bad man. He left us. I get it, I've heard it!" Although not shouting, Eli quickly becomes very agitated. Moving around as he speaks, making sure they don't have continual eye contact. Eli then takes a quick breath as he continues, "But he's changed. I promise he's changed. It's better now. He's better and he's sorry."

Instead of jumping down his throat, like it's clear she wants to, Alia takes short breaths of her own. Doing her best to internalise the many different responses she's trying not to show. Taking a small step towards him, Alia attempts to keep at eye level with him and control her shaking voice.

"Eli. We have to go. We shouldn't be here and we can't. You may think he's changed, but I don't want to hear it. He left us and it's over."

"But if you just give him a chance, please."

"No! Why should I? Give me one good reason."

"Because we almost died, Alia! You and me, at the Circus, and even after that. Hell, we could still die tomorrow and we'd be none the wiser now." He pauses, finally slowly his body and remaining still. "I don't want to die knowing that we didn't at least try to make things right." While still fighting the urge to argue further, Alia holds her tongue knowing that deep down, he does have a point.

Dying is never something that Alia thought much about before. Sure, it's known that people in Calla tend to die more often than the average, especially those in higher positions like the Force, but it's just a part of the deal. It is what it is. Yet being here, with the prospect of death hanging over their heads like a cloud, it's only when you think it's all over that you really remember what you hadn't and hadn't had time to do. Apparently for Eli, this is it.

"Please Alia, do it for me. He promised me he's changed."

"I guess I could," Alia suddenly frowns. "Hang on, have, have you been here before?" Eli goes quiet, creating more and more distance between them, as if afraid to be in a close proximity to Alia's shaking hands.

"Not much, just a little."

"What do you mean *just a little*?" She pauses. "Jesus Christ, Eli, why can't you just leave things alone?"

"Because he asked me not to!" Eli shouts this time. Both are suddenly aware of where they are, with the sun setting further by the minute, the rowdiness from the nearby crowds growing quieter but still loud enough to signify there are still people around. Anyone could walk out and see them at any moment, even the Royalist if they could be so unlucky. Trying to think quickly, Alia drags Eli around the side of the house, overlooked by a small roof, desperately trying to keep out of sight from as many prying eyes as possible.

Giving another cautious look at their continual empty surroundings, Alia takes hold of Eli by the collar of his uniform that slightly peaks out beneath their Orchid disguises and pulls him close. Their eyes now completely level.

"Spill or I will report you to the commander for letting the enemy escape."

"They'd want proof."

"Oh, screw that," Alia says, a little too quickly. "Just tell me."

Squirming a little under her grip, he rolls his eyes but doesn't speak. She continues to hold him, her grip getting tighter and tighter, as if all her anger is being radiated entirely through her fingers. Eventually, he winces and sighs in defeat.

"Okay, okay, you win." Dropping her hand, Eli smooths down his uniform before turning to her. "I've met him a couple of times over the years. Just short visits here and there, but more recently."

"Have you been coming here? To see him?" He nods slowly, as if suddenly ashamed.

"Most of the time, he's always made sure I had safe passage in one way or another. But he came to Calla once." He pauses, as if waiting for Alia to take the bait and comment. Yet she remains silent. "Please, can we not make a big deal of this. He's our dad, our family. He wants to make amends."

"After everything he did. To Mum, to me. I…" Eli smiles, letting out a small, almost fake kind of laughter.

"Why pretend you care now? After spending all this time convincing us all that you can do everything on your own." He pauses, as if waiting yet again for her to respond. To argue. To say anything in the silence in-between his words. "You've made it quite clear that we're all too naïve to ever really understand you. Just go back to your precious Commander and let me be. I'll re-join you all later. Tell them I'm following a lead."

Alia feels a tear prick her eye, yet she's not completely sure why. Although Eli can be a strange combination of quiet and stubborn, it's a rare occasion where he's completely honest. Especially when she has no interest in listening to it.

As if being summoned to try and break the rising tension, the side door that Alia had failed to notice before creaks open. A tall slender man steps out; his face clearly clean-shaven matching his bright ironed clothes, while his eyes remain old and tired. As if he's trying to be new yet failing to keep out the old.

"Eli?" his weak voice almost whispers.

Stepping further into the dimly lit walkway between the door and where they stand, Alia studies his face further. Through the lines that age his face, even more than his eyes, and the slight stiffness in his steps, he isn't the man she knew. Isn't the dad she knew. Like many people in her life that should feel like home, in truth, he feels no different to her than if it were a complete stranger standing there. A shadow embodying the shell of someone she once loved. And seeing it in person once more only makes it worse. Makes it real.

"Dad," Eli says, his voice suddenly lifted. He moves towards him and they smile towards each other, clearly anything but strangers. After a minute or so, her dad eventually looks up in her direction and finds himself smiling widely.

"Alia." He smiles. "It's good to see you." His voice is soft, as if trying to fade out all the rough edges that she always connected most with him. She stares, almost fixated, watching him as if doing so will make something happen. She focuses on his empty hands, watching the way his fingers gently curl around something that is no longer there, but how long ago was it since his skin had been at one with a bottle? Alia can't be sure. If Eli has been going to see him, then she can only hope that it's been months, maybe even years. Although the thought is a good one, maybe even one of relief or hope, she doesn't let herself believe it, not even for a second.

"We need to get back," Alia remarks as if they were in a completely normal situation. Deciding nothing else needs to be said, she starts walking away from the house towards the empty street. Looking quickly between their dad and Alia, Eli rushes to her, taking her arm as if to hold her back.

"Please, just stay. For a little while." Almost finding herself glaring at him, Alia forcefully removes her arm from his grip and takes another step away from the house.

"Do what you like, but I'm out." She leans in close to him, as if wanting him to feel her hardened voice. "Maybe you're right; maybe I am best off on my own."

"But you don't have to be." They exchange another glance, one that they both would prefer never happened but knew it had to be done. Neither of them is ready to face certain truths, especially coming from the other.

"Stay if you want. But if you're not back by morning, we're leaving you behind. And you'll move further down in the Academy." Her eyes slide once more towards the hollowed man keeping his distance. "He's not worth throwing everything away for."

"And she is?" Alia feels another tear worming its way into her eyes. Like always, she pushes it back as if it were a normal reflex.

"Enjoy it, it won't last." Letting their eyes meet a final time, Alia pushes her way past Eli towards the direction she's sure they came in before.

No matter how hard she wants to forget, she can't. But like most things, she has to leave it behind her. If Eli became one of those things, then so be it. She'd have to move on, just like before. Alone.

Sixteen

Alia isn't walking for long when she feels her pocket buzz. Having not actually used her phone since that morning Eli called her, Alia forgot she even had it on her, let alone that it still has some charge left on it.

Pulling over at the edge of the road she's currently on, everyone around her clearly packing up their stalls and heading home for the evening, Alia retrieves her phone to see a message from Commander Dormer.

Just seeing her name on the screen is enough to get Alia giddy, but in more of a doomed way than the usual excitement she feels. But opening it, she finds it to be a message that was clearly sent to all of them, and is nothing more than map coordinates which she can only presume is their next destination.

Putting her phone away, Alia takes a short glance back to where she knows her brother will still be but then decides quickly that this was his choice and she has full right to go on without him. Out of every realm they've been to so far, Orchid has seemed the safest.

Even though Orchid is one of the larger realms, it seems to be a place where everyone knows everyone, hopefully meaning that at the sighting of any stranger, who is clearly not the average traveller, they will know there's something wrong. But then she also knows that the Royalist could have had the same idea as them and borrowed certain clothing items in order to try and fit in.

As if suddenly realising her time pretending for the day is over, Alia pulls off the light orange dress that has been concealing her uniform and throws it off as if it were rubbish. She knows she should try and give it to someone who can use it, but she doesn't want to talk to anyone right now, even for such a trivial matter that won't evoke a lot of follow up conversations.

With every passing second, the sky grows a little darker, allowing the moon to shine a little brighter until eventually, it becomes the greatest source of light in the darkness of the night.

Walking back through some familiar and alien roads, Alia has almost forgotten that she isn't in the place she knows, but somewhere completely different. She never thought she'd miss the simple metallic roads and wired streetlights from Calla, compared to everything here which is a lot more earth and stone based.

The coordinates lead her to a deserted place that reminds her of Lily in the way the ground is dry, too dead for anything to grow again. She can only guess that this used to be one of their many working fields that has simply had its time.

The dried yellow blades brush her legs as she walks further through it towards the middle, now seeing a slight bulge in the earth that will likely be her destination.

Stepping close to the rounded earth, she bends down and grips the yellow ground, closing her eyes and feeling nothing but the ground beneath her. She listens closely, eventually making out the whispers of familiar voices and movements, each vibrating, like they were trying to channel an energy of their own.

As if sensing a change, the sky above suddenly rumbles a little before the clouds above open up, letting a sporadic downpour begin. Alia remains still for a minute, letting the water sink into her tightening clothes and loosely gripped hair.

She opens her mouth and lets droplets fall in, the liquid the closest thing she'd had to drink in hours, although she didn't realise it until the second she knows she needs it.

Slowly standing up, Alia takes a step away from the apparent camp and walks back in the direction that she came, sheltering under a few trees at the side of the landscape as she walks. She knows she should go back, yet she doesn't want to. Not yet. Not when she feels like this.

If it was only Kole on her mind, she'd probably have gone inside. But now with Marne and Eli also taking up more space than they should, not to mention how mixed she feels about the next time she has to see Commander Dormer. With everything currently swirling like a whirlpool inside her head, she just can't. At least, not yet. Maybe she'll shelter until Eli comes back and enter with him like they'd never been apart. Or maybe, she'll just wait until the rain stops.

It's moments like this where Alia used to lock herself away in the training room, using any excuse to stay there for as long as she could. Until now, she's never had to even think about doing anything else to settle her racing mind.

Even with the world at her feet, right now, walking seems like the most sensible solution.

Making her way slowly through the trees, she follows something that seems like a path, leading her deeper into the woods that she hadn't before realised surrounded the area of the camp. She takes cautious steps, her uniform sticking to her more with each one, prickling her now chilled skin. Although the days here are slightly warmer than what she's used to, even compared to their summers, Alia still forgets just how cold the nights can get. And changing from one extreme to the other so quickly can only be having a negative effect.

Continuing on the path, Alia looks ahead to the trees before her. Nothing can be heard aside from the sound of her footsteps and the pouring rain above.

Snap.

She spins around at the slightest noise, suddenly aware of all the dangers she's put herself in by walking this way alone.

The Royalist… She could be here.

Suddenly noticing how vulnerable she really is, Alia grabs a small torch from her leg pocket and points it in the direction of the noise. Nothing, yet she's sure she hadn't imagined it. She remains still, listening intently to everything surrounding her. The rain is beginning to slow, allowing dripping sounds to be heard from the large leaves of certain trees. But the dripping doesn't conceal another snap from another direction.

"Hello?" she calls out more from of habit of trying to be heard than using her intelligence trying to remain unseen and unheard.

Strangers probably wouldn't think anything of it but if it were anyone she knew, they'd be able to clearly identify something that is never usually found within her voice, fear. Plain and simple fear. But Alia knows she has to be brave, just like the commander would want her to be. Just like she taught her.

No reply is heard but the snapping continues without any hesitation. Each snap grows louder and happens faster, as if matching her rising heartbeat. Trying to control her quick, almost ferocious breaths, Alia takes more careful steps in her original direction, now rethinking her adventure away from the others more than ever.

And just like Eli predicated, it's only now that she starts to think about everything she knows she should have done differently.

I shouldn't have left him there on his own. I shouldn't be here.

The more she thinks the more she seems to panic, panting in the dark, pointing her torch in all directions, seeing nothing but trees each way.

But I'm here. And it's okay.

While she knows positive thinking won't cure anything, she'd still like to believe that it will help, at least a little. Right now, Alia feels so stupid for acting out like she did with Commander Dormer and opening her mouth about her doubts this morning. In a way, she even regrets not leaving on better terms with her mum, as if realising just how much all this will hurt her if she never comes back. Especially if Eli never goes back too. Or worse, if she is the only one to arrive home.

Taking long breaths, she briefly closes her eyes, piecing herself together and looks eagerly around, as if now wanting something to bounce at her just to get it over with.

Like someone has heard her wish, a bright, nearly clear, blue light peaks at the edge of her vision. Looking towards it, she winces as she puts her free hand to her eyes as a shield while her mind suddenly goes dark and her legs unbearably limp. Unable to think or do anything about it, Alia falls to the ground, motionless and still.

Seventeen

A fresh day dawns over all the realms. The sun rising up high at different points for each of them.

Whether due to the world or the realm itself, it rises earlier in Orchid than it does in Calla. The day becoming bright and warm only a few short hours after the first rays of the sun are initially seen.

The sun is nearly at its brightest when Alia's eyes open, wincing at the sudden light, especially when compared to the darkness she last remembers. Taking a minute to awaken her body, stretching everything as if to make sure it all still works, Alia sits up, feeling nothing but odd.

Putting a hand to her head, she winces further at the buzzing she feels within, like her body remembers but her memory is gone.

Looking up again at the bright sky, Alia gasps at the sudden realisation of morning, at least she assumes it to only be morning. Standing up quicker than she probably should, Alia feels herself continually gasping at where she is, her memory still blank as if she wandered here straight from leaving Eli.

Eli, she thinks, trying to remember while also trying to keep herself calm. *Why did I leave him? Did he make it back? Did he stay with him? Did Dad hurt him again?*

Her breathing remaining quick but somehow steady, Alia takes out her phone and almost throws it in sheer frustration at its black screen. The last of the battery finally gave out, she really is on her own now.

Looking around at the slightly singed trees circling her, her eyes land on the dry earth in the distance, peaking its way between the planted area. Focussing on solely getting back to someone, anyone with breath in their lungs, Alia races through the trees towards the tiny area she spies.

She breaks out through the trees quicker and with a lot more ease than she expects to. Alia sighs with sheer relief as she spies the rounded earth that she should have stayed in the previous night.

Attempting to run further, but finding herself out of breath very quickly, she continues to make her way further towards it, even at her slightly slower pace. Now nearly in direct eye line of it, Alia releases gasp of almost pure joy at the site of someone familiar.

"Alia!" Marne calls from the distance. He bounds towards her as she does him, his strides long and fast while hers are smaller and slower. "Alia!" he says again, now out of breath as he takes her in his arms, meeting her half way. Alia sighs again and lets herself be held, thankful for the simple contact of someone familiar.

It's only when he releases her and steps back a fraction that the confusion of what he can be doing here takes hold. Marne himself smiles widely before switching back to a serious glance, as if she would have missed it if she wasn't looking close enough.

"What are you doing here? I'm so glad you didn't leave, I am so sorry for spurting all that crap that you—"

"Forget it, it's fine. We're good." Although they're words of forgiveness, in some fashion at least, his harsh tone would make it seem like he wasn't forgiving at all.

"How did—"

"I'll explain later, I'm just so glad you're safe." He quickly embraces her in another hug but in the way that she can tell there's more going on than he's telling her.

"Marne, what's happened?" This time she's the one who lets him go and keeps her head up as he bows his own, almost like he's ashamed. "Tell me! What's going on?" She practically demands, her impatience kicking in. Eventually, Marne raises his head before meeting her eyes, his own bloodshot and tired.

"There's been an incident. Someone's hurt."

"Who?"

"The commander."

Eighteen

Alia rushes back to their current base, her mind suddenly too focussed on the present to think about the blank memory of the previous night.

Marne follows close behind her, making sure to use every available breath to grill her about where she's been. As they draw nearer, Alia can see the stagnant body of Cora who stands just in front of the entrance. Alia does nothing but smile as she rushes past her and down the steps that are far too obviously placed for somewhere that she presumes is meant to be a secret.

She follows the steps as they circle down into the ground revealing a small but not claustrophobic room. The walls, ceiling and even the floor, mimic the sandy illusion of a desert from the surface above between the trees.

Reaching the bottom step, Alia goes from face to face, trying to see who's still missing. A few people are continuously moving around while most are all centred around something, or someone, in the far corner. Going further into the room, she feels Marne step around her and walk quickly towards the scene. Alia follows closely behind him, ignoring a few surprised glances from everyone else.

Finally pushing her way to the front of the commotion, Alia sees a very limp looking Commander Peircly. His deathly pale skin made to seem even lighter compared to his ripped black uniform he still wears.

Several large rips are clear up and down his arms with blood covering the frayed edges. Larger and deeper cuts scar several parts of his ghostly face, spanning from his jaw right up to his eyebrow. His breathing is slow, his eyes are shut and his body is still. Like the only way you'd know he was even alive was by watching his slow but present rising and falling chest.

"What happened?" Alia turns to Lola who stands beside her. Quiet for a minute, Lola looks at her as if she doesn't even recognise her.

"Alia?" Alia is both relieved and nervous to hear the familiar voice echo from behind. Turning around, she doesn't quite know how to react so simply tries smiling normally at Commander Dormer, as if this were any other greeting. As expected, all she gets is a scowl in response.

"What happened?" Alia pleads, desperate to know if this is something else she can later blame herself for.

"Upstairs. Now, on the surface. Let's go!" At her unusually sharp words, Alia almost expects Commander Dormer to clap her hands to make her move faster.

As instructed, Alia leaves the crowd and goes back up to the surface, avoiding yet more obviously aimed glances, although now angled both at her and Commander Dormer.

While knowing to not lose her temper in front of others very often, after what happened before parting ways when they first arrived in Orchid, Alia can feel herself almost trembling at the shouting that is soon to follow. No one of any position, has ever made her physically shake before. Yet Commander Dormer does.

Alia has heard her shout on plenty of occasions and usually, she would just laugh, not being able to take her raised voice seriously. But when it's actually directed at her for something Alia knows she should have either never done or done better, it's a very scary place to be.

When standing once again under the bright cloud-filled Orchid sky, Alia breathes deeply as Commander Dormer appears behind her, anger present in her usually guarded face. Cora stands to attention, clearly not expecting them to appear so soon.

"Go downstairs Cora. We'll take over for a while."

"Yes, Commander," Cora responds timidly. Soon enough she's gone, leaving Alia alone with the commander.

Alia expects the shouting to begin as soon as they're left alone. But instead, there's simply silence and a lot of eye contact, an uncomfortable amount. The odd silence makes Alia think that maybe, she doesn't know quite what to say which if she plays it right, may just work in her favour.

Alia also knows that this is probably the end for her here. Even if Marne found a way to most likely sweet talk is way back in once everyone had calmed down, with her disappearing act, she's not likely to be so lucky. But then maybe, maybe that's okay.

As much Alia knows, it shouldn't be her priority, and she hates herself for thinking that this is the most important thing, but right now, she's not grateful that she made it out that woods okay, she's thankful that Commander Dormer is alive and not the one unconscious downstairs.

"So," Alia begins speaking. "I'm sorry—"

Before she has the chance to say anything more, Commander Dormer closes the short gap between them and pulls Alia into the hug she's been wanting so badly since the Circus, or possibly even before.

Instantly, Alia feels herself relaxing in her arms, as for a minute, as if totally unaware of the situation and imminent danger they're in. Too quickly for Alia's liking, Commander Dormer pulls away, her face clearly softening with every passing second.

"Never disappear like that again. Especially given where we are," she says, her hands still gripping Alia's arms, just as tightly as she did when she was angry.

"I promise," Alia replies, her voice breaking as if she's suddenly teary.

Commander Dormer pulls Alia's loose hair from its tie, letting it escape into several tangled ringlets behind her back. Alia takes a breath as Commander Dormer lets go of her arms and steps back, her eyes not leaving Alia's face, not even for a second.

"What happened?" Alia shakes her head, as if ashamed that she can't remember.

"I, um…" She pauses, trying to calm her rising agitation towards no one but herself. "I was with Eli. We were looking, but there was no sign of the Royalist. And then, I wanted to come back. But Eli. He—"

"I know what happened there, he told me," she cuts in. Alia stares at her, trying not to seem so surprised.

"He did?" Commander Dormer nods.

"Not everything, but he told me enough." She pauses. "I'm sorry you had to see him again."

"I don't even want to think about it." Alia tries to laugh but folds her arms defensively. "Wait, you've seen him? Eli. He's okay?"

Commander Dormer laughs; knowing full well that it took Eli to be mentioned by name for Alia to remember he even existed in their current world and was missing from the sea of faces she saw gathered around Commander Peircly under the earth.

Some sister I am.

"He came back late last night. Thought you were back already."

"Did you tell him I was gone?" Commander Dormer shrugs, knowing she doesn't have to defend her actions.

"Not until he came asking. I didn't want to panic him before I needed to, especially after the bollocking he got when he eventually did come back." As much as she knows, she shouldn't, Alia laughs. "He's been out with Commander Thornbe looking for you."

"Oh, god."

Shit, Alia thinks, only just realising how much trouble her absence has really caused.

"I would have called but my phone it—"

"You shouldn't have gone off in the first place, no matter how upset you were."

"I wasn't upset," Alia says, now being the one to get defensive. Commander Dormer raises an eyebrow at Alia's face. This time it's Commander Dormer who can't help but laugh.

"This isn't the Academy anymore, Alia. You can't just go off when you're in a mood and then come back when you feel like it. Especially when you're already on such thin ice."

"I know." She pauses, unfolding her arms and staring out briefly at the unknown world around them. "I'm sorry. For everything, this morning included. I just, I dunno, I snapped I guess. But it's past, all of it. Marne is back and, and I'm alive. I am sorry though, truly."

"I know." Commander Dormer takes a small step towards her. "I'm also, sorry about that morning. I shouldn't have grabbed you like that. You were just, speaking your mind, in a very unorthodox way but, I do think you may have a got a little of that from me. So, I'm sorry."

"I know." Alia mimics Commander Dormer's acceptance causing them both to laugh a little more.

There's a brief silence as they'd both much rather be laughing then trying to think about what's really important.

"So, what did you find out there?" Alia shrugs, her head suddenly becoming fuzzy once again at the hazy memory she still can't recall.

"I'm not sure," she stops, taking a breath before continuing, "one minute, I was walking through the trees trying to clear my head. And next, I thought I saw something. Well, I heard movements, the snapped of twigs and branches, like someone was there. But, I dunno really, I don't remember a lot of it very well." The commander nods. "But there was this kind of, um, blue light, I think. I remember seeing it and then the next thing I know it's suddenly morning and I'm lying on the ground. It wasn't raining anymore and it was a new day." Commander Dormer listens intently, not moving at first when Alia finishes speaking.

"Was it, her, do you think?" Commander Dormer shakes her head, taking a minute to look around the trees that circle them, as if the answer will just appear from within the isolated forest.

"It would explain it, just like what happened back in Anemone."

"You mean, we don't definitely know if that was her? But it must have been." Alia pleads, wanting the fire to have been caused by the Royalists, if only to help her come to terms with the fact that if it was, Alia has less to feel guilty about.

"The Council have ruled it as a Royalist event, at least that's what they're calling it. But—"

"You're not so sure."

"But," she enunciates her words as if to tell Alia to just let her speak. "I'm personally not going to rule out other potential factors." She takes a breath while Alia doesn't look away from her eyes, desperately trying to figure out what she's really trying to tell her. "We all know that the Royalist isn't the only one who would benefit from a war." Alia can feel her eyes widening, as if suddenly piecing together a lot of things that shouldn't be connected but might just be.

"That is, a theory."

"That you should keep to yourself for now." Alia nods, the familiar feeling of pride silently seeping in at the thought of being able to share in another secret. "I guess, we won't know for sure until we catch her." Alia smiles, suddenly feeling optimistic for the first time since they left Calla.

"We'll get her. We have to." Commander Dormer smiles back, reaching out and putting an arm over Alia's shoulders.

"I know."

As if to spoil a perfectly happy moment, their silent smiles are unexpectedly interrupted by Eli and Commander Thornbe's return.

They jog together in the far distance, getting closer with every passing breath. Commander Dormer doesn't attempt to move her arm from Alia's shoulders until they're nearly in direct eye line. At the wind-swept distance, Alia feels herself shiver in the disappointment that the moment of hope and comfort has passed.

"Alia!" Eli smiles as he jogs into her arms, clearly out of breath. Alia finds herself laughing at his sweaty exterior while finding herself tense as soon as he holds her in a normal sibling hug that usually brings them closer together. Letting him go, both their faces fall.

Commander Thornbe quickly makes himself scarce while Commander Dormer stays a second longer, brushing Alia's arm as she follows him down the steps.

Alia and Eli are quickly wrapped in a new form of silence. Both wanting to talk while avoiding the obvious conversation topic.

Although glad to see him alive, Alia can't help but feel cheated by the fact of how good an evening Eli seems to have had while she still can't remember anything vivid enough to make sense out of. Especially since he seems to have spent his time enjoying the company of their dad, a man Alia would rather never willingly associate herself with again.

"I'm not gonna press you for details if you don't want me to. But, I'm sorry for disappearing, really. I didn't mean to cause anyone any worry."

"Well, you did!" Eli snaps back. His warm, brotherly concern now completely evaporated. "The commanders say that Commander Peircly might not make it through, and even if he does, he still can't be moved for at least another few hours, his injuries are too severe."

"What happened to him?" Eli rolls his eyes, letting the corners of his mouth curl as if trying not to smile.

"I thought we said no details?"

"About us, not him."

"He," Eli pauses, shuffling his boots in the yellow grains. "He was out looking for you. He was gone for hours and then the next thing we know, he's limping back here with injuries that didn't look too bad but seemed to be killing him." Alia stands rigid, almost stunned about Eli's explanation.

He's injured and could die just because she decided to go walking in the trees to clear her head. Feeling guiltier than ever, Alia hides a building set of frustrated tears and sniffs back any overpowering emotion she feels rising within her still slightly chilled body.

"Does he remember what happened? I presume something attacked him, or maybe someone?" Eli's full attention instantly lands in her eyes.

"You think it could be…them?" Alia nods.

"Could be. It, it would explain a lot. I think." Alia squints, rubbing her eyes. Trying to remember anything to connect every part of this realm that seems random but isn't. "But even if that was her, she could have moved on by now. If she's been watching us, then she must have done." She pauses, still attempting to play a dot to dot with many of them still missing. "At least if it was her, I guess it counts as a lead." Alia smiles, trying to lighten the mood at least a little for both of their benefits. Eli smiles a little but not enough to make it look even the slightest bit convincing.

"We should head back in. See if we can do anything to help Commander Peircly," Alia says, swallowing her further rising emotion, taking a few steps towards the entrance of their current base. "I'm sure the General's already been told and is doing what she can from Calla."

"Course she is." Alia smiles again.

"Good." With that, she begins to walk towards the steps before turning back around. "One last question." While Eli doesn't look pleased at her continual voice, he doesn't say anything as she takes a breath between words. "Last night, was it only Commander Peircly out looking for me?" Eli shuffles his feet in the dried earth again, as if it will give him the right words to answer her question.

"By the time I got back, which was late and I got a hell of a beating for it."

"I'm aware," she says, smiling before she can stop herself.

"The commanders were only just starting to worry by the time they told me the truth. Commander Thornbe did a quick area scout but nothing. Then Commander Peircly went out to look properly."

"Alone?" Eli nods.

"They agreed it was too dangerous to send anyone else with him, especially if you'd been, well, you know."

"You can say captured, Eli, or dead. They're bad but they're not dirty words. It could have happened, anything could. You know, I'm not as indestructible as I make out to be. Well, most of the time." Eli laughs, as if forgetting their current situation and imagining them back in their realm as normal siblings rather than Royalist Retrieval group members.

"True, but still, we thought that's what might have happened." He shakes his body a little, as if trying to shift the sudden severity of their 'what ifs'. "Hey, we could have used you as bait."

"Charming." They laugh together. "Still, I'm glad no one else got hurt. I feel guilty for Commander Peircly though. If he dies then—"

"Hopefully, he won't," Eli cuts in, taking a few steps towards her until they're both lingering on the top step. "Besides, it could have been a lot worse. More people could have got hurt." He smiles, going ahead of her and walking down a few more steps. "And you know, Commander Dormer stayed out here all night, watching, waiting. Not letting anyone else take their turns. Not even me." Alia feels herself smiling more than she knows she should.

"She did?" Eli nods, smiling back.

"I guess, you really do mean a lot to her." He smiles again before turning around and going all the way down the steps and back underground to the rest of the group.

Trying to stop herself smiling further, Alia looks up at the bright sky above, taking a minute to watch the passing morning clouds.

Pulling her loose hair to the side, she hugs into herself as she imagines what could have been if she'd found her way back sooner, and what it would mean if the Royalist was really the one to attack her and Commander Peircly.

Although she shouldn't, with her eyes still on the trees that kept her safe during what must have been a long night, Alia can't shift the feeling that there's still more to all of this than meets the eyes.

Is Commander Dormer right about certain members of other realms wanting this war and possibly aiding situations that will get them the result they want?

Or is Marne's return and the Royalist's possible appearance too much of a coincidence to ignore?

Question after question, theory after theory, Alia can already feel her mind sinking at everything that could be when all she really wants to know is what is. Who can she really trust? Who has more than one agenda? Alia has always liked to think that she can not only see the good in people, but see when people are faking good for their own means. It's always been kind of a pride. But now, now she's in the dark the same as everyone else with no idea who is really lying and who is really genuine.

As much as she doesn't want to ever consider it, maybe even Commander Dormer is playing for more than one side.

Nineteen

As the day progresses into the earliest signs of darkness, everyone finds themselves having nothing to do but wait around. Waiting for something, anything, to happen.

Commander Peircly remains relevantly stable, slipping in and out of consciousness, never awake long enough to tell everyone what really happened.

A few members accompany Commander Thornbe for another scout of the realm; they find nothing worth reporting. While Commander Dormer is convinced that the Royalist has already moved on, Eli is somehow sure that she could still be around.

Alia spends most of her time with Marne. Practising and honing their skills as if preparing for what is yet to come. What could happen if they ever catch her. Although focussed on the task in hand, Alia finds her mind constantly falling back to Eli's words. *I guess, you really do mean a lot to her.* But is it in the way that she wants, or just the way that it is? The way it always will be.

Alia and Marne take turns in aiming their pistols and shooting at specified targets. Alia often wondered what their weapon of choice would be if they'd never had magic in the first place. After all, being able to insert anything, from a rock to pieces of dust, into the device and letting it turn it into pieces of metal that are actually dangerous when fired, would never have happened if it hadn't been for magic.

They take care to mute the sound of their shots as they fire, conscious of not causing Commander Peircly, or anyone else, anymore unnecessary discomfort.

A short distance away, Alia spies a glance at Eli who practises with Cora with their downgraded Academy pistoles. Alike in most ways to the ones that she and Marne hold, Alia can see that sine only having a limited number of metal shots, they're not firing, just aiming like they would.

The weapons system is one thing that even after working at the Bureau, limited time or not, is still something that she's yet to understand. The Academy pistols with limited shots and even a safety cap makes sense. It gives people a chance to train with something very alike to what they'll actually get to own upon graduation, but in a much safer fashion.

And then when out into the real world with a real Protector job, you get to use the proper version which is now something that Alia doesn't know what she'd do without. Although never firing at a real target, just having it and knowing it's a short reach away has become a comfort not just for Alia, but for everyone who has one.

Everyone graduates with the same weapon. In that way, everyone is equal. Yet if you get into the Force, you get to upgrade to learning and using how to wound people with a bow and arrow.

While Alia understands that it requires a lot more skill than their pistols, with the added factor of limited arrows, it still seems not nearly as effective, and quick for that matter, as it would be shoot someone with a pistole. But like a lot of things that Alia only has a vague understanding of, it's tradition and in Calla, traditions are kept and followed to the letter.

After hours of fake dodging and real shooting, Alia and Marne let themselves have a breather and crash on the yellow ground.

While she's enjoying it being just them, Alia can't understand why Lola hasn't tried to join them. Sure, she's probably still mad at Alia for getting Marne kicked off their team, but he found a way to come back and it's not like she chose to go with him over carrying on. So why is she still upset?

"So, you never actually told me what happened. How you managed to get back I mean." Marne pulls a face like he doesn't quite know what to say or how much he really wants to tell her.

"There's not a lot to tell really." He pauses, playing with the black painted pistol in his hands. "Once you guys all left, I went ahead and started asking questions. I thought if I could get jump start and find her first, or at least get a lead, then, it would be enough to convince them to take me back."

"And did it?"

"I can't divulge too many details, but let's just say I had a rather fortunate run in with some of Lady Dany's Guards when I helped them trap a street thief, nothing special really, and well, she's got pull."

"Nice." Alia laughs, relieved that he was able to find a way back in, no matter how extraordinary his story may be. "What's she like, Lady Dany?"

"Pretty cool actually. Imagine like, the exact opposite of Lady Talia, with the same sense of humour as us. She's amazing."

"Sounds it." She smiles as they continue to laugh. "Sounds like she really made an impression on you." Alia raises her eyebrows and nudges him, very much like when he teased her about Kole. But instead of him getting defensive, he continues to laugh it off.

"Well, all I'll say is that I'd never say no."

"Of course you wouldn't."

They simultaneously erupt into a new phase of laughing, drawing in the eyes of Lola who is now practising alongside Eli and Cora. As soon as she meets Alia's eyes, Lola looks away, an impressed look clear upon her face.

"Hey, is Lola still mad about the whole, you know, you getting kicked out thing?"

"Um," Marne longs out the sound of his attempt at a word as he quickly glances up towards Lola. "She just, takes a while to get over things, that's all. Don't take it personally."

"I'm not, I just, wondered, that's all." They both take a minute to look back yet again at Lola who is doing her best to avoid their eyes and keep her back to them. "I don't understand why she got so pissed though. It wasn't like she was in trouble and if she was that upset, she could have just gone with you but she chose to stay."

"I know, and believe me, I did try and explain that to her. But I think she just got scared, honestly. She may not let on but, this whole thing is terrifying for her."

"We're all scared." Alia points out. "Even if none of us admit it. We all know it."

"Yeah but, we've been best friends since our Academy days and, no offence to her but, she wouldn't be able to hack this if I weren't here. And honestly, I think I'd struggle without her too."

"Urgh," Alia exaggerates her disgust. "You guys are too co-dependant."

"Oh, like you can talk."

"Excuse me?" Although she's still smiling, Alia can feel something ticking within her as she realising exactly where this conversation is heading. "That's not, that's not the same. At all." Marne rolls his eyes.

"Yeah, you keep telling yourself that."

"Oh no really, it's nothing like that. At all, no. Never."

"Okay, okay, I'm sorry. It's just—"

"What?" Marne sighs, putting down his pistol and straightening his back.

"You guys just, it seems like there's a history there."

"So? Even if there is, it doesn't mean what you think it does."

"I guess you never really know what's gone on in a person's life."

"Unless they tell you, I guess not." For a moment, she feels like Marne looks at her in a way that no one ever has before. It's not the same as the way Kole looked at her, except for maybe a slight flicker. Whatever it is, Alia still doesn't like it. It's still, not what she wants, as much as she wants to want it.

Deciding the conversation has a hit a point where they both need to stop talking, at least for a while, both Alia and Marne relax into a comfortable silence before continuing on with more practise shooting and avoiding.

As the seconds of the day carry on ticking, they all can't believe when the sun finally sets and they've greeted with a blanket full of stars above, the first time since they left Calla that the sky feels as it should.

Sitting around another campfire, with Commander Peircly still safely tucked away beneath the earth, everyone tucks in to a variety of food, from berries to leaves to the scraps of meat they were able to scavenge throughout the day without wondering too far.

Just like it was before, the campfire is split between commanders, Bureau members and the younglings from the Academy. The two remaining commanders both eat very little, their attention constantly flying between everyone above ground and the withering Commander still below. Alia knows they have no choice but to move on tomorrow, even if it means leaving Commander Peircly behind which in a way, she's surprised they haven't had to do already. After all, the only realm they haven't been to yet is Aster which also happens to be their final destination.

"I don't see why we can't just drop him off at a hospital and be done with it," Marne says, clearly agitated that while he's used his waiting time wisely, he knows they should be out there doing more.

"I don't know," Alia replies, not as interested in the conversation as she probably should be. After spending all day within his company, Alia has come to find that Marne prefers speaking his mind, which alone doesn't bother her. But combined with his need to always be in the right, Alia is surprised that she hasn't hit him more times than she already has. Yet, he's still not as annoying as he could be.

"It's probably too risky. In case the Royalist knows he's alive and comes back to finish the job," Lola interjects, putting her leftover banana peel on the ground next to the few logs they sit on. While still not in the best mood with her and Marne, she's calmed down enough now to at least have a civilised conversation with them.

"But surely there would be some kind of hospital that's equipped for this kind of thing? You'd think so anyway," he continues. "Even Orchid will have appropriate hospitals. We should have just taken him there when this first happened."

"But then more people would know, or at least guess what's going on."

"Like they don't know enough already." Lola cuts in. "Did you even listen to the people out there? Like, really listen? They're scared and confused and know that something is going on."

"Yes, but they don't know what."

"Exactly! And that's just making them more afraid." Lola makes a sound that can only be described as being half way between a laugh and a grunt. "I don't see why we can't just tell them."

"Because you know how much panic that would cause." Alia can feel the irritation rising as she feels she has to state the obvious. "Besides, we don't know yet if the Royalist is completely to blame for all this."

"Of course, she is!" Lola practically erupts, clearly letting out a lot of built-up frustration she's been carrying out since the previous morning. "Come on, who else is going to want to harm the commander like that? And who would even be able to?" Alia rolls her eyes while sighing as she puts a hand through her loose hair.

"At this point, who knows for sure, okay?" Marne says, his voice oddly calm and obviously in peace keeping mode. "But we'll be okay though," he says quite happily, as if certain that nothing else can possibly go wrong for a while.

Continuing to smile, he slowly straightens his back and attempts to pull Alia closer to him. At first, she tries not to think anything of it and ignore Lola's dragon eyes. But as he tries to take her hand, in a rather obvious fashion, Alia leaps up and stands a short distance away from him, hugging her suddenly shivering arms to her chest. It takes a minute for him to decide what to do but in the end, he gets up and slowly makes his way towards her.

"You okay?" At even the touch of his hand lightly brushing her arm, Alia takes another step away from him.

"Just back off a bit, okay? I need some air." she rushes her words as she walks away in another direction, leaving him standing confused with Lola watching from the log.

Alia moves the edge of the small circle of wood around the fire. From a distance, they would all seem like happy campers who happen to all be wearing the same clothes, instead of an army trying to stop the looming darkness. She remains still, continuing to hug her arms close to her tingling chest.

"Hey, Alia," Eli says, appearing out of nowhere. Even in the presence of her brother, it takes Alia a minute to calm herself enough before attempting to reply.

"Yeah?"

"You okay?" he asks, placing a hand on her arm. She quickly moves it away.

"Yeah, I'm fine. I just, needed some distance." Eli laughs, although Alia can't see how he'd find it the least bit amusing.

"He was clearly just trying to get you to like him. Don't be so touchy."

"Excuse me." She moves her arms from a hug to a tight fold. Her eyes directly at him.

"He clearly has a thing for you. Don't knock him down just yet." Alia laughs herself now, not sure why Eli is suddenly defending him when he knows exactly why she overreacted at the littlest of touches. Or at least part of the reason.

"He's an idiot, Eli. Plain and simple. He should know by now that charm doesn't get you everywhere in life and not every girl is going to fall at his feet on command." Eli's smile fades as his confusion quickly turns to defence. "Plus, I never liked him like that anyway. Or the guy from the Circus before you bring that up yet again."

"Okay, fine. I was only joking." He pauses. "I just didn't think it would be the worst thing, you know, if you found someone."

"What's that supposed to mean?" her voice raises a lot quicker and louder than she meant it to. A few people look over at them but most know it's best to keep to their own business. "Don't make me sound so desperate and alone, Eli, I'm not the one who is going behind my precious mother's back and spending time with the man she loathes. Especially after we all promised her we wouldn't." Her defensive tone moves quickly to offence yet she doesn't care at all what Eli thinks of her in this moment. She's almost happy that she allowed her rising anger to take hold, as much as she shouldn't.

"You know what Alia, forget it. I'm not getting into this with you, not again, not now." He sighs, prickles of his breath appearing in the cold night air. "I'm going to get more firewood."

"Is that really your go to way to get out of arguing with me now?"

"And what if it is? I don't need to hear any of this right now, especially from you." Just like a few nights before, Eli says nothing else as he turns around and starts striding towards the edge of the woods.

Feeling a small sob creeping up her throat, she does her best to swallow it, taking long breaths, her eyes lowered. As soon as she opens them, Eli is completely gone from view.

While most people have gone back to their conversations as if there wasn't any disturbance, Lola now makes her way slowly towards Alia who stands clearly puzzled at her approach. When face to face, Alia feels the need to snap at her too but knows from the regret in her face that she should probably hear her out.

"Hey," she says, her voice unusually soft and not at all hostile like Alia was expecting.

"Hi," she replies, definitive caution laced around the singular word. It takes Lola a minute to clearly decide exactly what to say next.

"Sorry if Marne, you know, got a bit much. He can get a bit too excitable I guess you could say. And involved."

"It's okay," Alia says, still confused as to the sudden change in Lola's manor. "I didn't mean to step on your toes or anything. At least, make it look like I did."

"Oh god no, don't worry about that." Surprisingly, Lola finds herself laughing. "We're both just, very complicated. Together and apart."

"As everyone is turning out to be I think." Lola smirks, giving Alia a sense of reassurance.

"I am sorry though. You know, about everything that happened this morning."

"It's okay." She nods. "Now, I can kinda see where you were coming from. It was Marne that went too far. He should have known when to stop. Mind you, that would be a first." This time, it's Alia laughing at Lola's words.

"I'm sure he'll catch on eventually."

"Like Eli?" Alia finds herself nearly snorting.

"That will be the day."

"I'm sure it will come. From what I've seen, I think Cora could be a good influence on him."

"What?" Alia's eyes bulge. "You mean—"

"Don't take it as fact." Lola rushes her words, clearly not wanting Alia to get the wrong idea too quickly. "They've just looked a little, too familiar at times. It's just a guess really but—"

"No, I get it. I guess it wouldn't be the worst thing." Lola simply nods in reply, putting a hand to her mouth to try and conceal a sudden yawn.

"I think I'm gonna head inside but, we're good, right?" Smiling, and happy that she means it, Alia nods.

"Definitely."

"Good." Lola says, briefly returning her smile before turning around and walking in the direction of the stairs of the base, leaving Alia standing alone

As if sensing the start of an oncoming storm, everyone else soon begins to trickle back inside the safe house which Alia has decided is much more like a bunker. Leaving their last little bits of left overs on the floor for the animals of the night, it isn't long before everyone has abandoned the stars and ducked back underground.

Alia watches Marne as he heads inside, catching an odd but kind of sorry look he gives her before turning his head to the steps.

Grabbing one of the now available logs, she leans into the fire, getting so close she almost feels like she could reach out and touch it. She imagines the heat as something you can see, like a snake winding itself around her fingers, the way it would when preparing to take hold of its next victim. No matter what Eli says, maybe she is better off alone.

"Alia?" Looking up at the familiar voice, Alia smiles at the sight of Commander Dormer looking down at her, completely forgetting before that she hadn't yet gone back inside.

"Hello." Commander Dormer smiles, taking a seat beside her. Feeling herself tense, Alia continues to smile as she turns around towards her. "How's Commander Peircly doing?" The commander's face falls a little, clearly having no news that's good.

"The same, if not worse. Honestly, I don't know if he'll make it through the night. He was hurt pretty badly." Her voice fades throughout the sentence. "If he dies, he'll be the first loss of the mission, at least in terms of one of us." While

Alia knows they should all be preparing for the worst, it doesn't mean it will get any easier if it were to happen.

"It's my fault, and I can't say I'm sorry enough." Alia's face has now fallen too, her previous light expression replaced with one of complete regret and sadness.

"You can't blame yourself. She was bound to hurt someone sooner or later. If it was her, that is. It was all just, very unfortunate timing, that night. Can't be helped."

"So, you reckon it was definitely her then?" the commander nods.

"I know what I said before, but I can't see anyone else ever wanting to hurt him. At least, not that badly. He was known and liked amongst everyone I know, Calla born or not." Alia nods in agreement.

They slip into a comfortable silence, their eyes both watching the crackling flames in front of them. Although never a fan of silence, Alia breathes deeply at how relaxed she suddenly feels. How content, and how safe. The kind of feeling she hasn't really had since her time in the training room. The kind of feeling that she wishes she could have every day.

To Alia's confusion, Commander Dormer reaches out and touches Alia's hair, letting it slide through her fingertips. At first, Alia is alarmed but then finds herself laughing until they're both looking happily towards each other.

"If we're going to face the Royalists, you need to tie this back," Commander Dormer says with another smile, as if it's her turn to be completely unaware of where they are or what they're there to do.

"I've always wondered why we don't just all shave our heads. It would be a lot more practical."

"Not very flattering though." They laugh again, happy in their own little carefree bubble.

Without looking back to see exactly who, their ears prick up at the sound of someone emerging but only coming out for a second before heading back inside.

Although a little chilly, Alia doesn't want to move. Not yet. She's not ready to leave this rekindling comfort behind.

"I'll do it later. I doubt anything more will happen tonight."

"You can never be sure of that. Don't make me think everything I taught you has already been forgotten."

"Never." Alia laughs, knowing how true it really is.

"Want me to do it for you?" Commander Dormer offers, moving a little closer to Alia's side.

Her heart suddenly flutters, like there's nothing that she wants more in this moment.

"I mean, if you're offering?" she agrees, turning in her seat so she's positioned with the commander directly behind her.

Taking a few pieces of hair at a time, Commander Dormer begins tying Alia's bound of curls into two even braids that will fall half way down her back. Alia smiles to herself, knowing this shouldn't be making her as happy as it does. Knowing that she can't always have Commander Dormer just for herself.

In the distance, she spies Eli, taking a slow walk back towards the warm fire. At a quick exchange of eye contact, Eli shakes his head and walks instead in the direction of the underground steps. At his almost distant hostility, Alia feels herself tense. Sensing this, the commander goes a little slower, her eyes moving between Alia's hair and Eli. When he's completely out of view, Alia sighs, looking down for the briefest of seconds.

"Everything okay? You two can't be fighting right now." Instead of snapping or getting defensive, Alia finds herself laughing, feeling safe enough to finally tell someone the whole truth.

"We're not fighting. Things are just, tense, I guess. Like we can never please each other. Like, we can never be honest enough for each other."

"And this is normally a bad thing?"

"No," Alia responds quickly. "When we don't see or talk to each other too much, it all kind of works. Now, it's weird seeing and having to look out for him all the time. I've gotten so used to it just being, well, me." Commander Dormer nods.

"I get that." She pauses, taking in a long breath. Her hand movements slowly lessening. "When you've only known one way for so long, it's hard to kick the habit."

"Completely," Alia agrees, finding herself relax more as time continues to pass. "Especially when you're being forced to act one way when really, it's just all pretend." She pauses, suddenly feeling herself overcome with a new kind of emotion, one that she's only ever experienced when being completely honest with someone. The very rare occasion that it's happened. "I guess actors aren't the only ones who spend their lives pretending." Commander Dormer smiles softly, finding the last parts of Alia's woven hair.

140

"Poetic, yet true." She laughs softly, running her hands across her finished work before putting the braids over Alia's shoulders, causing her to happily turn around.

"Sometimes we pretend for them because we don't want to hurt them. And that doesn't make us cowards, it makes us human." Alia smiles, tears threatening to choke her because of how true the commander's words are.

"Like you'd ever have to pretend for anyone." She laughs, lightening the sudden serious mood.

"You'd be surprised actually. But there are some people you can never be fake to, no matter how much you try." They share another smile, one which seems to go on for longer than any smile should.

Enjoying another brief moment of silence, Alia turns her attention to the sky above, the soothing blanket of stars finally being taken over by a fresh wave of thinly spread clouds. Taking the time to look at the pattern of the remaining stars glaring above them, each one seeming random yet fitting in perfectly with another. Two that you'd never put together but somehow fit like they were meant to be.

Mirroring Alia's actions, Commander Dormer takes her eyes to the stars. Without hesitation, she puts an arm around Alia, letting her sink into her embrace. Instead of stiffening or running away, Alia finds herself relaxing even more, enjoying the rare feeling of pure contentment.

"Do you think we'll make it through this?" Alia says, drawing her eyes away from the stars and towards the commander's dimly lit face. The fire in front of them finally beginning to lessen.

"I don't know." Commander Dormer looks away for a second before looking back towards Alia. "But what I do know is you will be okay. And I don't just mean here. You're strong and you will get what you want in the end, no matter how ridiculous it seems right now. You fight for it, and you get it."

Alia can feel herself welling up, at the words and whom they're coming from alike. Even though they're sitting out in the open with fresh dangers constantly rearing their heads, right now, Alia feels the furthest thing from alone.

"And if the Royalist kills me first?" she jokes. Instead of laughing with her, Commander Dormer puts a hand on her head, smoothing down one last bit of hair.

"I won't let that happen," she says, her voice soft but genuine. Holding Alia tighter, Commander Dormer leans down and kisses her head. Alia closes her eyes, knowing she shouldn't feel as safe as she does. How herself she's able to be when really, she should feel like this when with so many other people. People that she's meant to feel like this with.

Maybe, blood isn't thicker than water.

"I'm sorry I wasn't there before. When you first left the Academy. I—"

"It's okay," Alia interrupts, sitting up to look the commander in the eyes. "You have your own life; you have your own problems without clearing mine up as well. I'm the one who is sorry."

"You don't have to be."

"Well, I am." Alia sighs, turning around and slowly sinking back into Commander Dormer's arms. "You're here now, that's all that matters." She pauses, looking around at the otherwise desolate land around them, as if just remembering that they're not really alone out here, as empty as it currently feels. Yet Alia wouldn't care if they were surrounded by a thousand people. In this moment, she feels like she could take on anything and not fall down when things get hard. As if she could finally get the safety net that she longed for, for as long as she can remember.

Twenty

The next morning draws in as quickly as the other one left. Alia finds herself waking up to a crowded room, everyone else already on their feet. Standing up, Alia moves over to the other side of the dimly lit room to find everyone yet again crowded around Commander Peircly.

Pushing her way to the front, Alia sees something that she doesn't think any of them are really ready to see. A body.

Like many children of Calla's realm, Alia thought she was always being told the truth when people spoke about death. They'd go in their sleep, their skin still pink but pale and their eyes closed as if they were sleeping. Yet a beyond pale white Commander Peircly lays before her, his eyes still open and formally light green circles growing darker by the minute. Maybe the only honest thing she was told that is true is just how cold he both looks and feels.

Eventually, the two living commanders appear from the surface and cover him with one of the few pieces of cloth they were previously using for a blanket. They quickly usher everyone else up top, advising them to pack their things quickly and be ready to go.

Within minutes of being guided to solid ground, under yet another warm sunny day, Alia stands alone, studying the shared looks of sadness and confusion across the faces of her allies. All except Eli's.

As if hearing her thoughts catching up with her, Eli suddenly appears in the corner of her vision, crossing from the surrounding trees. His face content, as if he's never been more relaxed. And in the middle of a looming war zone, it concerns Alia more than it usually would. When in close proximity, Alia moves quickly towards him, grabbing him by the arm harder than she initially intended to.

"Hey! Watch it!" He squirms, getting loose of her grip but chooses to not run away.

"And where've you been all night?" Alia can't quite tell whether he's putting on a confused face or whether it's real. Since being out here, Alia feels it's as if she was living somewhere else all her life and the hard truth is that she doesn't know her brother nearly as well as she thought she did.

"Asleep underground like everyone else." He gives her a look as if to say 'back down'. Yet she doesn't stop looking in his eyes.

"You went back to the surface not long after I went down and I didn't see you come back before I went to sleep."

"So, I can do what I want and it's not like you waited up for me." he says, his clear sarcasm meant to irritate her. "As if you care anyway."

"Eli—"

"No!" he shouts, a little too loudly even for her liking.

"Calm down. I'm just concerned like I'm meant to be."

"Well, don't be." He lowers his voice but not his rising temper. "I'm my own person now. I don't need you or anybody there all the time. I can handle things myself." Alia laughs, trying not to be mocking.

"What has happened to you? Really though?" She pauses, making sure minimum eyes are on them. "You come here and all of sudden you're all grown up? You finally start standing up to Mum and having your own thoughts and suddenly that's it? Cords cut and you're on your own."

"Better than coming here to prove yourself and regressing into a scared little child needing to be told that everything will be alright, rather than just believing it yourself."

Very much between wanting to shout at him and knowing there are core truths to his words, like always, Alia doesn't know how to react. Above everyone else, Eli always seems to be honest. Pacing back and forth for a minute, Alia drags her feet through the yellow earth, as Eli remains silent before her. Sighing, she puts a hand on his arm, without force this time.

"What happened last night? After we talked, I thought we were okay? At least on the way to being okay." While Eli doesn't move his body, he rolls his eyes before setting them over her shoulder. Turning around, Alia sees Commander Thornbe followed by Commander Dormer exiting the ground, their belongings on their backs.

We're moving on.

It takes a second for Alia to move her thoughts back to Eli who is already looking at her once again. Sniggering a little, he slowly removes her hand.

"We were. Until I realised where your true priorities lie." His eyes cross quickly between Alia and Commander Dormer. Alia does her best to not give in to the temptation and follow his gaze. "When the time comes, you'll have to choose." He laughs again, taking one step away from her. "And blood is always meant to be thicker than water." Smiling, his face filled with an odd combination of envy, yet complete content. Even happiness.

Watching him go, Alia feels her heart quicken. They haven't even started fighting the Royalist, or even caught them, yet she feels the most at war with herself than she's ever been. Maybe she was chosen not to come here to show her strength physically, but mentally. One thing people never tell you is how much war, however bad, affects the way you think about not only others, but about yourself and what you really want. When everything else has always been mapped out in front of you, sometimes it's hard to be given a blank canvas for the very first time.

Looking towards the commander, seeing her ready to give the first order of the day, Alia knows that Eli is right. That eventually, she'll have to make a choice. But for now, she has to remain focussed on the task in hand. Avoid any distractions and remember the most important thing, the Royalist.

"Everyone, listen up," Commander Dormer shouts, causing everyone looking towards her just like she wanted, even Commander Thornbe. "As I'm sure you all know by now, during the night, we lost Commander Peircly." There is suddenly a wave of muffled voices until Commander Dormer raises her hand and they stop as if hitting a sea wall. "We were to expect casualties, and we'll grieve his loss later. But for now, we move on and remember the true objective."

"Kill the Royalist!" Marne shouts, punching a fist in the air. A few follow his lead while others, including Alia, remain quiet.

"No," Commander Thornbe speaks up, allowing Commander Dormer to take a quick breath.

"Our instructions haven't changed. We're still to only kill her in the most extreme circumstances. But capture and contain her at all costs." She pauses, taking a minute to look at them all in turn, her eyes seeming to skim over Alia quicker than anyone else. "We've had a possible sighting at the border of Orchid. We should be there by nightfall."

"Are we taking another one of those ancient food carts?" Cora asks, oddly confident in herself today. Commander Dormer laughs, taking a step away from Commander Thornbe and into the sea of watchful young Protectors.

"Not today. This journey is a lot easier to walk. Try and get a sense of the journey she's made."

"Look for clues along the way?" Cora speaks again.

"Exactly." She smiles, holding the tight straps of the bag upon her back. "Now, onwards."

***

Although knowing how far their journey is, no one quite realises how far they've come until the sun is soon replaced with a high and shining moon. Its light reflecting like glass at different angles over every small lake they pass.

For the majority of the journey, they walk in silent whispers, only conversing as a group when examining something connected to the Royalist or deciding when to stop and rest. While Alia doesn't complain at some quiet hours to herself, throughout the day she begins to question more whether if and when the time came, would they all be able to pull together and take the Royalist down?

While their path is fast becoming nothing but a faded shadow, they continue to walk on. Bright city lights from the distance getting closer with each step, everyone is ready to be finished for the night.

Lola now walks with Alia, after having enough of most of her silent journey. Marne hangs back with the 'young-ins', as he calls them, from the Academy. Although Eli walks with them, every time Alia has looked back throughout the journey, she's noticed Eli's rather cheery but fake smile, his mind clearly on other things.

The commanders walk ahead, leading the way like they're meant to. Clearing the path for the rest of the team that they've sworn to protect. No matter what they face, they come first.

Throughout the day, Alia notices small but clear quick glances in her direction from Commander Dormer's eyes. Although she wants to smile and feel grateful for the attention, a part of her is now questioning why she feels the way she does. And how much she'd rather not feel anything at all, much like she does about other things she supposed to care about. The more she tries to wrap her head around it, the more she feels that every part of her is simply wired in completely the wrong way.

Alia keeps her eyes low until Lola appears at her side. Her unusually loose hair curling even more in the constant wind, making it seem thicker than Alia had ever noticed it to be. Especially compared to her own, which is still tied up nicely in its neat pair of braids.

They walk in silence for a long time, simply happy to be in each other's company. While not speaking much before, or even a lot since they left the Bureau, Alia finds that Lola is one of the rare people that she's felt comfortable around since they got to know each other properly. Unlike many of the others, as far as Alia can tell, she's here purely for herself and her own agenda. She's real and happy and idealistic. The definition of someone that Alia usually finds out to be fake. But good company until she's proven wrong.

"Is this road ever going to end?" Lola groans, only loud enough for Alia to hear. She laughs and they smile together. Happy to be doing anything but staring around aimlessly, watching the world go by.

"Agreed." Alia laughs again, making sure to keep it quiet. "I feel like we've been walking all day."

"Um, we have." They laugh again, a little louder. Causing a few heads to turn their way, including Commander Dormer's. At the connection of their eyes, Alia's face falls and she drops her gaze. It takes a minute for her to awkwardly lift her head again, making sure that the commander is no longer staring. Lola shuffles a little closer to her, a weird kind of smile on her face.

"What was that?" she whispers even quieter than before.

"Nothing." Alia tries to laugh off but Lola just stares at her, clearly unconvinced.

"You know you can trust me, right?" As much as Alia knows she does, the more Lola presses the more she can feel her skin getting hotter. Her ears twitching at the slightest voice.

"I know, but," she pauses, waiting for the right words to fall onto her tongue, "it's complicated."

"It didn't look it last night."

"What?" Alia turns to her quickly, feeling her pace slow down but not enough for anyone to really notice. She can feel her body gradually getting hotter, her heart beating the more panicked she feels. "What do you mean?"

"You know, you two, last night. You looked, I dunno, cosy."

"No," Alia responds quickly, trying to keep her voice a muffled whisper. "It wasn't like that, at all. It's never that. Why does everyone always think that romance is the most important thing when two people just happen to be close?"

"Okay, okay, I'm sorry," Lola apologises quickly, taking a minute before daring to speak again. "I guess it looked different to what it was. My bad."

"But yeah, it was way different to that. Completely different." Feeling herself beginning to get worked up, Alia takes a minute to breathe before turning back towards Lola, calmer than she would have been. "I'm sorry, you were only asking. It's just; it's definitely not what it looked like. Believe me, it never is."

"I do believe you, you know. I just thought I was being clever."

"In what way?" This time Alia looks towards her confused while Lola breathes deeply, averting her own eyes to the dark silhouetted buildings fast approaching them.

"You know the commander split from her partner, right? As in recently. Like right before we left."

"Seriously?" Alia knows she shouldn't already sound as invested as she does. But there are some things that you don't have time to fake. Some reactions just happen before you can think about how to pass them off as something else. Sometimes, honesty just takes over. "What happened?" Lola shrugs, as if suddenly uninterested by the conversation topic.

"No idea. All I know for sure is that something happened while the commander was on leave at the beginning of last summer. Something that caused her partner to leave."

"He actually left?" Lola nods.

"Not the realm, but yeah, he did. I'm pretty sure. But the rumours are that she found someone else. And for a minute, I—" She starts laughing as Alia's cheeks fade a little pink. Even in the shadowed light they're in.

"If you're about to say what I think you are, then you're way off. I can promise you, it had and still hasn't got anything to do with me. People need to stop assuming that the only way you can be close to someone is romantically. Not everyone has the sex drive of a Circus performer."

Lola laughs louder than she did before, although they're both surprised to see that no one looks their way.

"Damn right but wow, what a way to put it."

They laugh, seeming to do nothing else as they walk. But as the sound slowly diminishes from Alia's lips, she can't help but feel suddenly aware of what people might have seen, especially what they think they saw. Hugging her arms close to her chest, she can't help but wonder if enough people believe something, is that enough to make it real?

Twenty-One

By the time they reach the thinly marked border between Orchid and Aster, a low screeching can be heard in the far distance. Commander Dormer directs them to the dimly lit rusting tracks, running along the very edge of the line between the realms that share nothing but the metal between them.

Although neighbours in nearly everything, even from the edge, Alia can tell it's like stepping into a completely different world.

Alia crouches by the rattling tracks, breathing in the new scent of trees and life. Even from where she sits, she has a clear view of the distant city. Her eyes fill with so many lights it's almost like she can smell them. Like she can feel the brightness of the sleeping city leaking out into everything around.

Although they haven't travelled to a new realm as they're still technically within the borders of Orchid, it's never been a secret that due to its size, certain parts of the realm deviate from the more traditional values that they seek to uphold. For the northern parts of Orchid, the focus is less on the food distribution and more on helping keep people comfortable.

As the approaching train grows louder, Commander Dormer makes sure everyone is present and stands closer to the tracks, her bag on her back. Without having to say anything, everyone else follows her lead. Standing to attention and preparing for another train ride.

"So, now we're getting the train?" Marne asks, his tone sarcastic, although Alia isn't sure if he means it as much as it sounds.

"Yep, but only the second carriage. Unless, you'd all prefer to continue walking?"

"No!" everyone shouts together. Commander Dormer laughs, a sheer moment of happiness in her eyes. Commander Thornbe simply smiles, his eyes drifting between the commander and the direction of the train, which can now be seen at a distance.

"We're expected at the main hall tomorrow. We should get there just before sunrise, and then the real work begins." Alia and Lola exchange a brief glance, knowing full well that the worst is yet to come.

As if on cue, the train rattles across the tracks, getting closer by the second. Within minutes of everyone standing on the side, ready to move, the train is at their side and they each jump on.

To their relief, they've made it onto one of the proper trains with enough space to move around and several comfortable seats. While they didn't see exactly who, if anyone, is sitting in the first carriage, Alia presumes that it will be a collection of elderly members from across each realm, all having the same idea of moving to the north of Orchid to spend their final years. After all, it is known for making its residents comfortable above all else.

Regaining their balance, everyone stretches out across the carriage. Commander Thornbe quickly shuts the sliding door, blocking out the little light from the outside, leaving them with single flashes, the sparks growing more frequent the closer they get into the city.

This would be the carriage they forgot to add windows to.

While everyone takes their spots in the carriage, most taking the seats, with Commander Dormer and Lola left to take the floor, which neither of them seems to mind.

Commander Thornbe sits at the very front of the carriage, already enjoying the luxury of a softly padded seat as he splays himself out across it. Not far behind him, Marne does the same, whereas Eli and Cora also have a seat each but both lay like normal people and don't take up the whole thing.

Alia sits in the back seat, also enjoying the comfort and relief the padding is giving her tired and aching bones.

Most of them, including Eli, quickly slip into an easy looking sleep. And easy sounding from the volume of Commander Thornbe's snoring.

On the floor, Lola curls up in a tight but comfortable ball, using her bag as a pillow and seeming to drift off just as quickly. Soon enough, it seems that only Alia and Commander Dormer remain awake, both wide eyed and for the most part, alert.

Alia moves her body in all directions but fails to find the right way to sleep. Sighing, she sits up with her back to the carriage wall, rubbing her eyes.

"Can't sleep?" Even a whisper from Commander Dormer, who sits on the floor just behind Alia's seat, makes her smile through her otherwise agitated state. Sighing a little again, Alia turns her body so she's leaning slightly over the edge of the seat, her eyes on the commander.

"Apparently not." Their smiles are quickly interrupted by another irritatingly loud snort from Commander Thornbe's direction. While still trying to be quiet, they both can't help but snigger.

"And he said he'd take the first shift of staying awake. Classic Thornbe," she whispers before laughing a little again, her voice even quieter this time.

"I'm sorry about Commander Peircly." The Commander's face falls a little at the mention but she doesn't look away. "I still feel like it was my fault."

"No," she responds quickly, sitting up a little herself.

"It's sad it happened but then it's not surprising either. We all signed up for this. It was unlikely that we'd get through it without any casualties."

"That's true," Alia agrees, shifting a little, her eyes not leaving the commander's. "But I hope we don't lose anybody else." Commander Dormer smiles.

"We can all wish for that, but that's just life." She pauses, bowing her head. "When you lose enough people, it, it doesn't get easier as such but—" She stops again, a fresh overtake of emotions sweeping her like an unexpected wave. Alia feels a certain power in seeing the commander suddenly so vulnerable, although she doesn't think she wants to know why.

"Accepting it becomes easier," Alia finishes, feeling tears building up in her own eyes.

The Commander nods, sniffing back her rising emotion until her face is as controlled and still as ever before. She then smiles towards Alia, as if nothing had happened. Like she hadn't let down the walls that Alia never even knew were there.

"Eli's lying to me," Alia keeps her voice to a whisper, unsure for a minute why she suddenly changed the topic. "He's hiding something. And he keeps disappearing."

"I've noticed," she whispers back, taking a second to look around, making sure that everyone, Eli in particular, is still sleeping.

"Do you know what he's doing?" Commander Dormer shrugs.

"He seems to be good at keeping things to himself when he wants to. Just like you." Alia smiles no matter how much she doesn't want to. Her heart beating faster by the minute. "I'm sure it's nothing dangerous. He's probably just, taking time to himself. To do his own thing."

"I guess so."

There's a brief second of silence before Alia finds herself yawning, as if aware that she needs to be sleeping like everyone else. Yet she likes being awake when others aren't. Taking the time to watch everyone's individual breaths, Alia begins to relax at the continual motion of their rising and falling chests.

"You need to sleep. It's not like you have to stay up watching."

"I don't mind," Alia responds. Commander Dormer laughs as Alia yawns again, longer and louder than before.

"Sleep, now."

Rubbing her eyes, Alia nods before lying down again, disappearing behind the back of her seat.

She lies on her back, staring at the silver ceiling that when she narrows her eyes enough, she can tell it is slightly rattling along with the constant rolling motions of the turning wheels beneath them.

Laying on her back, in the quiet, somewhere relatively safe, Alia wishes she could see the stars. She wishes she could trace them with her fingers, feeling like if she reaches out far enough, she could touch them.

Closing her eyes, Alia does her best to think of anything but the images she sees whenever she closes her eyes now. The fire, the woods, Commander Peircly, lying there both dead and alive. She imagines what Eli would have looked like in his place. What would have happened if it had been Lola or Marne. Or even Alia herself.

Alia tries not to imagine everything that could go wrong when they reach the border and then when they inevitably reach Aster. In a way, Alia thinks that if she imagines the worst now, if it actually happens then it won't feel so bad. But then she knows as well as anyone that even if you try and prepare for something you think will happen, it doesn't mean it actually will. Deciding to cast out all the 'what ifs' that just seem to be making her mind spin more than before, Alia thinks back to sitting under the stars the previous night. Trying to remember just how good it felt to feel something that should be so easy, yet it's always so hard to find. Finally feeling herself relax enough to sleep, Alia pictures the stars and remembers how it felt to feel safe.

***

They're all awoken several hours later by small flecks of sunlight, each trying their best to break through the small gaps around the carriage door.

Their bones equally stiff and eyes still heavy, it takes everyone several minutes to adjust to yet another new morning.

The rattling beneath them eventually begins to slow, allowing everyone to regain their footing and remember where they are and where they're going.

It takes Alia longer than usual to fully wake up, stretching what feels like every bone before really ready to get up and face the day.

Moving her eyes to the continual fast-moving flashes of morning sun, Alia breathes deeply, controlling her quickening heart.

Everyone is now gathered by the door, a very similar look passing through each and every one of their eyes. Even the commanders are slightly more jittery than usual this morning. Studying each of their faces in turn, Alia tries to distinguish what exactly everyone is feeling.

Discomfort? *Maybe…* Fear? *Most definitely.*

Twenty-Two

The sun in this part of Orchid doesn't rise as high as it does in the south. Up here, after first emerging, it remains still, giving this part of the realm enough natural light to power the many little lights that when switched on can be seen from far away.

By the time Alia, along with the rest of her team, is entering the largest meeting room of the Council building, quiet rumbles of incoming thunder are beginning to echo outside.

While rare, they've all witnessed a storm at least before. Although this time, no one is quite sure whether this is one of natural causes or magical ones.

"Well done on all of you for making it this far," Captain Winter, the apparent military leader of Orchid, praises them. He stands on a small platform around a large circular table in the biggest meeting space in Orchid, several chairs pushed to the far corners of the room. Alia, along with the rest of her team, gather around, their eyes on the small thin oak object the Captain placed in the middle of the table.

Listening more intently as the edges of the previously normal wooden object begin to glow and curve until a large dome is created on top.

When did they get so fancy?

"This was taken from the only bit of surveillance footage we were able to save before the system shut down yesterday."

"When did everything go down? And how?" He already looks a little lost for words.

"It went down shortly after we got this and so far, it just seems like it was circuit failure. It happens from time to time."

Commander Dormer gives him a look like she's trying to tell him to stop kidding himself and pay attention, no matter how scary the truth may be.

He then presses a button causing the lights in the room to dim and an image appears in the middle of the dome. Everyone watches closely as the still image turns into a moving one.

They watch as crowds of people hurry through the town centre. Each one clearly interested in solely their own intentions.

Commander Dormer leans a little closer, her face so close it looks as if she'd disappear inside the projection is given a push. Alia hangs back a little, trying to stay alert while also trying to breathe through her tightening chest.

Something's wrong… yet she can't quite figure out what.

They continue to watch the footage play, looking for anything out of the ordinary. Captain Winter's exterior remains solemn, as if not wanting them to be swayed by his reaction before seeing it for themselves. His darkened skin appearing almost white through the leftover lighting.

Watching the pale figures move so fast through the video, it almost looks like they're dancing. So much so that it takes everyone a second longer than it should have to notice the slight ting of uneven lighting creeping out from a very particular person's hooded grey cloak.

"There!" Lola shouts it first, but everyone's eyes move to it simultaneously.

Captain Winter freezes the image, as they all look closer at the person frozen in a single second. The Royalist. Even with the image frozen, it's hard to see exactly, but at a more detailed look, Alia sees little colourful sparks reaching out of the cloak as if coming from a hidden hand.

Captain Winter surveys the image himself before turning off the projection and addressing all the curious faces now pointed in his direction.

"It was just after this that we had a small explosion, you might say, in one of our outer cities. Luckily, it was one of our smaller ones, far fewer losses than there could have been." Everyone turns to each other, trying to comprehend the most reliable information they've received since they left Calla.

"Why weren't we told about this before we got here?" Marne says, making it seem like the worst thing in the world that no one thought to inform them.

"We were already on our way. We couldn't have done anything and they knew we were heading here anyway." Eli speaks up, a new kind of confidence in his voice. Captain Winters gives him an approving nod, as if that's his way of thanking him for his support.

"Unfortunately, while we don't have that on tape, we do have the resonant readings from the explosion." He pauses, as if trying to build further tension. "It was magic. It was the Royalist, we're sure of it. She was here."

At this, everyone turns to each other once again. The commanders exchange a clearly worrying look while Alia and Lola just look surprised to one another. While knowing it was always their main aim to follow the Royalist and eventually capture them, alive, a part of Alia never thought they'd actually reach this point. A part of her never believed that any of this was really real.

Until now. Now she's sure. And she's terrified.

As if all on the same wavelength, Alia can feel a sudden panic flowing around the room. Like everyone else is suddenly thinking, and realising, the same things as her. All except Eli. Now standing alone in his own small square, he bows his head, shaking it continuously.

Looking up, Alia is careful not to catch his eyes but simply stare into them. Even from a distance, her heart quickens further as she realises that the look within his shining green circles is not one of fear, but of concern. Of sadness. But the type of sadness that you don't feel for yourself, you fear for someone else.

Twenty-Three

As soon as they leave Captain Winter, Commander Dormer assembles everyone together at the edge of the main city. While fear no longer remains in her face, Alia can still see it in her eyes, no matter how hard she's trying to hide it. Although it scares her, Alia finds it almost like a comfort that the commander is just as scared as everyone else.

"Just like before, we split off, but only into two groups this time, find out what we can, but we have to find her. No exceptions." Although clearly worried, the commander's voice remains strong and unaffected. "From what Captain Winter has told us, the Royalist is still somewhere in the Northern part the realm. Where exactly, we can only guess at."

"She's still heading for Aster, surely?" Cora speaks up, her voice louder and a little more confident than she'd ever heard it.

"That's her long game. As for the short game, I reckon, she's had to hide away somewhere. Keep her strength up. She knows there will be a fight waiting for her, and she'll make sure she's ready for it," Commander Thornbe responds. Everyone goes silent for a minute, clearly all with the same question lingering at the tip of their tongues.

Where is she hiding? And what is she planning to do next?

"Eli, Marne and Alia. You'll stay with me. We'll go through the east of the city. Commander Thornbe will take Lola and Cora. Remember, everyone must stick together." She takes a second to look sternly at Alia who tries to remain serious. "We'll meet back at the nearest safe house. Everyone has the coordinates, just in case."

"But what if she's further out than that? Can't we search the whole realm?" Cora speaks again.

"What do you think everyone else has been doing since she escaped?" Commander Thornbe laughs. Alia sees Cora shrink a little, back within herself. Commander Dormer smiles warmly towards the young girl, helping her relax a little while Alia feels her body suddenly tense. "People from every realm are out there every second of everyday, searching every corner of the world, trying to find her."

"You'd think someone would have found her by now," Marne says, taking the chance to insert himself into the conversation.

"You'd think so but—"

"It just proves that she's intelligent," Commander Dormer continues. "Intelligent with magic and an objective. Definitely a force to be reckoned with."

"So let's do it," Lola speaks, smiling equally at both the commanders.

Leaving the building, with only nods to encouragement from Captain Winter, everyone breaks up into the two separate directions, suddenly full of high spirits. Eli strikes on ahead towards the East. Alia hangs back a little, waiting for everyone else to go ahead, wanting to trail along behind, as if to try and gather all her strength, emotionally and physically. Lola brushes against her arm, their smiles synced when their eyes meet.

"See you on the other side."

"Good luck." With a short laugh, Lola leads the way for her group.

Marne follows closely behind Eli, clearly also wanting to lead the way. Taking her first step towards their direction, Alia is stopped by Commander Dormer at her side.

"I want you where I can see you, okay? I don't want a repeat of last time. No more loss."

"You know I didn't mean for any of that to happen," her voice comes out a lot quieter and whinier than she ever intended it to be. Commander Dormer studies her face, suddenly sad and almost lost. Sighing, she rolls her eyes before smiling towards Alia's childlike expression.

"Just stay close. And stay safe." Alia smiles.

"I'll try."

Without another word, Commander Dormer moves past her and jogs to catch up with Eli and Marne. Taking a long breath and a second to compose herself, Alia soon follows the commander and takes her position at the back of the group. Trying to feel ready for whatever will come their way.

***

For the remainder of the day, both groups go through each section of the centre, like trying to find a needle in a haystack. Literally.

The commanders kept in regular contact, talking back and forth about plans and strategies for when they eventually find her. If they find her.

Through the long, dry hours, Alia begins to lose hope. Every time they think they're getting closer, she still remains to be seen. It wouldn't surprise Alia in the slightest if the Royalist had used all her remaining magic to make herself invisible in order to reach Aster first. The more Alia suddenly thinks about it, the more she wonders if it's actually possible. And if so, why she didn't do it in the first place.

The more Alia turns all her thoughts towards the Royalist, her ideas and questions gradually churn quicker within her, as if she's surprised that she's never considered half this stuff before.

How much magic can she really have left? How does it all work? Are there limits? Are there things that require more magic than others? Can she actually just run out eventually? And if she does, will she be just like everyone else?

Question after question, thought after thought, Alia is suddenly overcome with an anger of no one else being more interested in the Royalist. All these things could aid them in the coming fight. Surely, if they knew more about her, then they'd have a far better idea of how to actually defeat her. Yet all anyone seems concerned about is beating the other team to the race just to have the home ground advantage before throwing the first punch.

For the longest time since they'd all ventured out into the complete unknown, Alia begins to feel uneasy. However, this time is not because she's afraid of just losing, but because she's now afraid of dying.

The Royalist could have the power to wound or even kill anyone by a single touch, whether her magic is dwindling or not. She's already, most likely, the cause behind the loss of Commander Peircly. So, who's next?

"There!" Marne shouts, bringing Alia out of her thoughts and back into the present.

They're in a narrow alleyway right at the centre of the city. The sun is beginning to set but as the sky grows darker, the thousand lights above them grow lighter. So bright, they could be seen to be brighter than the actual sun, depending on what way you look at it.

Marne runs down the smoothly paved street, followed closely by Eli and Commander Dormer. Alia falling last but still easily able to keep up. She wants Marne to have seen the real her, not another almost Royalist, like they'd been seeing all day. But this person isn't letting them catch her. They're running away.

They chase the hooded figure through several more streets, all brightly lit but still some were easier to follow her through than others. Eventually, Marne stops bounding at the end of one of the wider streets, right at a dead end with the hooded figure in front of them.

They're turned away, their breaths obviously quick. Their hearts trying to catch up.

Alia and Marne simultaneously point their pistoles in her direction, more as a threat than as an actual weapon. Although trained to use them in every known situation, it doesn't make firing the metal bullets in this confined space any easier. Especially for the first time they have a real moving target.

Commander Dormer follows their lead, one hand holding her bow with the arrow in the other. Primed to shoot on command. She stands a little in front of the others, as if trying to shield them from immediate harm. Just like the commanders are always instructed to do.

Eli hangs back compared to them, his gun in open view but not raised. His hand is set, his finger ready on the trigger, but his whole body is shaking. Shaking so much that Alia thinks he might just topple over at a simple push. But she can't worry about him now. She has to focus on the person ahead of them.

Hopefully, the Royalist. Or hopefully not.

"Take down your hood but remain where you are!" Commander Dormer shouts. Her voice full of so much fire and command, Alia imagines the words coming out of her a steaming red, almost like fire.

Slowly, so slowly as if trying to drag it all out, they raise their arms, holding both sides of the oversized hood. Just as slowly, they take down the hood revealing hair. Girl's hair. Hair that burns a deep auburn and is knotted into an almost eccentric pattern. Woven so tightly that from the back you couldn't tell it was there at all.

With their hands still raised, the girl moves her body anti-clockwise. Her feet taking small steps until her face reaches theirs. Her red eyes gleam with tears matching the clearly dried ones already living on her pale freckled skin. Her hands shake as she bites her lip, so hard that it looks like she could bite straight through it.

It's not her…it can't be…

"Who are you?" Commander Dormer asks it more like an instruction than a question. Her steady fingers not leaving her weapon.

"They, they made me do it. Made me run. Made me draw you here." the girl cries, her voice trembling, wavering between sobs and a kind of choking. "I'm sorry, I'm so sorry." She cries again, seeming to grow smaller by the minute, her legs slowly giving way.

"Who made you? Who are you?"

"They…" the girl speaks again between strained breaths. Alia lowers her gun a little, studying the girl's face.

She's in pain. They're hurting her.

"They made me dress like them. Made it seem like I was them. I didn't want to. T-they said they'd hurt my family if I didn't."

"It's okay." While not lowering her bow, the commander's words come out in a far softer tone. She takes a cautious step towards her. While nobody else moves, Alia can sense Eli's nervous stance. Of all the things to happen, she never thought he'd lose it. Even if this isn't a real battle. Not yet.

"Can you tell me where they've gone? Why she made you do it?"

"I—" The girl takes in a sharp breath, her eyes now on the sky. Her breaths quickening at an unnerving rate, she tries to take hold of the walls around her, digging her nails into anything solid. "She's gone! Run! Orchid flower! Orchid flower!" she screams the words before just hollow screams are left. Putting her head into her hands, she continues to scream and cry as if in agony.

Commander Dormer takes a few steps away, lowering her weapon. Alia and Marne mirror her, along with Eli who finally seems to be getting the hang of what to do.

Swiftly taking her phone from her trouser pocket, Commander Dormer vigorously attempts for someone to pick up on the other end. Holding the phone to her ear, she waits only seconds, but they feel like minutes.

"Dexter! I know where she is! Orchid Flower!"

Without any form of explanation, Commander Dormer leaves the girl, now crumbling in a corner, screaming as she collapses in on herself, running back the way they came and then in a new direction through the now nearly empty centre of the city. As much as Alia knows they have to move, a part of her can't quite believe that Commander Dormer willingly left that girl still in deep pain. Unless she knew that really, there was nothing they could do to save her.

Their path through streets and roads remains brightly lit, making the journey easier on all of them. Although all confused, everyone knows now is not the time for questions. Now is the time to run, and be ready.

So they run, weapons still in hand, until they reach a similar looking field to the one they were in yesterday. The previous safe house. *Safe house.*

They run further through now more of a grassy land. Their breaths becoming shorter as their fresh oxygen levels slowly deplete.

Moving closer, they spy a tall building. Designed very much like the other Orchid safe house, only this one seems to be entirely on the surface. The closer they get to it; the faster Commander Dormer seems to run. Gliding through the air as if she were flying. Alia, Marne and Eli follow behind, although not as closely as they were before.

Looking up at the slimly designed glass windows, Alia thinks she spies a shadow in one of them. A quick moving dark figure only seen for a second but seen nonetheless. For a minute, all she can think about is who could be in there.

Until the building goes up in flames.

Twenty-Four

Fire roars everywhere. Sprouting from the building as if it were a fountain, the flames dance around it, engulfing different areas of it one at a time. Almost like, they're dancing, spraying the very tops of the nearest trees with their pointed toes.

Commander Dormer is the first to be thrown backwards away from the house. At first it seems like it's just from the flames, until Marne tries to get closer and the same thing happens, only he's pushed back further by something more than flames.

"It's magic! This is her, it must be!" Marne finds himself shouting, fighting to be heard against the constant rumble of the growing infernos.

Alia runs herself running to the commander's side. Kneeling at her shaking body. The Commander squints in some kind of pain, taking deep and constant breaths while clearly trying not to panic.

"We need to get out of here," she whispers. Using Alia almost like a rope, Commander Dormer pulls herself to her feet and looks again at the raging house, now nearly swallowed completely by the spreading blaze.

"Is anyone in there?" Marne asks, looking helplessly between the still visible door and the rest of the shivering bodies around him. For a minute, everyone's silent, not wanting to get the answer they know is inevitable if they weren't the first ones to get here.

"Even if there were, it's too late. We have to go, now!"

Everyone starts to turn back the way they came, all their instincts changing into finding a way to get out alive. While Commander Dormer limps a little, everyone else seems to have escaped any physical pain. For now at least.

Weapons still out, they all find themselves panting, not knowing exactly what to do, before finally turning their backs on the building.

"Eli!"

A strained voice suddenly echo's through the flames. A familiar voice. A female one. "Lola!" Eli screams back.

As if now acting on full instinct, Eli whips around, running back towards the high rising flames. While he has a clear view of the entrance, all anyone else can see is fire. Usually, the bright oranges and yellows coming together is something people gather around to watch and sing around. But right now, they are the definition of hell.

"Eli, no!" Alia screams, as if suddenly realising what's really happening. She attempts to take a few strides forwards before Commander Dormer takes hold of her, pulling her back. Alia screams, more than she feels she ever has, thrashing her arms, desperately trying to be released from her hold. Tears spill in a constant rhythm from her wide eyes, almost like she's already anticipating the worst before it's even happened.

Marne looks between Eli's clear path and Alia's burning eyes. Pulling a face of clear determination, he smiles at Alia before turning and following Eli's lead. In just seconds, both Eli and Marne move out of site, swallowed by the raging fire.

Alia feels herself shrinking to the floor. Scared for Eli but also scared for Marne. Scared for Lola and ashamed of herself for not being brave enough to go in after them herself, to search for their friend rather than just leaving her to die. Even if it does seem like a suicide mission.

If she ever wants to be a part of the Force, or even a Protector at all, then she has to do better. Has to be braver, stronger, just like Eli has proven himself to be, now more than ever.

Commander Dormer holds Alia's trembling body, letting her scream and bow her head in her shame as the fire still roars in front of their eyes. They both know they can't stay waiting forever, but how long can they really wait?

"There's nothing you could have done," the commander whispers. "We got here too late."

"But I let him come, I encouraged him," Alia whines back, trying not to let herself completely fall apart. "I didn't stop him from going in, I failed him."

Their eyes don't leave the house as they listen out for anything, any sign that there could still be hope. Eventually, Alia is sure she hears the scurrying of something. Maybe something animal. Or maybe something human.

"Eli," she whispers, getting to her feet along with the commander, their eyes fixed on the smallest of paths that haven't yet been completely scorched. After waiting for what feels like an eternity, the faintest signs of human life finally appear.

"Eli!" Alia shouts as he fully emerges from the fire, his skin painted black with soot and his uniform burnt in many places. And he's not alone.

"Lola!" Commander Dormer rushes to their side and pulls Lola away from his reach, letting her lean on her while she continually coughs and sputters.

Alia reaches Eli just before he almost collapses, coughing even more than Lola, his throat burning from the sudden amount of clean oxygen now circulating around his body.

Commander Dormer leads them to the shelter of the nearest trees that aren't in immediate danger of being blackened. For a minute, they all slump next to the trunks, each catching their breath while inhaling as much fresh air as they can.

From a distance, the house almost looks like what a real sunset should appear to be. A small almost rounded burning orange light that stands out so clearly from the darkness around it.

Looking closer at the crackling flames, watching how they're taking each part of the building and suffocating it piece by piece, Alia is scared by the thought of how much harm one element alone can cause. If the Royalist's burn is worse than fire, then will they really survive this? Will anyone?

***

Before anyone can even begin to comprehend what really happened, they find themselves on the next possible means of transport heading in the direction of Aster. Inside yet another old wooden food cart that seems a lot more spacious, but darker, compared to the other times they've travelled.

Although none of them question why.

Everyone travels in complete silence, the sense of regret gnawing inside each of them. Eli sits towards the front but faces the wooden walls, tracing the circular engraved rings with his shaking fingers. Lola has curled herself up in a tight ball, almost like she was trying to sleep when really; she was trying her best to stop crying.

Alia sits across from Lola, her knees to her chest, arms wrapped tightly around them. As much as she wants to get more tears out, she just can't. While she doesn't cry very often, especially in front of other people, whoever they might be, Alia always found she's able to shed a tear or two when she really needs to. But this time, nothing.

Regret is more of a poignant feeling, deep in the pit of her stomach. Just like after the loss of Commander Peircly and even Kole, Alia can't help but feel like it was all her fault.

While this time everyone is thoroughly convinced that the Royalist is behind it, Alia still feels she should have done more. More to stop Eli so he wouldn't have gone in there, but then Marne would still be with them and Lola would be the one gone. Unless she'd been brave enough to go in there herself, then they could all still be breathing. Or she would be the one dead.

Alia's always hated 'what if' scenarios, but never one as much as this. While she knows that life will always consist of what ifs, she'd rather they didn't include the balance of people's lives.

Alia's eyes move to the other end of the carriage. The part that always seems to move a lot more than the rest, swinging neatly off course whenever they turn a sharp corner. She watches Commander Dormer strap up her leg, clearly wincing at the pain, no matter how much she tries to hide it.

Back on the grass, the moment she sat there, crying in her arms when she thought Eli was lost, although scared, she still felt safe. Safe when she was watching the burning elements that almost burnt her brother alive. Safe when she knew that there had already been so much loss. She felt safe while others were dying.

There must be something really wrong with me.

Alia hates herself for it, so, so much. In a way, she also hates Commander Dormer, for holding her back. No matter how much she knew it was the right thing to do.

Letting her watery eyes glisten in the dark, Alia can only sit back and wonder what all of this really means. Distracting herself most from everything she knows is still to come.

Twenty-Five

Like every morning since they left Calla, their new day begins with the sunrise. This journey, although shorter, finishes as the first bit of daylight peeks between the blanket of clouds above. But even though the sun is rising and the day is beginning, the first thing Alia thinks when she steps off the carriage is how dark Aster seems. At least when compared to the other realms.

They exit the train, in seemingly the middle of nowhere. In the distance, the main city of Aster can be seen clearly, the columns of tall business buildings and the bricks of many houses.

They're greeted instantly by two tired looking men. Both clearly Protectors of some kind, from their padded exterior concealing their triangle positions, and fingers lingering to their bulging sides. They converse around Commander Dormer, clearly only there as messengers.

What's left of their group stand back, letting the adults do their business in private. It suddenly occurs to Alia that they must now look like an amateur Academy trip rather than four trained individuals ready to do their part in stopping the rising war.

The two men's time with the commander is brief and they're soon seen walking away. Lola stands by Alia's side, sucking in her tongue, clearly trying as hard as she can not to be noticed. It's only in this light that Alia can see the similar singes of Lola's uniform. There as a constant reminder of everything that happened.

No one has dared press her on how long her group had reached the safe house before everything went wrong. As much as Alia wants to know, as well as if they saw or found anything when out exploring, she knows there will never be a good time and place to ask.

There's another, rather long silence, as they all watch the two men walk away. Even if everyone will put up the front of pretending they're okay, even if inside they're all screaming, she can live with that. They have to be strong in

168

order to carry on. Each one of them knows that if they crumble, or think too much about everyone lost so far, everything else might just fall apart. And no one can let that happen.

"Everyone, listen up." Commander Dormer's voice is hoarse but quiet. It takes a few forced coughs for her to be clear once again. "News about yesterday's events has reached the General and she's instructed us to stay put here, at least until tomorrow."

"You're kidding?" Eli almost laughs, his words mocking. Almost cruel.

"We have not come this far just to stop. If they're here, let's find them and just end this. While we still can." The Commander smiles, her face too softer a reaction. Maybe this is just the way she copes with loss.

"We're not stopping, not by a long shot. We will be the ones to end this and I'll be damned if I let the Royalist overcome us. Again." Alia smiles, happy that at least their leader hasn't completely given up. "General Jackin has decided that we can't keep this to ourselves anymore. Not now real lives are at risk."

"And the lives of Commander Thornbe, Marne and Cora weren't before? They were real people too! With real lives!"

"Eli!" Alia finds herself shouting. The Commander smiles slightly at her defence while Alia tries to avoid the many eyes now on her. "Stop." She sighs while the commander coughs again, getting ready to continue.

"You know that's not what I meant, Eli, not at all." She pauses, taking the time to look him in the eyes until he looks away. "We've been given the coordinates of an old bunker, the safest place they can think to keep us, for now. We will wait there until the General contacts me and says we're good to go. She'll give the order when Aster's been safely evacuated."

"But what if the Royalist attacks them before that? She's obviously still got a lot more power than any of us ever thought she did." Lola asks.

"It's risk we're going to have to take. But I don't think she will. She'll need the magic we're chasing her for if she ever wants to move against an entire realm, no matter how powerful she already may be. Plus, they've already positioned some of the best Force teams here and more are already on their way. We're not going down without a bloody good fight."

"Damn right," Eli speaks, his voice now a lot calmer. More like him.

"Exactly," Commander Dormer agrees, beginning to smile properly for the first time since the fire. "While we wait, we train. Train harder than we ever have.

Even not at full strength, we have to appear almost invincible if we're going to have a chance of defeating her."

"Alright then," Alia says, a part of her wanting to smile while the other wanting to cry. "Let's do it."

The remaining hours of the day are spent doing exactly that, training. And training hard.

Falling back with ease into her Academy role, Commander Dormer leads them through several training exercises that feel almost effortless to Alia as her body just seems to strengthen at the memory of having to do them before, so many times. Although struggling in parts, Lola and Eli both tend to keep up relatively well. While she's not surprised at Lola, who has after all already been trained and spent a year working at the Bureau. But Eli? Still very new to the Academy, let alone anything else, she's impressed. Maybe she has been underestimating him in more ways than one.

After all the physical strength tasks, they move on to further weapons training. At points, Commander Dormer even lets Eli use one of their pistols rather than the 'kiddy' version he still has to use.

Hours after the sun has reached its highest point and has already started sliding back down the clear skied day, they each separate into different parts of the open spaced land they stand in and take things at their own paces. When Alia feels like she can do no more, she takes a wander over to Commander Dormer who is still shooting arrows at a speed that is impressive but only before you remember she was a part of the Force for so long before. At times, Alia wonders why she ever left. Why she would ever give up that life for one of teaching and the never-ending spill of mundane days. Well, most of the time.

"You're a good shot." Alia speaks as Commander Dormer fires yet another arrow dead in the centre of a nearby tree. She smirks, turning around to face Alia head on.

"Well, it would be both embarrassing and unprofessional if I wasn't."

"True." Alia finds herself giggling as she steps closer. "It still doesn't look that hard though. I mean, surely you can hurt someone a lot more with an actual bullet rather than an arrow."

"I'd say don't knock until you've tried it, but then, I'm not going to encourage you to get shot by both an arrow and a bullet just to see which one hurts more."

"It would answer my question though."

170

"Yes, but please don't do it." They laugh a little as Alia continues to walk closer until she's able to reach out and lightly touch the commander's weapon.

To her surprise, it's smooth. So much so that she's surprised anyone is able to keep a tight hold of it without it slipping out of her fingers.

"Did you want to try?" Alia feels her head snap back up and mouth open a little.

"Are, are you serious? I can't, I'm not—"

"You may not be, yet. But the time will come when you are. And, there may come a time sooner where using it could be your only option." Alia nods, trying to smile without letting on how excited she really is.

Holding a bow and arrow, let alone being able to learn how to use one, is a privilege that has remained locked within Force members only for as long as she's ever known. Even after they've moved on from the Force and into other roles, much like all the commander's that are and were on this mission, who possesses a bow and arrow is always the clearest sign as to what type of life a Protector has led and what exactly they've been trained in.

"Are you sure?" Alia's voice is quiet, her hand once again moving lightly over the shining black bow. A smiling Commander Dormer nods.

"Let's see what you've got."

While Alia isn't sure exactly how long they're alone for, she does know that she relishes every moment. Trying her best to saviour every time the commander moves behind her, to slightly raise her arm or give her an example about what direction to look in, Alia feels for a second like she's back at the Academy within her favourite training room with her favourite Commander being in the leading mould in making her the best that she can be.

When she notices Commander Dormer starting to look around, Alia realises that they all still need to find something to eat and actually travel to the base that will shelter them tonight, Commander Dormer takes her bow away from Alia but smiles before walking away.

"I'm glad there are still some things I have left to teach you." Alia giggles as if she were a child being told there is still so much more to come.

"I don't think there will ever be a time when there's not." Touching Alia's shoulder for the briefest of seconds, Commander Dormer quickly leaves her to smile into the air and enjoy the buzz within her as to everything that's just happened. But the little tingle that swarms her body is put on pause as soon as she sees Eli approach her, his face almost expressionless, coated with some kind of hard varnish making it impossible for him to seem anything but serious.

"Hey." Trying to look past his odd exterior, Alia smiles as he gets closer. "You okay?"

"Not really." He pauses, taking a breath and running a hand through this hair. "How can you be smiling and laughing at a time like this?" Alia's smile quickly fades and is replaced by a hardened frown.

"Are you actually having a go at me for trying to stay positive and not give in to how shit scared I am?" Eli suddenly goes quiet. "Seriously, is that really what we're doing?"

"No, okay I get that, but—" He takes a breath, moving his mouth in all sorts of different directions before opening it again. "It just, seems like you've already moved on and forgotten them. And, I can't help thinking that you would be doing the same if it was me who didn't make it out."

"How could you ever think that of me?" Her words greet the air as a silent scream.

Does he really think I care that little about him?

"Eli, what—"

"Because you didn't come in after me" He says as if having to get out his words on a strict time limit. "Because, you didn't choose me."

"Choose you? I tried to come in after you, I did! And have you ever seen me crumble like that, well, have you?" This time she does shout, taking a small step back as if worried she'd hit him if she stood too close.

"No, I haven't. Because you never let anyone see you like that."

"Which is my business so really what is your point here? I tried to stop you, then I tried to come after you, of course I did. But the commander—"

"Of course. The Commander. Would you not go in without her permission?"

"She held me back and didn't let me."

"But you're strong, you could have got away and done it anyway."

"Then the likelihood would be that we both would have perished and wouldn't be standing here now."

"Not necessarily."

"But we're never going to know for sure so seriously, Eli, what is your problem? Just because I didn't fight to come and save you when in the moment, I thought you were already dead?"

"Because we both know that if the commander had been the one to go in then nothing would have stopped you going in after her. But with me, you'd rather have just let me burn, you chose her. You always choose her."

As much as Alia is ready to just scream in his face until he backs down and takes it all back, a part of her knows it's true. And she hates herself for it. So, much.

"That's not, that's not true." She whispers, clearly in as much disbelief at her words as Eli is.

"You sure about that?" He sighs as Alia already feels certain parts of her mind forming questions that she's still not ready to answer. "Look, I know I've never really understood what you have with her, but you need to stop. You need to wake the hell up and realise that she's there for you now, but she won't always be. But guess who will be? Me. Yet you'd still let me burn if it meant she'd live."

"You don't know what you're talking about."

"Oh yeah?" Eli practically laughs as Alia continues to feel herself spiralling, down and down with never ending questions and feelings she's never wanted to label.

"Just think about it. And think about why, what it is with her that no one else has ever been able to give you?" He pauses as she says nothing, suddenly feeling defeated and annoyed that he seems to know exactly what to say to throw her as much as he has.

"Not even 24 hours ago, we lost another one of the commanders, Marne, who was apparently your friend and clearly liked you in more ways than one, and Cora, who you didn't even bother to get to know."

"Well, it's not exactly like we're here having a get to know each other tea party is it? We're here to do a job!"

"Yes, we are. And you're too distracted without even knowing it. So figure it out, before it's too late." Before he has the chance to turn around, Alia finally asks something she's wanted to know even before they were actually in the situation.

"And if it were you." She moves back forward, closing the gap between them. "Would you have gone in after me?" Eli's eyes don't leave hers as he lets a silence form before giving her an answer.

"I would have gone in after anyone. It shouldn't matter who they are as long as they need saving." With that, Eli does nothing more but walk away.

Finding that she can do nothing but stand and watch him go, as she's now becoming accustomed to doing, Alia bites her lip as she knows she can't put off the whole Commander thing forever. Maybe it's finally time for her to be honest with herself, no matter how hard it all is to accept.

As much as she wants to disagree with her brother's words and think that there will never be a time when she doesn't have the commander at her side, she also knows she's kidding herself. Whether they were out here or back in Calla with no looming threat at all, there are some things that just won't last forever, no matter how much you try and force them to. Maybe the time has come for her to try and get answers so she can finally know whether everything she's ever felt is all in her head, or has been right there all along.

Wrapping her arms around herself, as if needing some kind of comfort without actually wanting someone else's touch, Alia holds herself and takes a breath, suddenly angry at both herself and Commander Dormer for ever making her feel anything that she could never explain.

***

When training for the day is finally over, Commander Dormer leads them to a bunker, similar to the underground safe house they found themselves inside last time.

They've managed to travel far enough that from the surface, they've moved far from any dustier dried out fields to a small beach, with grains of sand and noisy seas. Standing and looking out into the waters, Alia feels like she's on the edge of the world. Like she could dive in and swim out far enough that eventually, she could just tip off the edge of their little world.

As the night draws in after a long day, the waves around them become rougher. Alia sits alone on the ledge leaning over the crashing waves. Still lost within all the questions that she suddenly wants answers to but doesn't have the courage to actually ask, Alia separated herself from everyone at dinner. Made sure she sat alone and made it clear that she was not in any kind of talking mood. As expected, Eli and Lola left her to it while Commander Dormer sent a few puzzled looks her way, each one Alia doing her best to overlook and not respond to. If she's really going to get over this, whatever it is that she's made it out to be for so long, she can't afford to get sucked back in again as soon as the commander simply batters her eye lids and gives her more concerning gazes.

Hands on the cold metal railings dividing her from the water, she closes her eyes, breathing in the calming silence surrounding her. Finding the waters constant echo more comforting than any consistency since she left the Academy.

Shuffling a little, she removes a hand from the railings and grazes the grass she sits on. Her arms tensing and hairs standing upright at the tingle of damp grass across her bare fingertips. She moves her hand until she passes over something new. A stem. Looking closer, Alia finds it to be a flower. An Aster flower – literally.

Smiling at the very rare sight, Alia moves her fingers slowly over its small exterior. Marvelling at all the different shades of purple that have somehow been confined into one singular flower while the middle is still a prickled yellow.

Something's going to happen. Her smile fading the more she thinks about it. *They never grow without a reason.*

"Alia," a familiar voice speaks. Hearing her voice, Alia can feel her body beginning to shake, if only a little. Her breathing quickens, her face growing hotter by the second. Commander Dormer stands behind her.

Instead of standing to attention, just like she knows she should even now, Alia remains sitting but turns her head slowly. Without taking her eyes off the commander's face, she feels down in the grass again and pulls the flower from its root. Folding it before moving her hand back to the railings.

"Commander Dormer," she responds, more formally than she has in a long time. The Commander folds her arms, clearly picking up on Alia's unusual hostility.

"Can I have a word?"

"If you like." Alia sighs, getting to her feet. They stand for a second, several feet between them. Alia folds her arms, as if mirroring the commander's actions. But she doesn't move. She simply sighs, but she does so in a way that Alia has never seen before.

"We're on the very cusp of the beginning of a war. We've lost half our team to the hands of the Royalist and you're what?" She walks slowly towards Alia, their eyes not leaving each other's. "Sitting alone out here sulking?" Alia rolls her eyes, more by habit than initially feeling the need to.

"I was training. Enjoying a bit of quiet." This time the commander raises her eyebrows, clearly aware of the twisted words that left Alia's lips. "There's nothing wrong with that."

"No. But we should really be using this time to prepare. As a team."

"As you wish." Unfolding her arms, Alia walks past Commander Dormer. Using all her strength to keep a straight face. It isn't until she's taken a few steps past the commander that she can feel her turning around, her eyes on Alia.

"Alia!" the commander's voice raises to nearly a shout. Alia stops mid step; suddenly afraid she's finally gone too far.

Commander Dormer marches towards her. Eyes and face filled equally with something Alia believes she recognises as guilt, along with a bit of fear. Things that she's rarely seen present on the commander's face. Let alone at the same time.

Alia simply stares towards her, not attempting to say a word. There's so much that she wants to say, to tell her, yet the thought of actually bringing those thoughts to life is enough alone to shut her up.

"If you're trying to make a point, then well done, I'm listening."

"I don't know what you mean." Alia shrugs, concentrating on keeping her voice at least sounding steady. "I'm fine."

"I know you, and I know you're not. Spill."

"No!" Alia says a little too quickly. Swallowing her rising anger, she breathes deeply, continuing to look at her. "It doesn't matter. It's not as important as what we need to do here. That's what's important. That's what we have to focus on." She starts walking away again. Only this time the commander remains hot on her heels. Only a single step behind.

"It does if it's going to affect you," Commander Dormer continues, taking a gentle hold of Alia's arm. Making sure she doesn't move any further. "It does if you're not okay."

Alia does everything she can to blink back fresh forming tears. She feels her lips starting to tremble, knowing the affect the commander can have on her. Always making her seem like she can tell her anything and everything. Always making it seem like she has to be honest, completely, with every chosen word.

"It's just." She pauses, trying to once again even out her voice. The Commander lets go of her arm. Listening. "Why me?"

"What do you mean?" Commander Dormer asks. Her voice and expression clearly ones of confusion at Alia's question.

"Why was it always me? Why give me special training? Why help me more than anyone else? Why lend me those books? Teach me all the little tricks and let me play with bows and arrows? Why listen and give me advice about things that had nothing to do with the Academy?" By the end, Alia can feel herself shouting, the first set of tears coming to the edge of trickling down her heated cheeks. "Why be there for me when you didn't have to? Why make me feel so special?" Finally giving in to the tears, Alia briefly sobs before building herself back up to at least seem okay. However wobbly she feels inside.

Moving her eyes to the commander's, Alia spies matching tears in her own, highlighting the odd bits of gleaming emerald around her dark pupils.

As if acting on instinct, the commander reaches out, putting a hand on Alia's head. Her fingers moving to her hair, pulling a loose strand back from her near her eyes to behind her ear. Alia moves at her touch, although her reaction delayed.

Smiling in a kind of defeat, Commander Dormer sniffs back further emotion, putting her hand to her side.

"You are special, so special." She takes a minute, sucking on the air as if it were water. "Because you reminded me of myself. More every day." She pauses, giving Alia a second to try and catch her breath. "It was weird, but I loved it. Loved seeing it in you."

"Why?" The commander sighs, caught between trying to smile while wanting to be more serious.

"There are things that I still haven't told you. Things no one knows, not even my partner. Well, my—" She looks down for a second, pushing away further tears.

"I'm sorry, about him," Alia says, suddenly overcome with guilt for being upset at her in the first place. "I didn't know."

"No one did, not until recently."

"There were rumours though. Not that they're important."

"There are rumours about everything, over time." Alia nods.

"I guess." She pauses, considering whether it's worth leaving the heavy stuff, or getting it all out while she thinks it's possible. "I'm sorry as well, he clearly doesn't deserve you." Commander Dormer laughs, suddenly remembering how much Alia really means to her.

"You're a good kid." Alia feels herself flush at her words, although unsure why exactly. "But it was a long time coming. I honestly wasn't that surprised."

She pauses, suddenly overcome with yet another wave of emotion. "I made him choose, and he left. That's just life."

"You don't have to tell me, but you know you can." Alia smiles, nerves still ripe, but her body relaxing by the second, as if feeling like she's getting straight back into familiar habits. "I always meant to thank you, you know, for listening, over all those years. I don't think I've ever actually said it. Not aloud." The Commander smiles, wider than she has in a long time.

"You never needed to. I knew."

"How come you always know?" The Commander laughs. "No really. How?" Alia's voice falls as she thinks more about it. How Commander Dormer was ever the only person that knew anything real about her. How she felt. How she works. How hard it is for someone to look beneath the walls she doesn't even realise are there anymore.

"I told you, because I see myself in you."

"Is that why though, really? Why you always understood? Why you were the only one who ever got it?" The Commander nods. "Why you were the only one to never lie to me?" She continues nodding while Alia begins to smile, as if finally understanding.

"I had a daughter, once. A long time ago now, long before I knew you."

Is this it? Is this the great big secret?

"I was young, but I took care of her. I braided her hair and let her dance. Let her be happy." The Commander smiles, clearly lost in a memory that Alia is also trying to imagine.

"But before I ever really got to know her, she got sick, and, I lost her."

"I'm sorry." Alia finds herself speaking the most common words as she doesn't know quite what to say. To her surprise, the commander remains smiling, not teary or upset like she assumed she would be.

"While I see a lot of myself in you, I also see a lot of her, somehow. I've never quite understood it. So when I got to know you, and maybe just saw everything I wanted to see, but I vowed never to lose another kid again."

Alia feels choked. Suddenly guilty at how the commander must have really seen all her whining questions and puppy dog eyes. Guilty but confused at the fact that all this time, maybe she really was looking at Alia in the exact way she's always wanted her to. But maybe, she was never really seeing her at all. She was just seeing a memory.

"You make me sound like an imposter. I know I keep saying sorry, but if I ever unknowingly made it harder to not see her then I am, sorry I mean." Commander Dormer sighs, everything about her soft and vulnerable.

"You weren't to know. It's something that very few people do. So—"

"I promise, to keep it to myself." They both nod, knowing how much Alia means it. "So, I remind you of her?"

"Oh, in so many ways. She liked reading, a lot. And was stubborn as hell."

"Yeah alright." They laugh, trying to overlook just how serious the conversation has become. Yet Alia has never felt closer to the person she trusts the most in the world. "You know, someone once told me, you don't have to share blood in order to care about someone." Commander Dormer smiles while Alia blinks back further tears, still not being able to comprehend what she's actually hearing.

"Do you believe that?" She nods, putting a hand to Alia's arm.

"It's why you're special. It's why I care far more than I should." She pauses, squeezing Alia's arm just a little as a fresh tear escapes Alia's eyes. "It's why I can't lose you too."

"As long as you don't disappear again."

"Deal." They smile together, as if both finally understanding the truth between them. The truth that they both know, no one else can ever really understand.

Together, their eyes turn to the water close by. Standing side by side, they spend time simply watching the waves, each one seeming to climb higher but fall faster. Hitting the rising waters louder each time.

They know the worst is yet to come. They know there's likely to be more loss, more pain, more adventure. But in this moment, they're safe. They're together. And they both know the truth. Together, they believe they're going to be okay.

It's quiet when they return to the bunker. With just four people staying there, quiet becomes unavoidably inevitable. But coming back to complete silence unnerves even the commander as they step further inside.

Lola lies in a deep sleep on the far side of the room, wrapped up in the few blankets they have left.

It's a good thing the end is coming.

Alia moves towards her own sleeping area, right in-between Eli and Lola. Commander Dormer follows her, sitting at the other end of the thin blankets covering the surprisingly warm shards of reflective earth beneath them.

"Did you see Eli up there?" Alia asks, looking closer around the sleeping bunker. Definitely no Eli.

"The last time I saw him he was down here." There's silence as Alia begins to panic, feeling her throat begin to close up and her breath and heartbeat equally quicken.

"I should go and look for him!"

"Alia." She goes to stand before the commander pulls her back down.

Alia stares at her, wanting and trying to be mad at her. But she just can't. Commander Dormer pulls at her hair, freeing it from the tight braids she gave her what feels like a lifetime ago.

"You need to let him come to you. You won't always be there for him, as much as you may want to be. Some things, he has to figure out for himself." Alia sighs, knowing she's right. That she's always right.

"And why should I have to listen to you? He's my brother," Alia phrases it more as a joke than a question, leaving Commander Dormer to laugh exactly as she wanted her to. Lola turns, moaning a little in her sleep, but she doesn't wake.

"Well, you're already stubborn enough most days. When you listen, it's a real blessing."

"Excuse me, I always listen to you!" Although they try and keep their voices low, more high-pitched laughter escapes them both. Almost as if they can forget the constant linger of the coming threat. The coming battles of tomorrow.

Their short-lived happiness is quickly shattered when fast approaching footsteps echo down the stairs. They both turn, happy at what their eyes can now see.

"Where the hell were you?" Alia says, saying it more like a demand than a question. Eli remains quiet but walks up to where she now stands.

Sharing one last look with Alia, Commander Dormer excuses herself back up to the surface, leaving them alone in the candle lit room. Alia finds it easier this time to be angry at Eli. Easier to build up all her frustration and let it out on him. She knows it's not all on him, but she also knows how difficult he can make a situation that he doesn't truly understand.

Eli doesn't look in her direction until he kicks off his shoes and climbs under his sheets, not even taking his jacket off before wrapping himself up in blankets. He lies there quietly, staring at the grounded ceiling while also trying to steal a few looks in Alia's direction.

Copying is action; she takes off her shoes and lays next to him, a comfortable distance between them. She doesn't bother trying to hide her eyes in his direction. She wants him to know that she's looking. Wants him to know that she cares.

"Where were you?" she whispers it, but she knows he heard her. He twitches at the question but remains still.

Alia continues lying on her back, her eyes wandering back and forth across the uneven ground above her. Trying to see if she can depict which direction Commander Dormer is likely pacing above.

"How do you know if you like someone?" At the shock of not only his voice but his question, Alia finds herself laughing while sitting up straight, looking towards him.

"Excuse me?" Smiling, Eli sits up too and turns to face her until their eyes meet. Both their eyes light up when they smile. They glisten together in minimal light.

"It's a genuine question," Eli continues, his voice still giddy. Almost happy. "You're supposed to be my big sister, right? I'm supposed to ask you questions like this."

"Yeah, but timing, Eli." They laugh again, but their voices lowered as if suddenly wary of a sleeping Lola not far away. "Anyway, I've not been much of a big sister to you recently, have I?" There's a sudden silence from the blackened tone.

"You've been alright." Alia shakes her head.

"I should have been better. Protected you more. Got you out of situations. Made sure you didn't run into that damn fire." Although he laughs, Alia knows he's laughing isn't because he shouldn't be.

"You know you can't protect me from everything, you never have. And that's what I've always loved about you. You're there when you need to be. But other than that, you're off doing your own thing."

"You're making me sound like some kind of puppy." Eli sniggers.

"Well, you are only truly loyal to a few people. Don't know if I'm one of them though."

"Oh, lay off." He laughs as she shoves him, just like old times. Their smiles subside quicker than before.

"So, who is she?"

"She is no one, there is no she."

"Liar." They laugh again, more at the fact of where they're having this conversation. "You would pick the night before we risk our lives to ask the most complicated questions about love." Eli shrugs.

"I never mentioned love." This time Alia shrugs, trying to make all her reactions seem genuine.

"Goes with the territory," she replies, a lot quicker and easier than she thought she'd manage. "So, what do you want to know?" Eli takes a long breath, leaning a little closer to her.

"Nothing complicated, but how do you know if you like someone? As in, it's more than just a crush, but you're not sure that you're sure?" For a minute, Alia simply looks at him, caught between wanting to smile and being utterly confused.

"I dunno, it's complicated." She laughs a little while trying to think about how to give him an honest answer when she herself has never even had a crush, on anyone. "I guess you just have to really think about it. Think how much you think about them. How much you wish you were with them, all the time. How you feel when you're with them. How you feel when you're without them. How much you'd do for them. Maybe, question if you'd even die for them." Eli looks at her, completely transfixed within her soft words. It takes Alia time to realise what she's just said and how much she really means it.

"Wow," he speaks. "Are you sure you've never been in love? Because, that was something." Alia laughs, more at the thought of her ever being in Eli's clear position.

"Did you not pay attention to how many of Abella's admirers actually made it inside the house? Look at her history of romance close enough and you can learn anything." He nods, smiling again. Alia loves seeing him smile.

"Point taken." They further before engaging in another silence. But one neither of them find uncomfortable.

"Anyway, love comes in all sorts of shapes and sizes." She pauses, feeling a sudden warmth at knowing how much she means it and how much it's true. "Anyway, why'd you ask?"

"Because," he pauses this time, clearly trying to find the right way to phrase what he really wants to say, "what if you meet someone, the kind of person you never expected to. And they're amazing. They're like nothing or no one else, but they're not always good." Alia frowns, trying to understand while also work out whom he's talking about. "What if sometimes, they get angry and they do things."

"Define things?"

"I don't know. Like throw things or hit things or—"

"So they have a temper. Big deal. If you really like them, then so long as you're not in danger, or anyone else, then it shouldn't matter. If you care about, I mean really care about them, just trust yourself. Do what you think is best."

"When did you get so soppy-ing-ly insightful?" She laughs, more at his happy but confused expression than anything else.

"What's that supposed to mean? Just because I never brought a guy home. I mean, can you blame me?" Eli shakes his head.

"You? No." He laughs. "Although, I always had bets on you bringing home a really, um, out-there guy who you knew Mum would hate so you'd bring him back just to piss her off."

"Oh, believe me I thought about it." They laugh a little more before his face falls. No one has mentioned the people left behind. Not one of them. Alia always believed it was because they all wanted to look forward at what was ahead. But now, she believes they were just all afraid what would happen if they looked back.

"Do you miss her? Mum?" Alia holds her breath.

"If we're being honest, I don't know." She pauses, feeling herself relax, as he hasn't screamed at her for not saying yes. "I want to miss her, I do. Even when I moved out during the Academy, I always wanted to. And I always thought I would. But whenever I see her now, it's like, nothing's ever real. It's just fake smiles and I do my bit to play a part in her little happy family. As bad as it is to say, out here, as much as I wish we were here for different reasons, I can be myself. Without any walls or forced emotions. I can care who I want to care about and love who I want to." She feels a sudden tear in her eyes. Brushing it away, she tries to laugh, but her voice comes out as a faded croak. Eli remains still, watching her. "Anyway, this was supposed to be about you."

"Alia, I think it's fine that you don't." Her eyes go dead into his. "What?"

"I may be young, but I'm not an idiot. Yes, you have to love her because of who she is and what she's done for you in the past. But I know things haven't always been easy. That she's never seen you the way you've always needed, and wanted, her to see you. Not like other people have."

"What do you mean?"

"I'm saying, I get it. At least I think I do. And I'm also saying that I'm fine with the fact that you clearly idolise someone who seems to understand you much better than anyone else ever has, including Mum, and Abella and me. As long as you're okay with the fact that I like someone who has a damaged side. Maybe even a dangerous one."

"We're all damaged, Eli. There's no shame in that. There's only shame in what we choose to do with it."

Another silence consumes them, although this one is slightly uncomfortable. Alia can feel that something has changed. Maybe just in Eli or maybe in both of them. Whether it's a newfound acceptance or the aftermath of the most honest conversation, they've ever had, she doesn't care. She likes it. The change feels different, but it also feels right.

As if knowing that the conversation is over without anything else needing to be said, Eli lays back down, his own eyes now wandering the earth above. Alia does the same, a small smile planted on her face. If this is the moment she feels she finally has her brother back, tomorrow can't be the day that she loses him.

Twenty-Six

As the sun rises, signifying the official beginning to yet another morning, everyone in the bunker is awake but quiet. Waiting.

Eli stands by the door, twisting a knife in his hands, careful not to get his skin caught on the blade. His eyes move continually between what he can see of the outside world and the rest of the bunker. Out of everyone, he seems the most impatient to get out there and finish it. Almost a little too keen.

Lola sits on her bed, her eyes drifting between every part on the dust scattered floor. She sits with her legs crossed, her body tense. Wanting it all to be over.

Out of everyone, Alia seems the calmest. Perched at the end of her bed, she sits with her eyes lulling between needing to be open but wanting to close. She's never felt so tired, yet she's never felt so alive. As much as she wishes, she could be back in Calla, happily seeing everything from a distance like so many from the Bureau are, if she could go back, she'd still have chosen to come. Chosen to be a part of something real.

Commander Dormer sits further along Alia's bed, yet again taking pieces of her hair, although this time weaving them together to create something new. She takes her time while continually checking for any incoming signals from her phone, which somehow still has a little power left to it. But the bunker remains silent, for what feels like too long.

Eventually, Commander Dormer ties up the last of Alia's hair and sighs, smoothing it down once more before Alia turns around towards her.

Their eyes meet but nothing is said. Eli and Lola remain in their spots, feeling as if it isn't their place to intrude. Alia runs her fingers across the two braids that turn into one. She smiles, pleased to have had at least one more moment of being happily content.

"Thank you," Alia finds herself whispering. Commander Dormer smiles in return, not moving from her spot on her bed.

"Ready for battle?" Alia breathes in, her smile curving into a clearly anxious look. She wants to feel ready. In some ways, she believes she could be. But only time will tell for sure.

In trying to keep Commander Dormer smiling, and positive about the coming day more than anything else, Alia smiles, attempting to at least appear confident. But even with the knowledge that she won't be facing the Royalist alone, she still isn't convinced that even together, any of them really have any chance of defeating her. If she gains possession of the magic, then it could all be game over.

"As I'll ever be," Alia eventually speaks, her voice remaining quiet.

As if planned, Commander Dormer's phone then starts beeping and she quickly hurries out of the room, the device tight in her hands.

Everyone in the bunker tenses further at the noise, all knowing exactly what it signifies. They shouldn't be nervous, they signed up for this. They knew from the start of the dangers and possible outcomes. Yet in truth, none of them ever thought they'd ever reach this point. They never thought that anyone would be lost or that the public would ever be made aware. They never thought that they would actually come into direct sight with the Royalist, especially with the intention of them being the ones to walk out alive.

Scuffling footsteps sounds and everyone's eyes shoot to the narrow entrance to the right of Eli. Coming down the steps, taking the lower ones slower as if they'd break with too much force, Commander Dormer appears again. Her cheeks flushed and her eyes narrowed, clearly aimed on something.

"That was the General. It's time. We're moving out."

***

Leaving the sudden safety and shelter of the bunker, the remaining members begin their journey towards the suspected location of the Royalist.

Along the way, Commander Dormer informs them that the General has been told of a definite sighting of a young woman lingering around the grounds of the very meeting hall they went to upon their arrival the previous day.

While Alia wouldn't be convinced by a single sighting, when paired with the recent injuries and deaths of the majority of the original Aster Force team, she has no choice but to listen.

Reaching the outside of the hall, the damage speaks for itself. While from certain angles, the building just looks like it's been moved a little, as if the whole building has been picked up and put back down in a slightly different way. But sides of it show a range of burn marks.

But there was never any smoke, just fire. Magic.

A new Force team has assembled outside to see them in, each with a look of determination accompanied by fear in their eyes. This should make Alia more frightened, but it only spurs her on, much like the rest of her group. They need to end this and it has to end now.

Moving closer towards them, Alia smiles at a sudden familiar face amongst the sea of strangers.

"Emmett?" Her voice goes an odd pitch higher than her normal tone, like her smile remaining on her voice as she remembers they're not in a situation where a hug would be appropriate. "I didn't know you were stationed here."

"No one does," he says, returning her smile with his own. For a second, it's like they've both forgotten where they really are and are casually chatting in the halls of the Bureau once again. "It's a secret," he whispers which only makes Alia smile wider. With everything that's already happened, seeing an unexpected familiar face is more comforting than she ever thought it would be.

"Commander," a man a great deal older than Emmett speaks, his tone indicating that he is the one in charge here.

He stands directly in front of the main doors, offering Commander Dormer his slightly shaky hand when she's close enough in front of him. Commander Dormer says nothing but takes his hand, shaking it firmly. "This way."

Alia and Emmett exchange one last look before Alia is led away inside the opening doors along with the rest of the group.

From the entrance, you wouldn't think that anything had really happened. While a few slightly scorched marks can be seen throughout the room, at a quick glance, you'd think everything was normal.

Much like the majority of the realms, the building is deserted aside from a few Protectors, both members from the Force as well as other positions, standing at their posts in various parts of the large building.

The leading Commander of Emmett's Force unit takes them to what would have been the busiest part of the building. Walking through an empty meeting hall, Alia shivers at the ghosts she knows now linger here which only makes her think about all the ghosts that could linger in each realm, unless they stop her first.

They continue walking until they reach a small rounded door, slightly ajar. Through the crack, everyone can make out equally narrow stairs, spiralling down towards the very under layer of the building.

"The cameras lost sight of her down there," he says, his voice now slightly hushed. "We don't know where exactly, but it's not as big as it seems. It's mostly just used for storage." Commander Dormer moves past him, opening the door a little wider.

Everyone peers down, cringing at the slight creak the rusted metal hinges makes until it's opened as wide as it can be.

"Thank you," the commander says, exchanging one final glance with the Protector. He quickly leaves them; hurrying off as if the Royalist was right in front of them.

Commander Dormer takes out two small torches that Alia didn't even notice she'd been carrying. Switching them on, she gives one to Lola and takes her first step down. Alia falls in behind her, with Eli next and Lola at the back.

They reach the bottom step sooner than expected, their cautious footsteps each echoing more the further down they climb. When Lola joins everyone onto the level dusted floor, they all take a minute to catch their quick breaths and listen.

Silence.

Bending in all directions, pointing the torch around each corner, Commander Dormer gets everyone to move closer until they all feel like different parts of the same being.

"We stick together, she's around here somewhere. And remember, at any possible sightings, do not engage and certainly don't fire," Commander Dormer whispers, her voice so quiet it's almost like she hasn't spoken at all.

"But what if we have to?" Lola asks.

"In that situation, the General has advised me that we have the authority to take her down."

"No!" Eli's voice is still quiet but much more distinctive. The remnants of his voice bounce off each wall, creating a new type of sound. The commander pulls him even closer, their eyes inches apart.

"Yes. And that's an order." She tries to keep her voice calm and low but still makes it obvious that if they were in another situation she'd shout.

Straightening up, everyone is almost too focussed on Eli to notice the sudden rupture of colour and light coming from a room on their far left.

While they're still yet to hear any sign of movement, someone is clearly trying to get their attention.

It can't be that easy, Alia thinks as she follows Commander Dormer who leads their way towards it. *She can't want to be found. Unless, it's all a trap.*

The light leads them inside one of the first rooms they come across. It's dark, as expected given they're somewhere underground. As soon as they reach the doorway, the light and colours instantly vanish. Commander Dormer continues to lead, pointing her torch in every direction before stepping further into the room. Everyone remains closely behind her, all equally curious as they are afraid. Although trained by the best, there are some situations that no one can ever prepare you for.

Sliding the torchlight around the room, they each see stacks of old rotting furniture and equally decaying papers and documents. Everything seems normal, until they reach the far side of the room.

Someone is standing there, still as if trying to masquerade as a statue. Moving closer towards them, it's clear to see that they're hood is over their head, their back to them. Alia finds it almost hard to comprehend that someone who can appear so normal from one angle can still be capable of ripping the whole world apart.

"Hello," Commander Dormer speaks, taking larger steps towards them, as if proving that she won't be afraid. Alia follows her lead, as does Lola. They each take a side of the commander's, their fingers resting on the weapons in their pockets, ready to fight for their lives.

Eli hangs back by the door, like he has sudden stage fright, yet again, when faced with actually having the Royalist in front of him. But Alia can't worry about him now; his life is well and truly out of her hands.

At the sound of her voice, swirls of lighted colour spark from what they presume are the Royalist's fingers, hidden by the length of their dark cloak. Everyone pulls out their weapons, sweat teaming from their hands. They all trained for this, they're ready.

But the Royalist doesn't attack, doesn't even try.

Instead, they raise their hands towards their hood, the light still flowing from beneath their layers, but at a seemingly constant pace rather than a building one. As soon as their fingers touch the soft material that shields their head, the lights go. Only torchlight remains.

In one quick motion, the Royalist turns around, pulling down their hood, but their head is still bowed. Commander Dormer, Alia and Lola all prime themselves again, pointing each weapon towards them.

"No!" Eli shouts as the Royalist finally raises their head to reveal that they're not a girl. But a boy.

"I hear you've been looking for me."

Twenty-Seven

Stunned. Shocked. Surprised.

There aren't enough words to really describe the shared bewilderment as to what is currently happening in front of their eyes. Eli moves from behind them, making his way towards the Royalist. When close enough, he puts a hand on his arm before it falls to his hand.

The Royalist is really alive. The Royalist is actually a boy. The Royalist and my brother are standing, together.

"Eli," Alia's words come out as a whisper.

"Are you okay?" Eli whispers to the Royalist, no ounce of fear in his voice or his movements.

"Eli, please, can you just back away slowly?" Commander Dormer says, trying to take back control of the situation.

Eli says nothing, does nothing aside from stand hand in hand with the boy in long robes next to him. He doesn't even blink at the three weapons still pointed in their direction, as if he knows that none of them would ever really use them, at least on him.

"What the hell is going on, Eli? Get over here! Now!" Alia finds herself shouting, more from confusion than real anger. Eli remains motionless, as if immune to the glares and fear radiating from every other person in the room.

"Eli Alden, I'm arresting you for conspiring with the dangerous enemy," Commander Dormer's voice rings through, a new sudden authority in her words. Moving towards them, she puts her bow and arrow back on her back and takes out a small pistol from her pocket, identical to the ones that Alia and Lola both still hold. She points it at the Royalist's head, the metal on his hot skin.

Surprisingly, the Royalist doesn't react to this. He simply puts his hands above his head and lets her lead him away from Eli and towards the door they came through. She then glances towards Alia, a clear instruction in her eyes. Finding every new bit of courage she never knew was there, Alia makes her way towards Eli and mirrors Commander Dormer's actions. Although with a lot less kindness.

Alia pulls Eli towards her, her pistol against his temple, and walks him towards the door behind the Royalist and Commander Dormer. Lola follows along behind, breathing at the minutes she can allow herself to shake before they locate the stairs and head up onto the surface level.

***

Commander Dormer alerts the Protectors above of the situation as soon as they reach the ground level of the building. A new secured room is soon emptied and ready for them.

The Royalist and Eli stand on separate sides of the room, Lola in between them; pistole in her hand. Although it's clear that she isn't likely, even when provoked, to shoot either of them, Commander Dormer feels that a threat is better than nothing.

Every surrounding Protector takes their position somewhere around the small radius of the building while Commander Dormer tries to contact the General.

Alia remains outside of the room, finding she can do nothing else but pace. The more she tries to think about it, the more she can't believe that she's in this situation in the first place. Of all the things, she ever expected to happen while on this mission, she never thought anything like this would have ever been an option.

Commander Dormer soon returns, her cheeks pale but hands steady. She stops next to Alia outside the room, their eyes meeting as a form of hello. Without any words being said, Commander Dormer places her hands on Alia's arms as Alia closes her eyes, trying not to let any tears fall.

"I just don't understand," Alia whispers, trying not to let herself fall into the commander, fall into the comfort that she hasn't got time for right now. "How can the Royalist be a boy? How can Eli know him, let alone, like him? Defend him?" She takes a breath, trying to focus on one question at a time. "How didn't I notice any of this?"

Commander Dormer remains quiet, keeping her eyes on Alia, but her mind is clearly wondering. She wishes she'd seen it too. Wishes that she could go back and do it all again, but notice what she needed to. And do everything better.

"None of us knew, this isn't on you."

"It should be."

"Well, it isn't." She sighs. "This is on me. All of it. But now we're going to fix it."

"We have to save Eli. Show him what he, it, thing, is really capable of." Commander Dormer laughs, more towards Alia's unusual hostility.

"The General has already dispatched a control team to take care of it. They should be here by morning." She pauses, taking a second to look around, seeing if they're really alone. "Until then, let's see if we can learn the truth."

The commander pushes Alia in front of her, although not forcefully, as they head back inside the room that is now more of a prison.

The Royalist is chained to one wall and Eli to another. Their eyes meet but nothing is said. Lola still stands in the middle, clearly still uncomfortable. At their entrance, Lola backs away and all eyes fall onto Commander Dormer.

"Forces are on their way to contain you. There is no escape and this room can be instantly sealed if you try and use magic of any fashion." Her voice wobbles at the word 'magic' like she can't quite believe she's really saying it.

"He's not dangerous! He would never hurt anyone!" Eli says while remaining on his side of the room. Alia shoots him an estranged look, but if he sees it then he doesn't pay any attention.

"No, it's okay," the Royalist speaks, his voice calm. Controlled. "I have led you on, all of you, for far too long. You deserve answers. And I promise, I won't hurt anyone."

"Tell that to everyone we've already lost on the way!" Lola shouts, her weapon aimed firmly towards him. Even at the sight of a loaded gun pointed at his head, the Royalist doesn't even flinch. As if, he's clearly faced more in his life.

"I can explain, I promise. Just give me a chance?"

Alia looks between the Royalist and Commander Dormer. While she'd happily see him punished for everything he's already put them through, her curiosity, as always, overpowers any other constructive thoughts.

"Okay," Commander Dormer agrees, stepping forward to nudge Lola to lower her pistol. She then scurries to the back of the room to watch from afar while Commander Dormer moves closer to the Royalist. Eli stays where he is, simply watching, knowing it's best to not interfere. As much as he may want to,

"From the beginning."

Twenty-Eight

"When my family were captured, I was nothing more than a child," the Royalist, whose name is apparently Ree, begins. At his words, that seem almost hypnotic in a sense, Alia is drawn to the images he's creating, as if she'd been there too. While she can't be sure whether this technique is just another thing he can use magic to do, she knows that deep down, she does believe him.

"We lived the best we could. In there, in that, that hole." Alia thinks back to what she saw of his home. His prison. From the bumpy rounded walls to the limited space within what felt more like a bunker than a place to call a home. Even if it was a prison.

"Over time, they just started dying. All of them," Ree describes the decay, the pain. The loss. What it felt like to watch nearly everyone he loved reverse into helpless beings. Each one slowly falling victim to everything that even they can't run from.

"It took time. Even with the magic nearly gone, it still took longer than any one of your short little lives."

Charming.

"So, you're telling us that we weren't wrong? That everyone did die naturally?" Lola asks.

"Almost," Ree continues. "When nearly everyone knew their time was short, they all did something together, one last time. Did something kind. Something stupid." Ree laughs to himself, as if trying to relive the memory while still trying to understand what actually happened. "They gave me my ultimate wish. To be a boy."

Everyone takes a breath, their eyes darting between each other and Ree. Small tears are clear in Eli's eyes. Alia takes a long breath, knowing full well that she would be welling up too if it wasn't for who Ree really was. While she's never normally the sentimental type, there can always be exceptions.

"They pulled together their remaining power, knowing it would take their lives. But they did it, for me."

"Well, aren't you the special one," a familiar voice speaks.

Everyone suddenly turns around to the previously sealed door that none of them had heard even opened. A figure stands to the side of it, while clearly male, his face and features are clouded by shadows. He leans against a wall, seemingly knowing what's going on. Even from the shadows, it's clear he wears a cloak very similar to Ree's. He's not one of them.

Another Royalist?

Alia feels her heart quicken at just the thought of any more surprises.

Rubbing his hands together, the figure then steps out into the light. At first, all anyone can do is stare in complete shock.

It's Marne.

"What the—"

"State your name, position and realm. Try anything and I will shoot without any hesitation," Commander Dormer says, jumping into action and pointing an arrow towards him. Marne smiles, his arrogant, big as you like, genuine smile. He puts his hands in the air, his smile still wide.

"You're not really going to shoot me," he says, his voice bright and the furthest thing from panicked.

"Answer the question!" Commander Dormer shouts, her patience clearly stretched.

"Marne Howard, Surveillance, Calla." He continues to smile, his hands still in the air, "I'm real, I promise."

"No, you died!" Lola shouts this time, fresh angry tears appearing like bright shards of ice. "You died in the fire!"

"No." Marne laughs again, as if incapable of doing anything else. "I was meant to. I thought I was going to. But then, he saved me."

Everyone's eyes turn back to Ree. His head is bowed, but it's clear he's trying not to look directly at any of them.

"He saved me, and now, it's our turn to help him."

Eli suddenly moves from his position, so quickly it was as if he had finally broken free from a physical hold he didn't even know he was under. He goes to Ree's side and slides his hand into his. Together they stand. Together they fall.

"Everyone died after they gave him what he wanted. Apart from his aunt."

"You mean—"

"There's another Royalist still alive," Alia says, her words as quick as her racing mind. "But, but there can't be. They counted the bodies, they did reports, they…

…were tricked into believing that she died as well. It was the only way, it was…

…Magic?" Ree hesitantly nods.

Commander Dormer moves towards Ree and Eli. Standing so close that she can feel their conjoined breaths. In another instance, you'd question what she was doing. But anyone who knows her knows that she's only ever interested in what needs to get done.

"Where is she?" No one else speaks. Eli and Ree remain together, their hands gripped so tightly it's as if they really were one person.

With no further voices, the commander slowly reaches for her bow yet again. Primed to strike at any moment.

"It was never about the magic. It was always about her," Eli whispers. "He's not bad. We're just trying to do what's right."

"So tell me. Tell me so we can stop everyone out there from killing her on sight."

Ree sighs, finally looking up at the commander. Clearly not afraid of her, or her weapon. Or her courage.

Stepping towards her, releasing his hand from Eli's grasp, the Royalist takes a deep breath in before releasing it right in Ree's face. But she doesn't flinch, or back away. She keeps eye contact, remains solid.

"She's hidden, hidden deep within the trees where only one of you has dared to go." Ree's eyes land on Alia who shuffles uncomfortably.

"The woods," Alia whispers. "It was you." As if suddenly waking up, Alia raises her head, her eyes moving to Commander Dormer. "She's in the woods where I was attacked. The ones in Orchid that bridge the gap between there and Anemone."

Commander Dormer is out of the door quicker than Alia has ever seen her move. Lola is quick at her heels, which encourages Alia to then follow along. Eli is hot on her heels but stops when Alia remains still in the doorway.

"Alia, please."

"Don't," Alia whispers. "You made your choice. Just like they did." Eli shrugs, trying to find a smile that he can convince her to share.

"This is different. You know it is."

"Still doesn't change anything. You made your choice."

Without another word, Alia closes and locks the door in his face, truly separating them. She stands against the door for a minute before remembering now what has to be done. What she needs to make sure is done.

Find the other Royalist. Capture the Royalists. Get back to Calla. Join the Force. Live happily ever after.

A list. A set of goals. An end. If, everything goes to plan.

***

Leaving Eli, Marne and Ree still locked in the room Commander Dormer leads the way up several sets of stairs until they reach the top floor of the building. Looking down through one of the few gaps in the solid walls, Alia shivers at realising how high up they are and how far they could fall.

The commander takes her and Lola into the one other room on the floor. Going inside, the room is dark. But the kind of dark that seems to make everyone uncomfortable and constantly question whether they're really alone.

Towards the middle of the room, a light flickers. Pale and quiet at first, the beating white light grows brighter and more colourful as they approach until they're right in front of it and it's spraying out colours brighter than ones seen on rainbows. They each surround it, each reaching out towards it, as if trying to touch it. It's not contained, it's not in a glass box or tube, it's free. Yet it doesn't fly away, it chooses to stay.

Alia feels herself smiling the more she looks at it, as if it's filling her with a new kind of hope that she never knew she wanted to feel until it was right in front of her.

Looking at the others, she sees they feel it too. Something new and indescribable, but in the best possible way. The brightness in their eyes. The flicker of a smile that is simply just honest.

Alia's eyes cross Commander Dormer's, the shared light between them. They smile, now not only at the light but at each other. Knowing more now than ever before that maybe this is their time to leave everything else behind and give in to what they've always wanted more. Even if they didn't know it until now.

"It's beautiful," Alia whispers, her voice quieter than she intended. As if afraid that speaking too loudly would scare it away.

"It's magical," Lola says, making Alia smile even wider, a small laugh even escapes her lips. "I mean, I know it's magic but it's just so…"

"I know," Commander Dormer agrees. "It's like nothing we've ever seen, or even thought was possible." She pauses, tracing the moving lines with her fingers. Moving her skin so close that the colours reflect against her. "No matter what happens now, things are going to change. We can't go back from this. We can't ignore this forever."

"Are you saying you want to bring magic back?" Lola questions. Commander Dormer shrugs, her face still curved into a smile.

"Maybe it's just time."

"Maybe," Alia agrees.

They continue watching it, until more time passes than any of them really anticipated. The outside world grows dark, slight chilling winds occasionally cutting into the oddly open and spaced room. Alia shivers, hugging herself into her jacket.

Commander Dormer shortly leaves the room after her phone rings; it's gone quiet but consistent until she decides to answer.

Alia and Lola remain in silence, both secretly trying to listen to the conversation, knowing that it will be the General.

"Do you believe him? Marne, I mean?" Lola eventually speaks. Alia shrugs, not quite knowing what to say.

"I want to. But right now, it just seems like another thing to add to the list of questions and theories." She sighs, feeling the urge to say more but then knowing it's best if she doesn't. "I want him to be telling us the truth. And I want this to have changed him."

"We've all been changed by this. In one way or another."

"For the better?" Lola raises an eyebrow, as if finally seeing Alia, and their whole situation, for the first time.

"I'd hope so."

Commander Dormer barely enters the room before ushering them over. Alia and Lola do as they're instructed.

"That was the General. We're to continue to wait here until the team arrives to take Ree away." Her eyes close in on Alia. "And Eli." Alia feels herself gasp a little under her breath, although she saw this coming a mile off.

"And Marne?"

The Commander nods. "I'm afraid so."

"What about the other Royalist?" Alia asks, trying to think about anything other than Eli and what mess he's got himself into. Let alone how she's going to be able to explain it to her mum when she finally returns to Calla.

"She assembled a team to go and investigate, but we'll follow along once Ree and the others have been taken away." Alia nods, feeling herself beginning to shake. Commander Dormer smiles down at her, clearly trying to be comforting.

"We'll get through this. I promise." Alia returns her smile with another just as genuine. No one moves from their apparent statured positions until several thuds and noises are heard from below them.

Without any further words or questions, Commander Dormer takes the stairs back down to where they came from, Alia and Lola hot on her heels. When they reach the bottom, all Alia can really see is blood.

Footsteps, small puddles, everywhere. She doesn't have time to think much about it before Commander Dormer runs towards a slumped Protector against one of the few completely untouched walls.

While behind her, Alia and Lola keep their distance, not wanting to get too involved. It isn't long before they see his head slump and Commander Dormer return to them.

"We have to go, Ree and Eli are gone."

"And Marne?"

"Apparently."

"But how? When? Eli wouldn't just—"

"Well, he did and now we have to go. Now!" the commander shouts, hurrying them out the door as some kind of alarm starts to go off. "They'll be going to find his aunt. But we have to find them first."

Twenty-Nine

A cart awaits them back at where they first had left it when they had entered Aster's realm. A single, lone, wooden carriage blatantly sticking out against a landscape of grass and dust. But there's no one there to notice. The realm is empty, silent. Just like every realm will become unless they stop it. Stop him.

Running down to the carriage, each one primes their weapons as they see slender silhouette leaning against the carriage in the shadows. Even from a distance it's obvious who it is, but then, none of them really feel like they could deal with any more shouting, any more fighting, until their mission was complete.

Just like she did to Eli and Ree, Commander Dormer raises her arrows at Marne who seems to put his hands in the air before she even tries to position her weapon in his direction. Her breath is long, while his is short. Alia and Lola hang back, knowing that if anyone was to fire anything, it would be Commander Dormer.

"I know where they've gone," Marne speaks before any threats towards him can be made. "I can help you, I promise."

"So do we," Lola says, finding the courage to move closer to him, although her hands are shaking. "And why would we ever trust you again? We thought you were dead!"

"And I'm sorry about that, really," he continues, slowly lowering his hand although Commander Dormer keeps her weapon in place. "After he saved me, I had no choice but to help him. He can be very, persuasive."

"How?" Alia asks, her mind suddenly racing with theories about how to get Eli out of the mess he's now become the centre of.

"It doesn't matter," Commander Dormer interjects, lowering her bow and moving straight past Marne to the open-door carriage. "Get in or be left behind. We'll deal with you after we've dealt with everyone else." With that, she jumps through the door, disappearing inside. Giving Marne one last look, Lola follows without another word. Alia shortly follows, knowing that anything she has to say can keep until after they save Eli.

***

As expected, the carriage is silent throughout their long journey back to very bottom of Orchid. The carriage is dark, lit only by the few lighted pathways along the isolated tracks.

Marne and Lola sit together, exchanging words now and again before long periods of silence. Alia always wondered whether there was anything between them. Or there ever could be. Like many things, she knows it could never be simple. But out of everyone, she seems to be the one able to forgive him more. A quality Alia wishes she was able to have.

Looking over, Alia's eyes drift to Commander Dormer's still body. Her chest slowly rising and dropping in a constant rhythm. Almost like she was sleeping, but with her eyes wide open.

She suddenly turns her head, her eyes catching Alia's. But she doesn't smile like she normally would. Doesn't lift her head and go into a big commanding speech. She just continues to stare. Stare so close into Alia's eyes that she feels them sting with tears that have no need to be there. Yet they still are.

"I don't care what he's done, we have to save him," Alia finds herself whispering, suddenly very aware that they aren't really alone.

"And we will," Commander Dormer replies, her voice equally soft.

With that, the commander shuffles a little closer to Alia and holds out her arm, ushering Alia yet again into her arms. And as usual, she doesn't refuse. She can't. While she knows she should, she also knows a part of her will always say yes. When you've wanted something for so long, you know that there's always a piece of you that will take what it can get at every opportunity.

But even safe yet again in the commander's arms, Alia doesn't allow herself to cry. Not this time. Partly because they aren't alone, but mostly, because she can't cry anymore. When facing down in the final battle of the Royalist, she needs to be strong.

Crying is for the weak she thinks. *And I'm not so little anymore.*

"This will all be over soon," Commander Dormer whispers again, lightly brushing Alia's hair as her head rests on her shoulder.

"It's not the end that scares me. It's what will happen after," Alia says, sniffing back any riding emotion she knows she doesn't have the time to deal with. "It's the after, it's the rebuild. It's trying to build a future on the bones of the lost."

Thirty

It's light by the time the train comes to a halt and they step out once again into the cool open air. As expected, everywhere in sight has been abandoned. All they've really been told is that everybody in each realm of high risk has been safely evacuated to a secure location.

While she can wonder about it, Alia knows that it isn't her concern. Defeating the threat, now that's her business.

They walk and run in silence towards the very spot the General told them to go. Alia notices everyone closing their eyes for parts of the journey, they're all tired, but also tired of the running and the chasing. Even though it is what they signed up for, what they were chosen for, like many things, nothing can ever prepare you for what really awaits you out there.

As they reach the break between the inhabited land and the land of the trees, everyone stops, listening. They listen to the birds above, some occasionally squawking louder than others. And they listen to the branches, some noticeably louder than others. Almost like some want to seem heard as the midday wind swirls around them, plucking some leaves within its circles as if they'd been taunted to go.

They all listen as if they're waiting for a sign to go on. While the General may have given them this location, it's almost like she forgot everything else about it. How far these woods actually span. How lost you could get. How endangered, if you weren't careful.

Eventually, after hearing nothing more than nature at its calmest, Commander Dormer gives the signal for them to go on. Almost immediately, they're greeted by another group made up of people similar to theirs, some commanders, some from the Bureau and some from the Academy. The commander exchanges only a few words with them. Mostly along the lines of telling them they need to be ready to intercept at any time. They're then pointed in the right direction and carry on as if they know the way.

It isn't until Alia estimates they've reached halfway through that they stop. Something is occurring somewhere within the trees. While from the outside, they all see or hear nothing out of the ordinary, they can feel something. Like a warning, or a message. Or a signal.

At the very moment they're trying to decide upon which direction to carry on in, a shot is suddenly heard. It's loud. Close.

"This way," Commander Dormer instructs, leading them at a slight bend of a direction, but no one questions her.

They run until they reach a small clearing. The trees ease off until there's a large patch of damp earth beside a small lake that is small enough to be a pond.

As much as she wanted them to be there, Alia still can't quite believe what she's really seeing. Eli stands with Ree directly next to the water. They don't turn around at their approach. Their attention remains focussed on someone else. From an angle, Alia can see an elderly woman, barely able to stand, shielded behind Ree and Eli's backs.

Unsure of exactly what to do at first, whether it's worth risking a kind of surprise attack, Commander Dormer moves very slowly towards them. Her feet only stepping a fraction forwards at a time. Alia follows close behind, her gun held up right towards them, although her hands are shaking.

Marne follows their lead, clutching tight to the same weapon that he's managed to keep hold of since he left with everyone else. Although far enough behind them that she could still dart back into the trees at any minute, Lola remains. Her weapon also held high.

Before anyone has the chance to do anything, the old woman gasps, falling to her knees. Ree and Eli try to break her fall, taking one arm each, slowly easing her down. Commander Dormer remains still, indicating to everyone else not to engage. At least not yet.

Even from a distance, Alia can see that Ree is crying. Letting his tears come and fall as if it were just him and the woman who appears to be his aunt. As if even Eli wasn't there at all. In this moment, Alia almost feels sorry for him, but not quite enough to let her guard drop. She knows he could turn on them at any minute, so could Eli. He's unknown to them, he's something completely new and unexplained. Who knows what his triggers could really be?

"Ree, please. We can help you. Let us." Commander Dormer's words are soft, and genuine. Sounding true and the furthest thing from an act. While Alia knows she's always been a talented liar, in this moment, she can't be sure what purpose she's telling the truth for. "Please. We don't want anyone else to get hurt."

"I can take care of her myself. I can save her!"

"Not out here, not like this. She needs proper medical attention."

"And then what?" Ree snaps, finally turning his head towards them. Commander Dormer remains still, not letting his new direct contact unnerve her. "Lock her back up as soon as she can stand? And me with her? No." His voice breaks at his final words, another sob consuming him. Eli remains close by, trying to be the one to help. Even if it means betraying everyone that has helped him get this far.

"I won't let that happen. I promise," the commander speaks again, making her words sound honest. Even if she doesn't fully believe them herself. "We'll find a way. Just, let us help you. We can get you to safety."

"We don't need your kind of help! She needs magic!"

"And we have some. Back in Aster, all ready to go."

"You don't," Eli speaks this time, finally raising his head and looking at them himself.

"Eli, stay out of it," Alia responds, moving forwards until she's close behind Commander Dormer who prevents her from going any further. "This isn't your business."

"Like you'd know," Eli almost spits back, now eye to eye with only his sister. "You don't know a single important thing about me, Alia. Why do you think I couldn't tell you about any of this?" Alia feels her temper rising but keeps her breath controlled in order to try and remain calm. Now is not the time she can lose it. Especially over a trivial fight with her little brother.

"You know you can always trust me. I could have helped you." Eli shakes his head, tears now coming into his eyes.

Stay strong she thinks. *You can't let him play you.*

"Not with the important stuff. Not when you already have too many secrets of your own."

"That's different."

"Hardly."

"Enough!" Ree shouts, suddenly making Alia aware that this isn't the best time for the type of conversation that was brewing. "I stole the magic. It's all in me, flowing through my blood. Every last drop."

"That's impossible," Marne speaks this time, although his voice so quiet it's barely noticeable.

Ree laughs, his voice an odd distinguishable blend between mockery and a type of sadness.

"None of you have ever seen real magic before. Easy enough to fake when you know how."

"Give it back!" Lola unexpectedly shouts. "Give it back now!" she continues shouting, pointing her gun towards him. Her face hard, even from a distance. "It wasn't yours to take! We could have used it!"

"Let us help you and we can work together. To bring back magic. To save your aunt, to save your people!"

"It's too late for that!" Ree shouts back, mirroring the rising anger of everyone within close proximity.

"Ree," Eli speaks again, placing a hand on Ree's back, "I think we're too late."

Suddenly ignoring everything else, Ree's attention goes back to his aunt who is now lying limp on the wet bark covered ground. Her eyes are open, her mouth closed. Chest still.

Motionless.

"No! No!" Ree screams, more out of fury than shock.

Clenching his fists, colour suddenly begins to erupt from him, creating various shapes and patterns around them. If they were in another situation, Alia would almost find it mesmerising. The power and beauty that can come from an element long thought to be extinct. But here it is, in this moment, so alive.

While all eyes are on Ree, Alia can see Commander Dormer finally lowering her bow and dropping her arrows to the ground. While she keeps hold of the bow around her body with one hand, with the other she searches for Alia's hand, sliding her fingers into hers. Alia breathes deeply, feeling like Commander Dormer knows what's about to happen. And that it can't be good.

"Be strong. And know that I love you," Commander Dormer whispers, still holding Alia's hand tighter than she ever has before.

"No! No! No!" Ree screams, as another blast of colour seems to explode from his fingertips as he continues to lean over his aunt's still body. Only this time, it's not only colours that erupt. A powerful blast of something that could easily be mistaken for a silent bomb ripples from Ree, first knocking Eli violently to the ground.

Before Alia can even take in what she's seeing, the ripple of magic moves over them like a tidal wave. Without a second thought, Commander Dormer pushes her way in front of Alia, letting the full shock of the ripple hit her, ramming her to the ground.

Alia and Marne are thrown a little as it only skims them, causing a little pain but more shock than anything else. Although they don't hear her, when they both manage to sit up and look around, they find that Lola is gone.

"No!" Alia screams, finding every bit of strength to run to the commander's side.

Tears quickly consume her vision until for seconds she can see nothing but blurry faces and the wet ground. But it isn't until she hears Ree's growing sobs that she notices another body.

"Eli!" Turning to him, more tears come quickly. Putting a hand to his face, Alia almost feels him to be the person, the brother, she once loved and cherished.

"Alia!" Marne shouts, his trembling stature knelt over Commander Dormer's body. "She's not dead! They're not…" He quickly rushes over to Eli, nearly pushing Ree out of the way. Feeling for any sign of life, not matter how small, Marne smiles at the discovery of two weak but present heartbeats.

"They're both alive, but their pulses are weak."

"We have to save them!" Alia sobs, trying to control herself enough to think clearly.

"There isn't time!"

"Then make time!" she cries, looking between them. "I can't lose them!"

"I can save them," Ree says, his previously still body bent between his aunt and Eli. "I-I can use magic. Use the rest of what I have. Even if it means, well, I will be less like me and more like you." He pauses, almost like trying to catch his breath. "I can channel what I have left to take my long life and shorten it, into new life energy. For them."

"Then do it!" Alia almost can't believe her luck, but feels it's too early to be able to breathe from relief. "This is all your damn fault you better make it right, now!"

Ree quickly snaps to attention, going to each of them in turn, placing his hand on their hearts. Alia watches closely, feeling herself panic as his face falls.

"What?" Alia asks, her words rushed.

"Their pulses are weak. They both absorbed too much."

"So? Fix it!"

"I can't! At least not for both of them."

"What?" Alia sighs, feeling a new rush of panic climbing its way up her throat.

"I only have enough power left to save one. The other well…" His words trail off as he looks between them. His eyes staying longest on Eli's little body.

"One is better than nothing," Marne says, clearly trying to be helpful, but from Alia's scowl knows he's being anything but. "We can't let them both die. If this is our only option, then we have to do it."

"So, you're what? Asking me to choose?" Alia shouts, looking back between them before looking back at Marne. "You can't ask me to do that." Her voice breaks at even the thought of it. Having to choose between the brother she's grown up with, her only light in a family of shadows. And the woman who's taught her everything she knows. The woman who took her in, in more ways than one and showed her the true meaning of being able to choose your family.

"I can't do that." She continues to sob. "I'd rather just go with them."

"Well, I won't let you do that," Marne says, his voice almost forceful. He bends down next to her, his eyes sad but clear. "Never."

"And it's not your job to choose." They both look up as Ree speaks. His eyes full of bold determination as he makes his way towards his chosen body. "It's mine!"

Thirty-One

Greif is a very funny thing. It manifests itself differently with everyone. Sometimes coming out straight away and other times, it stays dormant until you least it expect it to. In many ways, it can be described as a shadow, waiting for exactly the right light to emerge and cast the dark reflection it can hold over someone. It's always there, but it can only be seen when it wants to.

For Alia, the grief is of course, the odd in between.

The initial tears come first. Sitting in the forest, now swarming with Protectors of nearly all job descriptions. Some focus on containing Ree, binding his body which has instantly withered with all its magic gone. While others draw their attention to the bodies, the living and the dead.

Several Force members arrive, taking the lead on securing the area from further threat. But Alia knows the threat died with Ree along with any chance that magic could ever be brought back into their lives. At least, that's what she believes.

Several Force members accompany Alia and Marne on their carriage ride back to Calla. Clearly sensing she's in no mood for any type of conversation, they let her be as does Marne who stops spurting seemingly random stings of words when nothing even comes close to tainting the dullness that consumes her face.

Back in Calla, Alia is surprised to see Emmett greet them from the station. While hugging him and being thankful that he's there, Alia still does not allow any further emotion to cut through her dead eyes. She's also grateful that Emmett is the one to lead them to the same meeting room where she believed this all began. Only this time, she's on the other side of the wall, a place she never thought she'd ever be.

Inside the room sits the Council, all wide eyed and ready to debrief Alia and Marne as well as listen to everything they have to say.

Although their voices are each rather soft, obviously trying to get across their condolences without actually saying it out loud, every member of the Council continues to speak as if Alia and Marne were officials who've just come back from a real war, rather than who people who are currently trying to do their best at playing adults. While paying attention, Alia finds her mind glossing over everything that they say.

Medals. Deepest thanks. Bravery. Any role you want. Anything else, you need.

They say everything she expects them to and is almost relieved when they do everything by the book. She knows she should be more excited at the thought of being there when history was made and completing everything she ever set out to do. Barely a month working at the Bureau, she was chosen for something real and helped make it all a reality. She has become a part of history that children will be taught for many years to come and has already gained a reputation that will not undoubtedly, eventually proceed her until she's nothing more than a name in a history book. Yet now she's here and it's happened, Alia begins to wonder if it all was really worth it.

When released from the Council's hold, with being given immediate leave from the Bureau until everything goes back to normal, Alia is more than relieved. Shortly after they exit the room, Lady Dany appears with an offer for Marne, fulfilling her end of the proposal that was clearly talked about during their time where their paths previously crossed. Happy that he's now got something to do, Alia finds it easy enough to slip away and in time, out of the Bureau.

As much as she knows she shouldn't, Alia finds herself back at the Academy. With everything that's just happened, the whole building is empty, like a real-life ghost town. She's never seen it so quiet and almost misses the bustles and voices of how it was for as long as she knew it. How was it when everything around her felt so alive.

Pushing open the door to the training room where she thinks this all really began, Alia shuffles over to the punching bag and starts to hit it, over and over. Unlike all the other times before, Alia starts with quick hard punches that she keeps up until her arms inevitably slow down as she's starting to burn out all the left-over bits of adrenaline she didn't realise were still in her system.

When the movements finally dwindle down to simple, light taps, Alia squints as she finally feels ready to let the emotion in. Now with each gentle tap, she sobs so hard she wonders how she's still standing.

Behind her, embedded deep within the casting shadows that she grew to love so deeply, Alia almost feels as if she's there, watching her, just like she always did. But Alia doesn't want to look behind as she knows she isn't there as she never will be again.

A ghost, a spirit, each feels like the wrong words to describe the familiarity about the dancing shadows. If she closes her eyes and wishes hard enough, Alia can almost feel a hand on her shoulder, squeezing it as if reassuring her that everything happens for a reason and that in the end, she'll get over this.

Sniffing as she finally learns how to swallow further tears that are burning her eyes, Alia takes a deep breath and closes her eyes before finally turning her head in the direction of the shadows. Exhaling, while trying to tense her fingers to stop them trembling, Alia finds the courage to open her eyes.

The ghost has gone, but there's something in its place.

Making her way towards the door, knowing that this time, it really is goodbye, Alia bends down and picks up the bow that she's only ever held once before. Much like that day, she marvels at its shine that still hasn't yet dulled. She holds tightly as she puts it over her shoulder along with arrows that it goes with. A perfect pair.

Taking one last look into the room, that this time is littered with small droplets of tears rather than sweat, Alia finds herself smiling. Although it's small and not what she expected to be doing, she does it. She does it knowing it's what she would have wanted and what she needs to do to finally close the door on the part of her life that she loved the most, but has to now let go of. She needs it to become just another one of the many memories that has made her who she is and that she has to say goodbye to.

Finally feeling ready to walk away, Alia knows she has to leave one last thing inside. One last thought, one last question that while she knows she'll never get an answer to, she needs to leave there in order to never ask it again.

"I hope I made you proud."

Epilogue

The sun rises, signifying the mid-point of another warm day in Calla. Winter has finished, the danger passed, yet plenty of guilt still remains in the air.

Alia stands in a cropped version of her Bureau uniform, her bare legs tingling under the direct rays of warm sun. She breathes deeply, trying to lose herself in light rather than open her eyes and face the day ahead.

The graveyard is quiet but not eerie. The kind of quiet that is peaceful, allowing you to remember things that always seem too hard to think about in the presence of other people.

Bending down, Alia lets herself get teary but keeps them all in as she almost strokes the corner of the headstone. She tries her best to remember what it was like to feel her breath, her heartbeat. Her touch.

"You okay?" Marne's voice appears out of nowhere.

Alia keeps quiet, her eyes not leaving the stone. Marne slowly leans over her, touching it lightly himself.

"First time this place has been quiet in months. You know, I've always wondered who would come and visit me if I were the one in the ground." He tries to laugh but soon learns that it's best if he doesn't.

"She deserved better than this." She pauses, her eyes not leaving the carefully carved name at the top of the stone. "It should have been me."

"You know she never would have let that happen." Alia feels her throat closing up, doing its best to swallow the sob that she can't let ever get out. "She loved you."

Alia abruptly gets back to her feet, her hand not leaving the stone.

"I know," she says, her voice low and soft. "But I still feel far from ready to carry on without her."

Her eyes then travel from the stone into the distance. The church close by is surrounded by colours, laughter and people. A woman in a pink dress stands arm

213

in arm with a woman in a similar purple one. Together, under the falling petals of confetti, they laugh together, as if nothing else in the world really matters.

Mum and Fiona. They finally did it. Without me.

They stand surrounded by people of equally colourful nature. Their smiles contagious but all genuine. To the far side, Alia spies Eli and Ree in matching suits, applauding the happy couple. Even from a distance, Ree could now be mistaken for any other man. Standing in his suit, a smile on his face, he could pass for anyone, like nothing had ever happened.

Besides him, Eli sits in a wheelchair. His smile equally happy and real. Through everything that happened that day, through how much anger Alia still has towards everyone, a part of her is still happy that Eli was the one to survive.

Although now without the use of his legs, he was still luckier than some. And if he hadn't lived, then Ree wouldn't have been given a second chance. After months of treatment and rehabilitation, he made his decision to be human again, or at least try his best to be. Aside from the people who were a part of his story, past or present, no one would think twice to look at him now.

As much as Alia hates him more than most, she can't deny that he has brought himself back from the edge of something worse. Because he was helped, there will be no war. And maybe because he was helped and proved to be of a somewhat good nature, magic may one day return to the realms. Only this time, to be used properly.

And wisely.

Alia then turns to Marne, her eyes sad but equally alert.

"I'm sorry about Lola. Maybe, we'll see her again someday." Marne smiles, happy at her mention.

"I hope so." He pauses, using every spare and silent second to look at her.

"I didn't love her, not like that. It was different," Alia speaks again, slowly lowering her eyes and turning back to watch the wedding, happier by the second that she's able to watch it from a distance rather than be there in person. As if sensing her emotions building, Marne leans down and pulls something from his feet that Alia hasn't even noticed was there.

"You made it through. You've got your place in the Force. You can choose your own path now," he says, all the while slowly placing the bow belonging to their previous Commander over her head. "I think she'd be proud of that."

Fresh tears consume Alia's eyes. She quickly wipes them away, trying not to let herself feel more than she can handle. She knows Commander Dormer's death should never have hit her this hard. But then again, it wasn't until just before the end that she realised what she truly meant to her.

"She told me she was proud, once." She pauses, laughing at the memory. "It was the first time that anyone had truly believed in me." Marne smiles, knowing how happy it makes her to be able to talk about their Commander so honestly after years of keeping it all to herself.

Together they now stand, looking out at the happy events unfolding in the distance.

They will rebuild, the realms will heal, people will live on. While all those that started didn't make it through, their names will be spoken for years to come. Their legacies, never ending.

Taking one last look out at her family, Alia knows that one day, when she's ready, she'll go back and mend all the broken bridges. But there's time for that. For now, she'll let them live their lives and go on with their way of living, leaving Alia to try and find her place in the new world they are set to live within.

"What do we do now?".

"Stay with the Force. Be the best we can. Prepare for whatever else is out there." He pauses, taking a deep breath. "Prepare ourselves for the return of magic. I wonder what kind of world that will be."

"I'm not sure I want to know anymore." They laugh, moving slightly closer together. Still keeping their eyes and concentrations ahead, Marne moves his hand towards her, lightly brushing her fingertips. She takes a breath, letting him take her hand in his. Letting there be someone there to keep her upright, although in exactly what way, there is time to decide.

They stand together, hand in hand, thinking of a better tomorrow. With Dormer's bow over her almost like a blanket and for a minute, Alia almost feels okay. Like, maybe she won't be alone. And that actually, even without her commander, she'll be okay.

Wow. You made it to the end of the book, thank you! I still can't believe I've had to write one of these, and not just in my head. Of all the scenarios that have got me this far in life, I never imagined this one actually coming true.

I'd firstly like to thank everyone who has literally been involved in making this happen:

I want to thank my editors, all the proofreaders and everyone at Austin Macauley for taking a chance on me and my little story. I always wanted to have something interesting to say and while I never thought I would, I also never thought I'd ever have an audience who'd want to listen.

On the topic of people who helped make this whole thing real, thank you to One4Six Coffee for unknowingly employing me to both serve coffee and write this book when no one was around. It's a good thing I'm pretty good at multitasking.

And now, for some more thanks.

Thank you to my mum, dad and the rest of my family for your support and encouragement over all these years, I am eternally grateful for all that you do.

Thank you to all the friends who let me talk their ears off day after day about how amazing it is to tell a story. In particular, to Rhian and Kara for being there from the very first draft of my very first attempt at a novel all those many years ago when we were still sitting in uniform, not really knowing where our lives would take us.

To Matt for being my first nerdy friend and helping me realise that liking odd things can be normal but in the best possible way. Next stop is world domination, right?

To Erin for being my first writing buddy and helping me learn to love what writing can be. Maybe we should finish that puppy book someday? To Emma for all those long radiator talks and pick-me-ups that you're ever so good at.

To all my convention and theatre friends. There's far too many of you to list but you know who you are. Thank you for letting me in and becoming a part of the crazy convention and cosplay world we share. I definitely wouldn't have finished this and thought one day it could really be something if it wasn't for all those times I've shared with you all. I promise if I ever really make it in this world, I'm bringing you all along with me for the ride.

To Eve for all those little pep talks and wise words over several small convention tables. You're one of the few people I actually believe when you say I can do something; I hope you now know how much that means.

To Vicki for giving me more than a second on more than one occasion and helping me find some of the most supportive people in my life.

To all the fictional characters who gave me a home in their stories with the door always wide open. Of course there are far too many to list, plus my list seems to get longer every day, but thank you for the guidance and giving me oh so many unreal life expectations that I'll never stop fighting for.

And now to the first person who I actually witnessed to get as excited as me over the little fandom things and made me feel better for feeling the same way. Thank you, Miss Spencer, for far more than I have pages to say. Six years ago, at least at the time of writing this, you told me that one day I'd write a book and have the opportunity to share it with the world. Although I didn't believe you at the time, apparently I've done just that. You were right (obviously) and while I still can't believe I've really done it, I know without you I never would. Thank you for all the DVDs (I still think of you fangirling every time Spike comes on screen), all the fandom and bookish talks and general words of wisdom. Growing up we're all taught to respect and look up to our teachers. Looking up to you was looking up to everything I one day wanted to be. Well, aside from the actual teaching part because I think we all know that that just wouldn't end well for anyone involved—teenagers still stuck so high praise to you.

Well, I think that's it. Of course, there are so many more people that have had a handle in this little story but I'd like to think that you all know who you are.

Thank you again to everyone that has read this far. Thank you for taking the time to get to know my characters, I hope they treated you well and welcomed you with open arms.